CASH DELGADO IS
LIVING THE DREAM

CASH DELGADO *IS* LIVING *the* DREAM

A NOVEL

TEHLOR KAY MEJIA

DELL
New York

A Dell Trade Paperback Original

Copyright © 2024 by Tehlor Kay Mejia

Published in the United States by Dell, an imprint of Random House, a division of Penguin Random House LLC, New York.

DELL and the D colophon are registered trademarks of Penguin Random House LLC.

ISBN 978-0-593-59879-5
Ebook ISBN 978-0-593-59880-1

Printed in the United States of America on acid-free paper

randomhousebooks.com

2 4 6 8 9 7 5 3 1

Book design by Fritz Metsch

CASH DELGADO IS

LIVING THE DREAM

1

THE THING NO one tells you about being a single parent is that you will be running late for the rest of your life.

No matter how early you set the alarm, how generously you appoint transition time, or how much you prepare the night before, you will still find yourself standing in the entryway of your house at 8:05 yelling *Are your socks on yet?* as you anxiously watch the seconds go by.

I know, because I'm here now, yelling those exact words for the fourth time today and at least the thirtieth time this week. My lifetime count is probably in the thousands.

"I can't find matchies!"

"It doesn't matter," I call, trying not to let the frustration show. "Matching socks are boring, anyway."

This appears to be today's golden ticket, because my daughter, Parker, bounces down the stairs seconds later, beaming from behind her no-break soft plastic glasses.

"Look!" she says, gesturing down. One of her feet appears to be getting eaten by an ankle-length frog, and the other hugged by a smiling, rosy-cheeked sloth.

"Perfect," I pronounce, forgetting the ticking clock for a moment as I look down at her.

The other thing they don't tell you about being a single parent is that you'll love your quirky, nearsighted, perfectly herself oddball child so much it will make every stressful countdown worth it. And then some.

Despite the ticking clock, I take out my phone and snap a picture. My best friend Inez's contact is at the top of my suggested list, of course. I don't trust myself to remember the nuance of the outfit when I see her later, so I send it with the caption: *Fashion Icon.*

"I thought we were late," Parker says pointedly.

"We are," I say, stowing my phone with a chuckle. "I wanted to show Auntie Inez your style, but now we'll probably be last in the drop-off line again."

"I like being last," Parker says, unruffled as she pulls hot pink rain boots on over her mismatched socks. "I get to make an *entrance.*"

She flounces out to the car before I can respond, tutu bouncing over her jeans, green dinosaur sweatshirt completing the ensemble.

Oh, to have the confidence of a six-year-old, I think as I grab the keys and follow.

We are indeed last in the drop-off line. The doors to Ridley Falls Elementary are so close, and yet so far away. This morning the school is wreathed in mist with the town's trademark ponderosas looming over it.

In the backseat of the Jeep, Parker belts along to the radio. When your car was made before the new millennium there's no aux cord, and there's something pop-rocky playing that I recognize from working a thousand karaoke nights.

It makes my brain hurt. I pray for the serenity not to lean on the horn at the PTA moms lingering at the front of the line.

"If you took a chance! If you let me in!"

"How do you know this song?" I ask, glancing at Parker in the rearview mirror. She's using one of her rain boots as a microphone.

She gives me a withering look. "*Everyone* knows this song. The Walking Wild? Madison's mom *knows* them."

This is probably true. When Ridley Falls became the home of the Pacific Northwest's most beloved indie record label five years ago, name-dropping within city limits reached an all-time peak. "Put your shoes back on," I reply wearily. "We'll be at the front in just a minute."

It takes ten, but we do eventually reach the promised land—marked by traffic cones adorned with the school mascot, the mighty porcupine.

No matter how late we are, I can never bring myself to rush this part. I get out of the car, unbuckling Parker and grabbing her backpack, checking for missing shoes, glasses, lunch box, etc. and pleased to find everything where it's supposed to be for once.

"Have a good day at school," I say, down on one knee in front of her.

"I always do."

"I know. You're pretty awesome, you know that?"

"Duh," Parker says, flipping one of her short brown pigtails. "You tell me every day."

"Get used to it. I'll still be doing it when you're a hundred and five."

"Deal," Parker says, sticking out her tiny hand for me to shake. A little knot of kids call her name from the doorway then—none quite so flamboyantly dressed, I note with pride—and she bounds off without so much as a goodbye.

There's a thread of tension that runs through you from the moment your kid wakes up in the morning until the second another qualified adult takes over, and mine snaps the moment Parker is in the building. Suddenly, the four hours of sleep I got between closing the bar and the alarm ringing for school don't seem like enough.

My phone buzzes before I can even pull out of the drop-off lane. Inez, of course, replying to my photo of Parker from earlier. Cash Delgado, the message reads. Your daughter is officially more fashionable than you are.

I try to be offended, but then I look in the rearview mirror. At the rumpled T-shirt I threw on over yesterday's jeans. The short curly hair that's more a riot than a style. The bags lingering beneath my eyes.

Touché, I text back. But you have to give me some credit for being so behind on laundry that she's forced to be creative.

Three eye-roll emojis precede her next text. I'll meet you at your house in fifteen and we can get through a few loads before we have to open the bar.

To some people, this would seem like extreme altruism. Volunteering to help your single parent best friend do laundry before your shift? Inez deserves the Nobel Peace Prize. But I know Inez, so I know better.

Wow, I reply. You must really not want to be there when your girlfriend wakes up.

She's not my girlfriend, she insists. And I'll get you coffee if you don't bring her up again.

I start the car, feeling marginally less exhausted at the thought of coffee I don't have to wait in line for. You have a deal, I text her back.

I don't even have time to restart the slightly damp, severely wrinkled clothes in the dryer before Inez breezes in without knocking.

"Honey, I'm home!" she calls.

Inez always looks much more put together than I do, no matter where she's coming from or how late she was up the night before. Today she's wearing a pair of dark jeans that hug her hips. A black tank top with one of those breezy shawl things over the top. Her dark hair is in a topknot that looks messy on purpose.

She was the first person I met in Ridley Falls, fresh off the bus from Portland when I showed up to work at Joyce's, leaving my whole life behind. I'll never forget that day—Parker and I were lost, Inez was coming out of a coffee shop and dropped her cup on the sidewalk. It splattered all over my shoes. She insisted on buying me new ones, and Parker ogled her with her little baby smile, and we all ended up eating lunch together.

Sometimes I remind her she still owes me a pair of shoes.

"You'll never guess who was at Ponderosa's," she says, closing the door behind her with one foot, balancing the coffees and an overlarge tote bag she takes on dates that have overnight potential.

"Who?"

"That couple who comes to karaoke once a month or so—the guy always has like three too many pretentious-sounding beers and stares at my ass?"

I know who she's talking about immediately. The blessing and curse of running a small-town bar. "The wife drinks white wine and makes a face after every sip," I confirm. "It's like, if you hate it so much . . . why do you order it all the time?"

"Exactly. They were in front of me in line, just falling all over themselves to look like responsible adults in the light of day. I swear she said the words *vow renewal* four times in five minutes. As if her husband didn't once ask if he could bounce a quarter off my tits."

I laugh, taking the coffee, drinking half of it in one fortifying gulp. "And you wonder why I'm still single. I'm telling you, for those of us afflicted with heterosexuality, it's bleak out there."

She hangs her bag on my coat closet doorknob, kicks off her shoes, and collapses into my creaky old corduroy chair, which is the same root beer–brown as the carpet. Interior decorating isn't high on my list of priorities—the place came furnished and I didn't ask too many questions.

"I'll never understand how you do it," she says and sighs.

I take my own cup to the matching couch, sitting beside the pile of laundry I'm afraid might become sentient if I don't deal with it soon. "I don't do it," I reply, trying to think of the last thing I did that counted as a date. Did rattling the storeroom shelves with an ex-coworker count? "And anyway, it can't be so blissful in La La Lesbian Land if you're here this early in the morning."

Inez glares at me over her to-go cup lid. "You promised not to bring it up."

Holding up my hands in surrender, I allow her to change the subject. I know all I need to know about Chicken-or-the-Egg Lady, a woman Inez met last month at some young farming professionals meetup in the next town over. They've been seeing each other ever since, but it's clearly moving much faster for one of them than the other.

"*Anyway,* Granny O'Connor called me right before I texted you," Inez says now, swinging her legs over the side of the chair to examine her bright green toenail polish. "She was at the school this morning, and she said you look dead on your feet."

I groan. "Granny O'Connor needs to mind her business."

Inez cackles. "Try telling *her* that. I swear she only volunteers at the school library so she can gossip about all the parents. I get three calls a week at minimum just about the happenings in that parking lot."

Inez's grandmother has been retired for a hundred years. She used to run a farm a couple of miles outside town, but she moved into a guesthouse on the property a few years ago and turned the operating over to Inez. Mostly Granny volunteers around town just to keep her finger on the pulse of Ridley Falls gossip.

"Some old people play bingo," I mutter.

"I didn't even say the mean part yet," Inez replies, taking her hair out of its bun and shaking it out. Always in motion. "She said if you don't find a man to delegate to soon, Parker is going to grow up *troubled* and you're going to get wrinkles."

"Rich, coming from a woman who is seventy-five percent wrinkles by volume," I say. But as Inez and I begin tackling the laundry pile—her separating items by color and me making trips to the laundry room—I'm forced to acknowledge that Granny O'Connor's comments hit closer to home than I'd like to admit.

For as long as I can remember I've been on my own. My parents kicked me out at seventeen when I shaved my head and joined a punk band and I never looked back. No siblings. No extended family to speak of. For the first part of my adult life I thought I'd found a chosen family in my little group of Portland restaurant industry degenerates, but relationships based on attending basement punk shows and building pyramids of beer cans tend to fizzle when the pregnancy test turns pink . . .

. . . Even the one with the baby's father, as it turns out.

Of course, I know it would be easier to share the unending responsibilities of life and parenthood with someone else. That it would probably be better for Parker to grow up with another role model. But there's the hypothetical, and then there's reality. And the reality is I haven't met a man in her lifetime (or maybe even mine) who would be remotely worthy of a place in Parker's life. The last person I slept with was so unsuitable he never even met her.

Inez comes out of the kitchen as I'm folding socks and hands me a plate of scrambled eggs and toast. "Eat," she says. "We gotta get to Joyce's in an hour."

As I gratefully take the plate, finally noticing my growling stomach, I think for the millionth time that we have Inez, at least. That I'm not entirely alone in this.

But one day Inez will meet someone much more interesting (and much less clingy, I hope) than Chicken-or-the-Egg Lady. She'll want to have her own family, maybe. So I can appreciate her, and I do, but I have to remember that my being the most important person in her life is probably not a permanent state of affairs.

Once we've finished breakfast and the final load of laundry is in the dryer, Inez spreads the contents of her overnight bag across my coffee table, applying mascara and lip gloss and whatever other magical potions make her face look like that.

For my part, I spray some water on my hair, put on a fresh Joyce's T-shirt I'm able to extract from Parker's leggings, and tuck it into my high-waist jeans. Mondays are usually slow, I think, pulling on my boots. Hopefully we can coast through, close early, and I'll get *five* hours of sleep tonight instead of my usual four.

Inez takes off to pick up our weekly order from the cash-and-carry as I walk across the dirt lot to the back door of the bar. I let myself in and turn on the lights, smiling.

Working open to close isn't ideal, but the owners of Joyce's let me take off for a couple of hours in the middle. Pick up Parker from her after-school program, have dinner, and get her into bed before the babysitter comes.

It might not be the job I always dreamed of, but between the schedule flexibility, the health insurance, and our free half of the duplex out back, it's a good deal. And as divey a place as Joyce's is, it's strangely peaceful when you're the only one here. Before the old geezers show up for darts and tallboys at eleven, and the chatter and the smacking of pool balls and the jukebox get going in the late afternoon.

For thirty minutes I run through my opening routine. Vacuum, wipe down the tables and the bar, fill the ice and the garnish tray—mandatory, even though no one will order anything but tall cans of High Life until at least six.

I make a note of which beers need restocking, which syrups are running low. It's all very methodical. The same every day in a comforting way. Once I turn the sign on, anything might happen. First dates, fistfights, a dissertation on the migratory patterns of gray whales, family reunions or estrangements. Minor explosions, metaphorical or literal. Once, memorably, an actual wedding.

But before the customers arrive, it's just me and the dark wood paneling. The ghosts of karaoke performances past. This place has so much potential, I think, gazing at it from behind the bar. With a real stage, an updated kitchen, an actual menu . . .

I cut myself off before I can get too deep into the fantasy. The Joyce's owners aren't interested in expansion, and even if they were, they don't have the money. I've suggested half a dozen fixes over the years, small updates, but the answer is always the same:

The timing's not right. Maybe if things pick up over the summer. Etc., etc., etc.

George and Linda are good people, but they inherited the bar. They spend their money on cruises, enjoy their retirement. This place was never their dream.

When Parker started kindergarten and I suddenly had *any* free time, I drew up a business plan for an upgrade. Thought maybe I could get a loan on my own, or convince George and Linda Joyce's would pay for a lot more cruises with some changes made.

But Parker got the flu that week, when the plans were only half finished. She was home for four days, and sometimes I feel like life hasn't slowed down since.

Someday, I always tell myself. *Maybe someday.*

Inez returns ten minutes before opening, backing in through the front door with her arms full of frozen potato products and her phone wedged between her shoulder and her ear.

"I know," she's saying soothingly. "I should have left a note. I just remembered I had an order to pick up early for the bar and I didn't want to wake you."

I meet her halfway across the room, taking the grocery boxes and smirking at her as she apologizes to Chicken-or-the-Egg Lady.

"How am I going to make it up to you?" she asks, rolling her eyes dramatically in my direction. "Let me think on it, okay? We've gotta open in a few minutes."

A pause. I take the fries to the freezer.

"Cash?" Inez is saying when I return. "No, of course there's nothing going on. We're best friends, we run a business together. But unfortunately for me she's straight as Highway 46."

She winks at me. I roll my eyes as her expression changes rapidly to one of apology.

"No, not *unfortunately* like I wish she wasn't. It was just a joke. Look, I'll call you later, okay?"

When Inez lowers the phone, I can still hear the voice on the other end echoing tinnily out of the speaker. It does not sound pleased.

"I think I have to break up with her," she says dejectedly, hanging up and sticking the phone into her back pocket.

"What gave it away?" I ask. "The fact that you're completely not into her? Or was it the part where she got jealous of you going to work?"

Inez tosses a bar towel at me as she sets up the register for the day. "She's not jealous of the job," she says, waggling her eyebrows.

I feel my face heat up. "What's Highway 46 anyway?"

"The straightest highway in the continental U.S.," Inez says with a fake sigh. "A hundred and twenty miles without a single curve."

"I can tell you're still taking the tragedy of my heterosexuality very personally," I deadpan, making my way over to click on the sign. In a flare of fluorescent pink and green, Joyce's is officially open for business.

2

TRUE TO FORM, the geezers are in the door before I can make it back to the bar, and they're already arguing.

"*Jaws* came out in seventy-three!" Charlie shouts, his fishing hat pulled down low over his eyes. "I wouldn't forget that! I took Cindy Trebucci. If you'd ever gone out with a girl who looked like her you wouldn't forget it, either."

"You better start doing your crosswords, Charlie, your memory's going. It was seventy-five, I'm sure of it."

"Seventy-three or I'll eat my hat!" Charlie cries.

"Morning fellas," I call out over the bickering. "What can I get you today?"

"Get Mo here a big helping of crow and look something up for me, would you?" Charlie asks, taking their usual table by the dartboard. "Make use of that smartphone while you can still see the letters."

"High Lifes," Mo says with an eye roll. "And keep 'em coming."

"You got it," I reply, heading back to the bar before I can be badgered into looking up the release date of *Jaws*.

Of course, Inez is already on it. "Sorry, Charlie," she calls with a grin, waving a chili fry at him. "Mo's right, it was seventy-five!"

I leave the two sweating cans of Miller on the table amid the crash of Charlie's dismay at Mo's triumph.

"I don't trust the damn internet," Charlie grumbles, despite having been the one to request consulting it. "You know anyone can edit that thing? How do I know you didn't get on there first just to trick me."

Mo fires back, and the argument carries them through their first round of cricket. Blessedly, it doesn't require any further intervention from Inez or me. She rifles through receipts while I dust the tall shelf of liquor bottles behind the bar. It's a comfortable rhythm. There won't be more customers until at least lunchtime, and Mo and Charlie are low maintenance. Two more cans every forty-five minutes or so is hardly taxing even when you're *dead on your feet* as Granny O'Connor so charmingly described me.

So when the bell on the door rings again half an hour later, all four of us snap our heads up at the intrusion.

"Oh, shit," Inez croons at me when the mystery patron's identity becomes clear in the low light. "Speaking of heterosexuality . . ."

Her words echo my thoughts exactly. Because haloed in the too-bright light streaming through the door is none other than the Guy Who Wasn't Worthy of Being Introduced to Parker himself—Chase Stanton. Former manager of Joyce's, and the only person I've slept with in the better part of a decade.

It takes me a moment to realize Chase is really here and not a mirage brought on by lack of sleep and Granny O'Connor's cutting comments about me and men. But Inez can clearly see him, and now Charlie and Mo are on their feet, greeting him like a long-lost son with hearty handshakes and claps on the back.

This whole *hail the conquering hero* bit gives me time to scope out how a year in Seattle has changed him. And how it hasn't, too.

For one thing, he's still absurdly handsome. Square jaw, piercing blue eyes, dark hair that has a little more gel in it than it used to. When he worked here it was all jeans and flannels and work boots, but he's wearing a suit now. Expensive. Tailored. He clearly knows exactly how it makes him look.

Once he's finished catching up with the boys, Chase makes his way over to us. He's smirking just a little—an expression that led to more than one after-hours session in the storeroom when we worked long hours here together.

"Well, well, well," he says. "Cash Delgado."

"Chase," I say, like he waltzes in here every day. Like it hasn't been forever since I last saw him. "Seattle kick you out already?"

"Nah," he replies. Effortless. Casual. "They handed over the keys to the city last week, in fact. Just came back to tell my parents."

"Right," I say without missing a beat. "The hair product lobbyists probably had a lot to do with that. I heard the whole industry would still be floundering if you hadn't shown up just in time."

His eyes flash in a way I recognize. This is how we ended up in bed, I reflect—or on the bar top, anyway. I didn't even know I was flirting with him, but according to him our banter was pure sexual tension.

"I missed this," he says, laughing. "I always said you're wasted on Ridley Falls, Cash."

Without asking, he slides behind the bar and begins mixing

himself a drink. An old-fashioned. Before noon. His hands move smoothly and confidently, like they always did.

"Hey," Inez says. "No interlopers allowed."

Chase doesn't stop what he's doing. He squeezes an orange slice, flips open the garnish tray for a cherry. "Inez," he greets her. "Nice to see you two are still joined at the hip. When did you start working here?"

"I decided it would be good to hire someone the customers actually liked," I tease, falling back into the old rhythm like no time has passed. "It's been a nice change."

"You can't fool me," Chase says. "I know you miss me." He leans across the bar, turning the full force of those mountain-lake eyes on me. I'm forced to realize that our last goodbye was also the last time anyone saw me without my clothes on.

I can feel Inez's amused gaze following this back-and-forth, which puts an end to my musing.

"It was the end of an era when you left," I say, a little brisker than I mean to. "But managing a swanky city bar seems to agree with you. You look great."

He raises an eyebrow at my change in tone, but takes my lead. His hand is very close to mine across the bar top. I struggle with feeling like it's been a day since he left and an entire lifetime, simultaneously. Is the version of me who gave in to the banter still in here somewhere?

"Listen, I only came in to make sure the place is still standing," he says. "I've got a couple people to see today. But I'll be around the rest of the week—let me buy you dinner for old times' sake?" He drains the old-fashioned, leaving the cherry in the glass.

I'm about to remind him we've never had dinner together. That the entirety of our affair happened inside these walls or at one of our apartments in the dead of night. That neither of us ever felt compelled to make more out of it.

Unfortunately, before I can say any of this, Inez leans over the bar and says, "She'll call you."

Chase smiles, that boyish small-town charm breaking through before he throws out a smooth city-slicker wink. "Same number," he says, puts a ten-dollar bill on the bar, and walks out without looking back.

I round on Inez the moment he's gone. "In what universe was *that* a good idea?"

Inez smiles, her red lips stretching mischievously. "The one where I'm your best friend, and the dating world is bleak for straight women, and a no-strings-attached lay is exactly what you need right now. You can thank me later."

"I'm not sure . . ." I say. "I mean, I know it was only a year ago, but it feels like ancient history, me and him." I'm not sure how to articulate how it felt to see Chase. Like I was suddenly so aware of the chasm between who I was a year ago and who I am now . . .

"Then you get a free dinner out and no means no," she says. "But trust me, Cash, you need to change out of your work clothes. Go out. Be objectified. You're a hot-blooded woman, not just a manager and a mom."

"You just want to tell your girlfriend I'm dating a man so she stops thinking we're having a secret affair," I counter, but I can't deny the logic in what she's saying. I literally can't remember the last time I wore anything but a Joyce's shirt. The last time I went to a bar when I was off the clock.

My mind strays back to last year. Me and Chase and the convenience of the after-work quickie. The charged banter that got us through the long shifts.

I remember my surprise when he kissed me that first time. I hadn't even known he was interested. Assumed a guy that looked like him would have a type more resembling a Barbie doll than whatever makeup-less look I was rocking.

But he had always been a guy who got what he wanted, and I felt the glow of being chosen by someone who looked like they could play a bartender in a movie. Would it be so bad to feel that way again?

"You're right," I say, with as much certainty as I can muster. "Dinner. Objectification. You don't mind watching Parker?"

Inez smiles angelically. "Why do you think I orchestrated all this in the first place? I want her all to myself."

Chase is free the following night, I find out when I text him after my shift. They're the first messages we've exchanged since he left.

Above our quick confirmation of time and place, our last back-and-forth sits like a justification of what I'm about to do. I read over it in bed, doing my best to put myself back there. To awaken whatever drive made me choose him over precious sleep time and time again.

CHASE: Goddamn I want you so bad right now
ME: You have a line of eight customers, stop ogling
CHASE: The second that door locks I'll be doing a lot more than ogling . . .

There's something there, I think. Some little spark rekindling. Maybe dinner will be enough to coax it into the no-strings flame Inez predicted.

I drift off to sleep in a state of mild anxiety about tomorrow night. That, I tell myself later, is probably why I have the most bizarre dream I've ever had in my life.

It starts where most of my dreams start: Joyce's. I'm wiping down a table after closing when I realize I'm not alone. Inez is behind the bar, and she's wearing lingerie. Bright red, heart-shaped, lacy lingerie like some Victoria's Secret Valentine's Day ad.

"*You better get dressed,*" I tell her. "*Chicken-or-the-Egg Lady isn't gonna like you wearing that around me.*"

Inez leans over the bar. The Valentine's Day lingerie is barely equal to this position, and I find my eyes drawn to the places it's struggling. My mouth is suddenly dry. "*I don't care what she thinks,*" she purrs, in a voice totally unlike the one she usually uses with me. "*What do you think, Cash?*"

Her hair cascades around her shoulders in glossy, dark waves. Her skin glows against the red lace. Her eyes are heavily made up, and she flutters her lashes at me. Even in the dream I know I would normally crack a joke here, but I can't think of a single one.

Instead, I step closer. "*I probably shouldn't say what I think,*" I tell her, like I'm watching myself from above. Someone else at the controls. Someone who isn't nearly as straight as Highway 46.

"*But I want you to.*"

I'm on the other side of the bar top from her now. Close enough to touch. My whole body feels electric, like I'm a dryer sheet and she's a staticky sweater and we're destined to come out of this tumbling cycle together.

"*It might be easier to show you,*" I say, leaning across the bar top, our lips just inches apart.

From all around us, music starts to play. A cascade of sounds like bells. At first it's nice, but it gets louder and louder and I want to kiss her so badly but I can't stand the noise anymore.

"*It's your alarm,*" Inez says, a little sadly.

"*What?*" I ask. "*What alarm?*"

"MOMMY, IT'S YOUR ALARM!"

I wake up with a gasp. For a moment I'm so disoriented I don't know where I am. Where's Inez? How did I get home?

But then I hear the music. The cascading bells of my phone alarm getting louder and louder on my bedside table. Parker is standing in the doorway in her pajamas.

"I'm sorry," I manage, turning off the sound at last. "I guess I slept through it. Go get dressed and I'll get your breakfast, okay?"

She agrees sleepily, and I flop back onto my pillow, my heart pounding. The dream still feels so vivid. The swells of Inez's curves beneath the lingerie, her glossy lips so close to mine.

I probably shouldn't say what I think.

But I want you to.

It's all so absurd that I laugh. Loudly. In my room by myself. "The subconscious is really something else," I say out loud, grabbing my bathrobe and going to turn on the shower. After a second's pause, I turn the nozzle all the way to cold. Just to be safe.

3

THE DREAM, AS silly as it was, isn't the reason the rest of my day is terrible. But it is. Terrible. Inez has the day off, she's taking a crew of rescued mini donkeys to a petting zoo in Aberdeen. I could have called Eduardo, our backup bartender, to help out. But I decided I'd rather be alone.

Of course, it's dead as a doornail all day long. I reorganize the storage closet and all the cabinets and drawers behind the bar before noon, and then there's nothing left to do but try to avoid thinking about last night's dream or tonight's date.

I fail stunningly on both counts.

The Joyce's sign officially clicks off at six-thirty, when it becomes clear the old woman who came in for a glass of red wine at three was an anomaly. Parker is already at home. I relieve the neighbor kid who watches her after school early and tell Parker to get ready for her sleepover with Auntie Inez.

My body is filled with energy that feels like buzzing bees—they could just as easily sting me as make honey.

I try to picture myself across a candlelit table from Chase. The planes of his face, those blue eyes that used to hook right behind my belly button and tug. Instead, all I can see is my idiotic dream.

Inez in that ridiculous lingerie. I shake myself and open my closet, resisting the urge to go inside. Curl up in a ball among the sweaters and extra blankets and pretend something came up.

"Mom! Where are the twinkle lights?!" comes Parker's voice up the stairs.

"Nothing that plugs into the wall without supervision!" I call down, and she makes a frustrated *humph* sound. If it were up to her she'd be using power tools by now.

I turn back to my closet with a renewed sense of urgency. Nothing like an unsupervised, bored six-year-old to light a fire. But the next obstacle is immediately clear: I don't have anything remotely suitable for a date. My closet is a series of relaxed-fit jeans and a million faded black T-shirts. Almost all of them prominently feature the Joyce's logo or a beer slogan.

There's a pair of slightly nicer jeans I wear when I have to do conferences at the school, or the Joyce's owners are in town—are those date appropriate? I think of the couples I've seen at the bar recently. The women in sundresses or floral print rompers or whatever. I can't picture myself wearing any of that.

When was the last time I went out? I ask myself. And have I *ever* been on a date? Parker's dad and I met while we were dishwashers at neighboring bars in Portland, getting to know each other during smoke breaks by the dumpsters, covered in fryer grease.

"Parker?" I call, starting to hyperventilate a little. "You're not using plugs, right?"

"Nope!" she calls cheerfully. "Glitter twinkles much better anyway."

I laugh, and it comes out a little wheezy. I'm not dressed, I'm going to be vacuuming pink glitter out of my living room carpet until Parker graduates high school, and this is all a horrible mistake.

The front door opens and closes downstairs. I hear Inez greeting Parker enthusiastically and suddenly I'm considering a new angle on this whole best-friend-sex-dream thing. What am I going to tell her? Do I tell her anything? Am I gonna act all weird and give it away?

I throw my afternoon shift jeans and T-shirt back on, vowing I will show up just like this and damn anyone who tries to convince me otherwise. Chase was never bothered by my grungy bartender attire when we were hooking up at work—why would a change of venue make any difference?

But my panic only increases when I descend to find Inez holding *clothes* in *garment bags*.

"What is that?" I ask warily, by way of greeting. At least this wrinkle is enough to make me forget the dream. Instead, the dresses and rompers from dates I've seen at Joyce's are dancing through my head again.

"Options," she says. "I figured you'd either be freaking out in your underwear or"—she gives me a once-over—"wearing that, still."

"Two for two," I mutter as she hangs the clothes on the back of a chair and turns to survey Parker's creation.

"*Love* what you've done with the place, P," she says. "Are you ready for the best sleepover ever?"

"Best sleepover ever!" Parker shrieks, breaking into the kind of dance only a first-grader anticipating pizza, sugar, and princess movies can possibly pull off.

"Okay," Inez says, getting down on her level. "You've gotten a great start here. But what I need you to do is find every single pillow and blanket and sheet and towel that isn't in your mom's room and make a pile of them on the floor right here. Can you do that?"

Parker nods breathlessly before zooming off at top speed. At least I won't have to worry about her tonight. Me, on the other hand . . .

"Look," I tell Inez. "I'm sure whatever teen movie makeover montage is happening in your head is lovely. But I haven't worn a dress since my eighth-grade graduation, and I'm not about to start now, so just—"

"Oh my god, we did not just meet," Inez interrupts with an affectionate eye roll. "Would you have a *little* faith in me?"

She leads me upstairs. I glance through Parker's door on the way by, where she's busy obeying Inez's orders with little thought to the structural integrity of her bedroom. But at least she's busy. Inez lays the hangers on my bed. "None of my stuff would work, obviously, so I borrowed these from Mars."

Mars is one of Inez's three roommates. When she took over Granny O'Connor's farm a few years ago, it was double-mortgaged with a ton of debt. Gossip around town was that Inez wouldn't be able to keep it through one tax season. But she rented out the other three bedrooms to queer friends around the valley and turned the place into this adorable little cottage-core commune.

They host shows and skill shares and do all these cool trades with local businesses around town, not to mention the herd of rescue mini donkeys they take to county fairs and town events for the kids to feed and pet.

Inez is looking at me expectantly now, so I dutifully survey the wardrobe options. She was right to ask for faith. There's not a dress in the bunch. I find a pair of cuffed, dark-wash jeans that look a lot nicer than even my school-conference pants. Some slim dress slacks. A variety of quirky, short-sleeved button-downs.

"Okay, you're still my best friend," I say by way of apology.

She grins. "Take it or leave it, I'm sure Chase will gobble you up regardless. But I meant what I said before. I want you to try to have fun tonight. I figured a costume change might get you out of your head."

"What would I do without you?" I ask, thinking of the night ahead with something other than dread for the first time all day.

"Let's hope we don't find out." She boops my nose. This close to her, the memory of last night's nocturnal antics comes back full force. I can feel my face flush as I realize what a stupid, patriarchal fantasy it was. Red lingerie? Cleavage? I'm clearly not creative enough to be an actual lesbian.

"You good?" she asks, obviously noting the blush.

For a second, I consider just telling her. It's probably the secrecy of it all that's making my stupid subconscious feel like a bigger deal than it is. I'll tell her, she'll make a joke about how she *does* have a nice rack, and we'll be laughing about it in seconds.

But she leaves me to get dressed, and I don't say a word.

Within twenty minutes, I look like a slightly shinier version of myself. The dark-rinse jeans work with my belt, and a button-down with little sharks embroidered on it is fun and slightly dressy without being over-the-top. A pair of Inez's bright white sneakers tie it together, and I even let her spray some citrusy-smelling stuff in my mop of curls.

"Okay," I say in the mirror twenty minutes before I'm due to meet Chase. "This isn't terrible."

"Not *terrible*?" Inez asks, offended. "You look hot! I'd take you out myself if we didn't both have other plans." She winks. It's pretty commonplace, these jokes of hers. Safe because we both know they're only jokes.

But for a second, in my dream-addled brain, I'm thinking of her across the candlelit table from me—and it's a lot easier to imagine this way.

"You *do* look cool, Mama," Parker says, wrapped up in a pink blanket in the doorway of what is now an impressive fort.

"Thanks, pal," I say, shaking myself free of my ridiculous thoughts. "Not as cool as you, though."

Her tiara wobbles dangerously from where she's set it on top of a feather boa tied under her chin. "Maybe next time," she says, yawning widely.

"She tuckered herself out with the glitter," I say under my breath to Inez. "She won't make it halfway through *Frozen II*."

"I'll make sure she gets some pizza in her before the crash," Inez assures me. "Hawaiian is already on the way."

"Okay, she doesn't like—"

"Canadian bacon. Only pineapple, and not too much sauce," Inez finishes.

"You're the best," I say, relieved.

On my way to the car, I think about the times before Inez when there wasn't a single person I could trust with Parker. I have to remember not to take Inez for granted. Or to ruin our friendship by being weird about a dream that obviously meant nothing.

There are three restaurants in Ridley Falls that don't have wheels.

Sassy's Diner out by the freeway exit is open twenty-four hours for truckers. They have spectacular food—as long as you want a breakfast combo with bacon (not sausage, trust me) or Monday meatloaf. It's owned by a woman named Claudette Perkins who is at least a hundred years old and seems to have some magic barrier around the place that allows her to pass her annual health inspection. There's no other explanation.

Ponderosa Café is a cute little place downtown that does breakfast wraps and sandwiches but closes after lunch. About five years ago it took the place of a hardware store, which everyone in Ridley Falls called a harbinger of doom for the town. It's run by Ginny and Bradley Peterson, a married couple in their thirties from Seattle—hence the predictions of the end times. But after a rocky few months, the community decided they liked the lattes and cortados more than they liked complaining about the city slickers. Ginny rescued a three-legged dog who started hanging around the shop during the day, and all has been mostly peaceful since.

Lastly, there's Badger's Bistro, which is kind of the catch-all for everything else. It's owned by a grumpy old lesbian named Robin Knight, who dresses like a lumberjack and only comes in to scowl. She and her wife are kind of Ridley Falls' original queer power couple—Kendra Knight is the editor of the *Ridley Falls Gazette*.

Badger's, of course, always gets rave reviews.

The restaurant sits at the end of Main Street, surrounded by looming pines, with an excellent patio that looks out at downtown from a comfortable distance. Their menu is doing too much, in my opinion, but there are a few mainstays on it that aren't trying to fuse two cultural dishes into one, making it the only truly viable option for dining in town on a non-Monday after three o'clock in the afternoon.

Even with the glitter and the wardrobe crisis, I'm a few minutes early. The place is mostly dead—par for the course on a Tuesday night. An elderly couple sits at a candlelit table near the door, finishing dinner, a few twentysomethings I recognize from karaoke are having beers on the patio.

It's a casual, seat-yourself type of vibe, but the idea of waiting in my fancy date outfit for Chase is intolerable, so I approach the bar instead, where Sasha Winters is wiping a glass, looking bored out of her mind.

Sasha has been at Badger's for almost as long as I've been at Joyce's. She's another transplant—cool in that platinum blonde pinup girl kind of way. We're not exactly friends—who has the time? But when you work in the same pocket-sized industry there's a certain level of camaraderie that builds whether you choose it or not.

"Hey, Cash," she says. "Get you a drink?"

"Sure, I'll take a Corona. Slow night?"

She shrugs, turning around to fish a bottle out of the fridge behind her, long red nails clinking against the glass. "Typical Tuesday. I'm almost hoping those kids outside get in a fight just to break the monotony."

"Relatable," I chuckle. "But the cleanup is never worth it."

She pops the top and slides the beer across the bar. The first sip is nice—despite the job title I maybe have a beer a month. Between work and Parker and trying to get a human amount of sleep there's never any time for that, either.

"You must be dead at Joyce's too if they let you out from behind the bar," Sasha says.

"Yeah, well, old friend in town. We'll see if there's an angry mob demanding tall cans by the time I get home."

As if on cue, the door opens behind me. I can tell it's Chase by the way Sasha's eyebrows shoot up. "I always knew there was something going on with you two," she says as he makes his way over. "No way you could be shut up with him all those long hours and not at least try it. Good for you, Cash."

I roll my eyes. "This small-town gossip is beneath you, Sasha."

"I'm just saying, I wish more of my *old friends* looked like him."

"Ladies," Chase says, sidling up beside me at the bar. He smells good. Something subtle and cedary. And there's less gel in his hair, I note; it's falling loose over his forehead. Best of all, he ditched the suit for jeans and a sweater. Nondescript brown boots. All in all, he's looking a lot more like the guy I remember following into that storeroom than he was yesterday.

"Welcome back," Sasha purrs. "Figured we'd lost you to the big city for good."

"It's great," Chase says as she pours him a house red. "But I have to come back every now and again to check on this one. Make sure she's not running the place into the ground in my absence." Drink in hand, he turns to me. "Should we sit?"

"Let's," I say, borrowing Sasha's envy. This is what I remember loving about being with him. The aura that surrounds someone this handsome and confident. The way being chosen by them functions as certified proof that you're doing something right.

We sit. We sip our drinks and size each other up in the low light.

"I like you better like this," I offer when the quiet stretches. "Ridley Falls Golden Boy. That whole sharp-edged city guy thing doesn't do it for me."

"Well, good," he says, his voice a little lower. Huskier. "I dressed down just for you."

The half a Corona is doing its job. I feel warm and loose. I smile. "And I dressed up. Looks like we met in the middle."

"It's nice, but you know I like you better *un*dressed," he says, low enough that no one else will hear.

I can feel my skin flush pleasantly. "Yes, I think I remember that about you."

Sasha comes over then, I order a flank steak and mashed potatoes, Chase gets a burger. She lingers at the table, batting her eyelashes at him, which amuses me. Especially when he's only polite to her. When his gaze returns often to mine.

When she finally leaves to put in the food order, Chase turns the full force of his attention on me. "So, are you seeing anyone?"

"Ha," I say. "Between single-parenting a six-year-old and running a bar I don't exactly have time for dating."

He leans across the table. "Good. You know I like to have you to myself."

I remember this about him. The intensity of his focus. It was one of the things that appealed to me back then. I'm in charge in every other aspect of my life—but when Chase and I were alone, all I had to do was follow the map he drew to my own pleasure.

"Now," he says, sitting up straight. "I suppose we should make appropriate small talk before I get arrested for public indecency."

"Right." I smile at the thought that I'm having this effect on him. "What do you suggest?"

"Tell me about the bar."

"It's been good." I lean back, sip at my half-finished beer. "The weekend crowd has picked up since that profile in *The Seattle Times*—did you see it?"

Chase nods, a little of the predatory gleam fading from his eyes. "I did. It looked nice in the photos; they must have picked their angles."

I ignore the slight dig in the name of diplomacy. And Corona. "The profiler was here for days," I say. "Every business in town was trying to get them to pass through. Mostly they hung out at Max Ryan's studio retreat and the Verdad Records offices, obviously, but they meandered around a bit, too."

Chase smirks. "How hard did you have to campaign to get them in for karaoke?"

I shrug, like it was no big thing. Like I didn't ask Inez to call one of the local queer farmers she skill-shares with who happens to be Max Ryan's new wife's childhood best friend. "When you're the only bar in town, you don't really have to campaign," I say, leaning back in my chair, looking up at him with what I know is a cocky smirk.

He leans forward again, and I can almost see what he's seeing. The table cleared. The restaurant empty. Me on my back.

Sasha, who can really pick her moments, arrives with the food then. We make casual conversation about the tourism and the industry and profit margins, but our hearts aren't in it—a fact that becomes obvious when Chase extends his legs under the table. Starts rubbing his foot against my thigh.

My phone buzzes a few minutes later and I reach for it, thinking maybe it's Inez with a question about Parker. But it's Chase, who's smirking at me from across the table.

CHASE: How soon can we get out of here?

The heat spreads. When was the last time someone touched me who wasn't passing me a five-dollar bill across the bar? When was the last time someone looked at me like I was desirable?

"Sasha?" I ask when she walks by from the patio. "Can we get the check?"

I still have half a steak left. It doesn't matter—we both know conversation and the delights of Badger's cuisine aren't the real reasons we're here.

In the deserted parking lot out back, Chase grabs my hand, pushing me up against his sleek Seattle-young-professional car, his mouth a hair's breadth from mine.

"Kiss me," he demands, and I know the girl I was a year ago would have obeyed. But something inside me bristles at the order.

"Kiss *me*," I counter, and he chuckles indulgently before closing the distance.

Teeth and tongues tangle. I used to melt for him, but I find myself exerting equal pressure now. Competing instead of collaborating.

"I like this side of you," he says, as I break our kiss to graze my teeth across his neck. He opens the car door smoothly behind him without letting up, pivoting so that when we find our way inside I'm in his lap.

My legs hang out the open door. His hands move to my chest, groping frantically at my barely-there breasts in their sports bra beneath the shark shirt. Ridiculously, I think of my dream then. Inez's ample bust straining against the red lace.

Suddenly, my body is electric again, the image refusing to leave my mind. Chase's fingers make their way toward the waistband of my borrowed jeans and I'm hungry for him in a way I wasn't a few minutes ago, considering having it out right here, the dream and the reality a hopeless tangle in my mind.

"Wait," I whisper, needing to untangle it. Needing to not have an orgasm in a parking lot while thinking of my best friend in a holiday negligee. "We should probably take this somewhere a little more private, don't you think?"

"Why not both," he says. "I'll take care of you here, and we can finish up properly in my hotel room."

In my mind's eye, Inez's negligee loses the battle at last. I push Chase's hand away. "I have a child," I tell him, a little irritably. "I can't be seen finger-banging in a car in a parking lot on a Tuesday night. I need walls and doors." *And a few minutes to get my head on straight*.

He backs off, but it's clear the moment has shifted. "You're bossier than you used to be," he says. This time it doesn't sound like a compliment. "I'll have to get used to that when I'm back."

I stand up, hitting my head on the car and swearing. I'm not sure which part of this is more upsetting. "What do you mean *when you're back*?" I ask when he joins me outside. The whole point of this was that it was supposed to be no strings. Suddenly this isn't sounding at all like that.

Chase, eyes still heavily lidded, runs a hand through his hair. "I didn't want to tell you like this, but I have . . . a surprise. The real reason I'm down here."

He waits, all but daring me to ask him to explain.

"Well?" I say, when waiting him out doesn't work. "This kind of suspense doesn't make great foreplay. What's going on?"

"Kings is thinking of opening a franchise here," he says, and my whole body begins to freeze one muscle at a time. "That's what I'm doing in town. Taking the temperature. Looking at a few possible locations."

"A Kings franchise? In Ridley Falls?" I ask, hearing my voice as if through a long tunnel.

I hate everything I know about Kings—the cookie-cutter hipster bars/venues Chase was hired to manage. They have no personality. No charm. They don't support or depend on their communities. They're all owned by some huge restaurant corporation and they hire people with perfect teeth to manage them.

But to open one here? It would be the end of Joyce's. We barely scrape by as it is, and that's just because we're the only bar in town. If we had real competition, backed by Seattle corporate money, it would be game over.

"Yeah," Chase is saying, as if this is some delightful secret he's letting me in on. "It's like you said in there, this town is getting some great publicity with the label and the studio retreat. The *Seattle Times* piece got the attention of the money guys. They say there's a boom in tourism coming over the next few years and they want in. It's exciting."

My frozen head is spinning now. I'm a human margarita machine. Everything Chase is saying is true. It's also in my perpetually half-finished business plan for renovating Joyce's. Building a legit stage for live music, creating some ambiance, developing a real food menu sourced locally from all the amazing farms.

I've been telling myself for two years I'll pitch it to the owners. And now it might be too late.

Chase is still talking in that smooth, confident way of his, seemingly oblivious to my tumultuous inner monologue. "My boss knew I was from Ridley Falls, told me to come here and get some pictures of available venues, see if we'd have support from the locals. If he likes what he sees I'll get to make the pitch myself. It could be a real step forward for me."

He turns toward me, smoldering again as though I'm not a solid block of ice.

"And of course, the idea of seeing you again was icing on the cake. Tell me it wouldn't be great. Me, back here running a Kings franchise. You and me, picking up where we left off?"

Finally, the ice shatters. I take a definitive step back from Chase. "A Kings franchise in Ridley Falls would *kill* Joyce's," I say. "Like, flat-out murder it. You have to know that."

Chase, catching sight of my expression, finally seems to understand that I'm not thrilled by this news. He shifts into pacifying mode and I hate it. "I'd never do anything to hurt Joyce's," he says patronizingly. "They'll have completely different vibes. I'm sure it'll be fine."

From frozen, my blood begins to boil. "You're *sure* it would be *fine*?" I ask. "I work there, Chase. I live in the apartment out back. The owners pay for my kid's health insurance. I'm not really stoked about gambling my entire future on your best guess about the *vibes*."

"Cash, there's no need to get so upset. You're way too good for that place, anyway. If the worst happened, you could get a job anywhere. Hell, I'll hire you at the new Kings, how about that?"

I don't know which desire is stronger—to explain exactly how offensive that statement is or to get out of here as soon as possible.

"You're unbelievable," I say, shaking my head, turning to walk back to my car.

"You can't be serious," he calls after me. "You're not leaving over this."

"Watch me," I say over my shoulder. Then I get in my car, pulse pounding, and drive home long before I ever expected to.

4

WHEN I PULL up to the house, it's not even ten. I know I closed Joyce's myself at six-thirty, but the sight of it, closed up, sign off, depresses me even more now that I know what Chase is planning.

I can so easily imagine there's already a Kings across town, music blaring, parking lot filled to the brim as this place—*my* place—withers away like a lime slice in the garnish tray.

For a second after I turn off my car, I consider starting it back up and leaving again. I don't want to admit how the date ended to Inez after she worked so hard. But this is Ridley Falls on a weekday night. Where else am I going to go?

Don't freak out, I text her before I get to the front door. I'm about to come in.

I ease the door open in case Parker is asleep in the living room, expecting chaos and glitter and pizza boxes. *Frozen* playing on mute. Instead, it opens to reveal my living room. Cleaner than it's been since before I moved in.

Parker is nowhere to be seen, and neither are the hundred blankets and pillows—or, from what I can tell, a single speck of pink glitter.

"How . . . ?" I say wearily.

"Damn, you're so early!" Inez exclaims, closing her book and hopping up off the couch. "I wanted to have the rest of the laundry done!"

The stuff we washed yesterday is all folded, and so are at least half of the blankets, pillowcases, sheets, and towels in the house. Walking in farther, I see that even the kitchen is spotless.

Weirdly, between the high emotion of Chase's revelation, the little sleep I've gotten this week, and the shock of seeing my kitchen table for the first time in a month, I'm fighting back tears. "Thanks," I say, facing away from Inez so she won't catch on. "This is really amazing."

"Are you *crying*?" she demands, clearly not fooled by my attempts at deception. She stomps around to stand in front of me, looking furious. "What the hell did that asshole do to you? I'll kill him!"

The tears give way to laughter. She relaxes a little.

"No, no, it's not like that. I mean, I don't honestly know what it's like." I struggle to find the words to encompass everything that happened tonight. The feeling that I wasn't the same girl who enjoyed Chase's handsome guy aura last year. The dream, and the way it cropped up at the least opportune moment. The Kings franchise . . . Joyce's, doomed.

I hadn't even planned on telling her about that last part yet, but suddenly another secret between us seems like a choice. So I collapse onto one of the kitchen chairs—newly cleared of laundry—and cover my face with my hands.

"Turns out Chase wasn't just here for a social visit," I say through my fingers.

Inez plops on the chair across from me and gasps. "Wait, let me guess—he's getting married! Or, wait, he's already married. He has a secret baby. That was actually his twin!"

"He's here to open a Kings franchise in Ridley Falls," I say, largely to stop her from listing soap opera tropes. "The *money guys* think the attention we've been getting from the rockstars-in-residence and the *Times* piece are pointing to a surge in tourism. They want to get in on it."

For once, Inez appears momentarily speechless. She opens her mouth, then closes it, then opens it again. "But . . . that's exactly what you always say when you talk about renovating Joyce's," she finally manages. "A Kings franchise—"

"—totally kills that dream?" I finish for her. "And probably kills Joyce's? Yeah, pretty much."

Another long pause. "How far along are they?"

"He's here scouting potential venues and *gauging community support* to strengthen the presentation they're making to the board."

Inez whistles, long and low. "That's not a lot of time."

"Time to do what?" I ask, spreading my hands out helplessly. "Joyce's only survives because it's the only place in town. Chase will find them a more convenient location. The company has money to run a bunch of opening promotions. Bring in big bands. You think our karaoke-night crowd will keep showing up if they have the option of real shows? A sound system that isn't held together with duct tape? Fucking . . . fusion appetizers and signature cocktails? We're toast."

Inez has a familiar sparkle in her eye as I run out of steam. One that usually means she's got a wild idea I'm going to futilely protest until she ultimately gets her way.

"Cash, you need to finish your business plan," Inez says, leaning across the table in a way that I *refuse* to let remind me of my dream. "Now that George and Linda are facing real competition they'll have no choice but to invest or lose the place. This is your moment to strike!"

To my immense surprise, I don't hate this idea. In fact, it actually seems kind of perfect.

"They don't have the money," I protest feebly. "Not for a renovation that will make Joyce's competitive with a place like Kings."

"But it's not about the money," Inez says. Her cheeks are flushed. Her hair, adorably, gets twice as big when she's feeling passionate about something. She gets up and starts to pace around the kitchen as I slump even lower into my chair. "Joyce's is a community hub! A gathering place! It's the *soul* of Ridley Falls!"

"That might be overstating it a little . . ." I say, feeling my face flush, too. But I don't hate the picture she's painting. Of a place that's something more than just tall cans and karaoke. More than the only bar in town.

"You are as good a bar manager as stupid Chase or anyone else in stupid Seattle." She stops abruptly, leaning across the table again. "We have to try, Cash. We have to *make* George and Linda say yes."

This time, it's impossible not to think of the dream I had about her last night. The way she leaned just like this across the bar in red lingerie. And now I'm remembering more than just the dream. I'm remembering being in the car with Chase, and thinking of Inez, and how my body responded . . .

"I'll pull out the business plan," I say, a little hoarsely, when I realize she's waiting for me to respond. "I guess it can't hurt to try, right?"

"Anything's better than that slimeball stealing all our business,"

Inez practically growls. Thankfully, she stands up. "Oh, sorry, I didn't even ask how the date went."

There's no way to extricate it all, I realize. Chase and Kings and Joyce's.

"It was already pretty tepid before he told me he's here to ruin my life," I manage. "I don't think there would have been a second date even if he wasn't here to ruin my life."

"Sorry," Inez says with a sympathetic expression. "We'll find you someone. I'm sure there has to be *one* man out there who isn't a total asshole."

"You're sure?" I ask, raising an eyebrow skeptically.

Inez tosses her hands up. "I'm a lesbian!" she cries. "I'm doing the best I can!"

I laugh, trying not to look too closely at her. I don't know if I can handle any more reminders of that dream or anything that came after it. I must look tired, because Inez starts collecting her stuff.

"I should let you get to bed," she says. "Parker ate a slice and a half, passed out around nine. The last load of towels is in the dryer. Her clothes are picked out for school tomorrow, and we made her lunch. It's in the fridge. Get some sleep, okay?"

"I love you," I say, overcome with relief. It's not the first time I've said it, obviously, but it's the first time I've said it within twenty-four hours of a dream where she's in lingerie. My face gets hot again. I hope she doesn't notice.

"I love you, too," she says casually, checking the contents of her bag and pulling out her keys. "I'll see you tomorrow, yeah?"

"Yeah."

When she's gone, I flop down on the couch, utterly spent but knowing there's one more thing I need to do before I can trust myself to sleep.

I open my phone's browser and type into the search bar, looking around furtively as if there's anyone here besides me.

Is it normal to have lesbian dreams when you're straight?

The first thing that comforts me about the results is that there are thirty-three million of them. Apparently I'm not the first person to have this question, or this problem. The second thing that comforts me is that everyone from psychiatrists to advice columnists to gynecologists to lesbians on reddit say it's not only normal, it's common.

And it doesn't mean I'm queer—though it might mean, according to one particularly New Agey site, that I have a deep fear of being judged by society. Which seems a little off the mark for someone who once had her buzz cut dyed leopard print, but that's not really the point right now.

I feel a thousand times lighter as I make my way up the stairs toward bed. I'm just a regular straight girl who had a regular sex dream about my lesbian best friend. No big deal at all.

I'm washing my car in the parking lot of Joyce's. It's a hot day, unseasonable for this time of year, I think as I dunk a giant sponge into a bucket and begin wiping the grime from the windshield.

The Jeep is really filthy, and I'm not even half done when Inez walks out the backdoor of the bar. I freeze with the sponge in my hand. She's wearing a virtually microscopic black bikini. One of those stringy ones that ties behind your neck.

Her hair is piled on top of her head in a curly bun with a few tendrils escaping around her face. "Need a hand?" she asks, smirking as she approaches the bucket and reaches in for another sponge.

My throat is too dry to respond. I can only nod as she wrings out the soapy water and steps in front of me, leaning over the hood of the car, moving the sponge in rhythmic circles. I know I should get back to work, but I find I'm rooted to the spot, transfixed by the sight of her curves. The creamy expanse of her skin. Her hips swiveling along with the movement of the sponge . . .

"Fuck," I mutter under my breath. I know there's some reason I shouldn't be staring at her like this, but for the moment I can't remember what it is. I can barely remember my own name.

Inez hears me. The swiveling stops. She looks over her shoulder. "What was that?" she asks, but her teasing tone says she knows exactly what I said. Exactly what the sight of her, barely dressed and gyrating, is doing to me.

I clear my throat. She turns, leaning her back against the car, extending her arms. "Maybe there's something you'd rather be doing than washing a car," she purrs, and it's all the invitation I need.

Stepping forward into the circle of her arms, I can feel her breasts in her damp bikini pressing against my T-shirt, her hips now grinding into my shorts instead of my front headlight. Our mouths hover inches apart. All my circuitry is overloaded. I can feel my pulse in places I've never felt it before.

"Kiss me already," she dares, sending another jolt through the inner workings. Diverting every ounce of electricity from my thinking brain.

But before our mouths can meet, before we can keep the promise made by the tension between our bodies, I hear Parker calling my name.

"*Mommy, I had a bad dream,*" she says, even though it's the middle of the day.

Something's wrong, but still it costs me something to pull away from Inez. From the taut urgency of her body perfectly matching up with the drumming of my pulse.

"Mommy, wake up."

And I do. In my bed, alone. The clock on the bedside table reads four in the morning. My heart is racing. The electricity from what I now know was a dream lingers on the surface of my skin.

Parker is standing over me, eyes wide, chin wobbly. "A bad dream?" I manage, even as my own dream stubbornly clings to my waking mind. The feeling of Inez's body against mine.

It's normal, I remind myself. *Perfectly normal. It doesn't mean anything.*

"Can you check the closet for monsters?" Parker asks.

"Of course."

I get out of bed, holding her hand on the way back to her room. I'm on autopilot as I turn on her light, getting down on my knees to peer under the bed, then into the closet, then in every corner. I look in the chest pocket of her pajamas when the room has been thoroughly swept, and she giggles.

"Sometimes our subconscious plays tricks on us when we're sleeping," I tell her as she wriggles back under her covers, her expression peaceful.

"Why does it do that?" Parker asks sleepily.

With a bikinied Inez still swiveling her hips in my mind's eye, I can only shake my head. "I don't know, pal," I say. "But we're a lot tougher than some imaginary monsters, right?"

"Right," Parker says with a huge yawn. She's asleep before I close the door behind me, and as I crawl back into my bed, more afraid to fall asleep than a six-year-old, I wish my own tricky subconscious could be so easily subdued.

5

THE NEXT MORNING, with Parker's clothes picked out and her lunch premade, we are in the front half of the drop-off line for the first time ever. Even Granny O'Connor gives me a thumbs-up as I pull away from the school.

I return it, trying not to think about my R-rated *totally normal* dream about her granddaughter in case she somehow reads the details on my face with those owlish old lady eyes.

Back at home, the hours before I start work seem much more significant without a mountain of laundry and dishes to do. But without my normal catch-up work to distract me there's little to do but obsess. Yes, the internet says same-sex erotic dreams are normal for straight people—but two in as many nights? And about your best friend?

I'm honestly afraid to google the specifics at this point.

Instead, I sit down at my clear kitchen table with my laptop and pull up the business plans for Joyce's expansion. The document says it hasn't been opened in over a year, but the plans still seem sound—if unfinished. I make some tweaks to what I already have before picking up where I left off.

The planning makes for a surprisingly good distraction, and before I know it it's time to open the bar. This gives me heart as I pack up my laptop, shower, and change. At least if my subconscious gets out of control, I have one effective strategy to subdue it.

Too bad I can't work on business plans in my sleep.

Inez's shift doesn't start until opening, so I spend the first hour in Zen-like solitude, stocking and wiping down tables and generally steeling myself to act normal when she arrives.

There are five minutes to go before the sign clicks on when the Wednesday Stitch-n-Bitch ladies arrive ahead of schedule.

"Sorry, Cash," the ancient Mrs. Blair says when I open the door to her frantic tapping. "I know we're early, but can I use your restroom?"

"Go ahead," I say, laughing as I let the rest of them in. "Y'all can go ahead and get set up, I'm ready for you."

Stitch-n-Bitch is a Wednesday Joyce's tradition that I think dates back to Joyce herself. When I first started here it was just a few of Ridley Falls' oldest biddies bringing their knitting in and complaining about the aches and pains of advanced age, but it's really blossomed since then.

Today, the crowd is all over the age and gender spectrum. They take up the big community table in the middle and several of its satellites, spreading out sewing, knitting, and crochet projects, greeting one another warmly.

A few of the moms from Parker's school are here, and the wife of Inez's farmer friend who put in a good word for us while the *Times* profiler was in town. She stands out with her platinum boy-band haircut and her full sleeve of tattoos, but everyone seems to love her—even the old folks.

"Brook!" they call, when she comes over holding a large basket. "How's little Zephyr?"

"A holy terror, thanks for asking," Brook says with a smile, then she veers toward me, basket in hand.

"Can I get you anything?" I ask, trying to suppress my delight that the Wednesday crowd is skewing bigger and younger than usual. That has to bode well for my plans.

"Absolutely," the woman says with a dazzling smile. She's wearing a button-down that reminds me of my borrowed date shirt. "I think we'd love as many mimosas as you can fit on that table. But I actually have a favor to ask you. A lot of the ladies here can't do fried food, so if I pay you a table fee would you mind if I hand these out?"

She opens the basket, which is full of an incredible assortment of what appear to be handmade pastries. Muffins, scones, turnovers, even croissants.

"Uh, sorry," I say, smirking. "But that's illegal and I'm gonna have to confiscate absolutely all of these. Also, if you see me stuffing them all in my face back here, no you didn't."

She laughs. "Maybe I could get you to look the other way if I gave you first pick?"

Pretending to look both ways furtively, I reach in and take a chocolate-dipped croissant. "This never happened."

"Pleasure *not* doing business with you," she says with a wink. "I'm Brook, by the way."

"Cash," I say. "You're new to the Stitch-n-Bitch, right? Welcome to Joyce's."

"Thanks," Brook replies with a smile and a hair flip. "I'm awful at knitting, so I need to butter the ladies up. If my wife doesn't think I'm making progress on a non-cooking, non-parenting hobby she's gonna tell our therapist on me."

I laugh, and she turns back to the table. Once I've provided the group with a stack of paper fry boats, napkins, and two pitchers of six-dollar champagne and orange juice, I sit back and watch. The scene before me further strengthens this morning's resolve to finish the business plan. At least fifteen folks that might never have come together under any other circumstances are trading tips on their fiber arts projects, proudly showing off their work, asking for advice and support.

It's amazing, I think, that Joyce's is the place they've chosen to gather. I need to find a way to protect it. For them, for Inez, for me and Parker and our future . . .

Near the register, I see my phone light up, interrupting my emotional moment. But before I can make my way to it, Inez bursts through the front door in a whirl of bag and hair and jacket, already apologizing.

"I'm *so* sorry," she says. "Granny swiped a stop sign. I had to pick her up in the Bug, which had a flat tire so Gladys and I had to change it while she was just waiting with the car. It's already been a *day*. What can I do to—?"

Before she can finish, Granny O'Connor comes in behind her. She doesn't look any worse for wear in her floral print crewneck and lime-green pants. A sun hat tilted back over her purple-tinged white hair.

She's got her knitting basket swinging from her shoulder— she's never missed a Stitch-n-Bitch, and apparently no minor vehicle damage is going to change that.

"Hey, Mrs. O'Connor," I say, still avoiding eye contact in case she can somehow sense the content of my dreams.

She turns those bird-of-prey eyes on me and I shudder at the feeling I'm being x-rayed down to my bones. "Cassandra," she caws. "I saw you with that little girl at the school today. Would it kill you to match her socks?"

"It's Cash," I say firmly. "And Parker likes her socks like that. Apparently it's the style these days."

I'm expecting admonishment, so I'm pleasantly surprised when her eyes soften. Drift toward Inez. "Well, it's good to let her express herself," she says. "You try to hold them to your expectations and you won't change them, you'll only lose them."

Inez has never told me the gory details of what happened between herself and her parents. All I know is that they used to live in Ridley Falls. Raised her here. And some time very shortly after she came out to them in eighth grade she went to live with Granny O'Connor on the farm for good.

"That's good advice," I say. "I'll keep it in mind."

She makes a little *humph* sound, then the sentiment clears from her expression and the eagle eyes are back. "Well, she has an excuse, Cassandra. No one expects a six-year-old to have a fashion sense. *You* on the other hand could do with some sprucing."

Mrs. Blair flags Granny down before I have a chance to respond, thankfully, and she toddles off to take her seat.

Inez returns from greeting everyone then, somehow draped in a rainbow knitted scarf and holding a massive blueberry muffin. Her cheeks are flushed. She's smiling and my face heats up as I remember the car wash. The black bikini . . .

"Sorry," she says, stashing her bag under the bar. "It's a circus over there."

"Granny seems in good spirits," I say, *perfectly normally*.

"She's all good," Inez says. "Though we're going to have to

have a tough conversation about driving this evening. Plus, the Bug has a new tire, which it's been needing for weeks now."

"And you expect me to believe *you* changed it?" I ask, unable to help it.

She waves a hand, as if to dismiss the minor details. "Gladys helped. And by that I mean she did most of it and I . . . supervised. But we got it done, that's the main thing."

Gladys is another one of Inez's roommates—a lesbian woman in her sixties who moved two counties over to live at the farm when her wife passed away last year. Parker adores her, and as far as old ladies go, I vastly prefer run-ins with Gladys to the unavoidable ones with Granny O'Connor.

"I'm glad everyone is okay," I say, shaking my head. "But next time you can call, you know. I could change a tire in my sleep."

"Duly noted," Inez says, then narrows her eyes at me. "Anyway, I expected you to be all mopey Eeyore this morning, but you seem . . . okay? Did I miss something?"

A very juicy dream about you sudsing a car barely dressed, my unhelpful brain supplies.

I open my mouth to mention the business plan when I'm interrupted by an exclamation from across the room.

"Ah, that's it exactly!" It's Mrs. Blair, as one of the moms from Parker's school finishes some complicated-looking yarn-twisting maneuver. "Thank you, dearie! I've been doing that wrong for fifty years!"

At the other end of the table, Granny O'Connor is eating a scone, regaling Brook and a few other ladies with the tale of today's mirror-meets-stop-sign conflict.

Looking back at Inez, I'm pleased to be thinking about Joyce's and not bikinis or cheesy lingerie. "You were right about the business plan," I say. "I started working on it this morning. I think I can have it finished in the next day or two if I work hard, and then we can pitch it to George and Linda."

Inez's face goes from confused to shocked to beaming in a matter of seconds. "Are you serious?" she asks. "I thought I was going to have to do *so* much more convincing."

I know it's just some misfiring from the dream, but my face flushes again at this.

"Uh, nope," I stutter, clearing my throat. "Nope. When you're right you're right. We can't just lie down and let Chase and Kings take over Ridley Falls. We may be the underdogs, but we have to try."

"Yay!" Inez squeals, before throwing herself into my arms.

We've hugged a thousand times, obviously. Mournful hugs and celebratory hugs and greeting hugs and parting hugs. How is it possible that this is the first time I've noticed what her hair smells like? Chamomile and roses. I pull away before I can compare the way her body is pressing into mine to the way it did in my dream.

Inez smiles again, dazzlingly bright. "This is going to work," she says. "I just know it."

When she leaves to get more mimosas for the table, I take a quiet moment to bury my head in my hands. I need to figure out how to get my subconscious under control before it ruins the best thing in my life.

6

INEZ INSISTS I let her handle closing tonight while I go home and work on the business plan. Normally I'd protest, but she's right. This should be the priority. And I need to put my overactive imagination on ice anyway.

I leave the bar in her capable hands when it's time to pick up Parker, and Inez promises to come by the moment the sign goes dark.

I'm sitting in the pickup line at school when I notice a text I must have missed earlier. It's from Chase—who I haven't given a second thought to since my save-Joyce's wheels started turning last night.

Hey, the message reads. I'm sorry about last night. I really didn't know Joyce's was such a big deal to you or I wouldn't have sprung it on you like that. Maybe there's some kind of compromise here—would you be willing to talk about it? I promise this isn't just because I want to pick up where we left off last night. Even though I do . . .

It's easily the most words he's ever sent me at once. I lock my phone, flopping my head against the seatback in frustration. The fact that he thinks there's any chance of us picking up where we left off after last night is insulting, obviously.

But maybe there is some way to compromise. If he really understood what Joyce's means to the community, to me, maybe there's enough love left for this place in that overly shellacked heart of his to convince him to end all this . . .

Back at home, I call next door and let the babysitter off the hook. I'm shocked all over again by how clean my house is, and how much time it frees up when I don't have to take care of it myself.

I push thoughts of Chase and Joyce's and the business plans entirely out of my mind as Parker eats her snack and tells me about her day. I wouldn't miss this for the world. Her little legs kick rhythmically as she devours crackers with peanut butter between lengthy explanations of the day's dramas.

". . . So then *I* said we shouldn't leave anyone out, but then *Madison* said no one could come in if they weren't wearing pink and *I* said that's being mean and *she* said if I couldn't beat her at jump rope we had to do it her way and *I'm* not very good at jump rope but I said okay but then the bell rang so we have to jump rope tomorrow and I'm *doomed*."

"Wow," I remark as she takes a very crumbly bite of cracker. "Madison doesn't sound very nice."

"Yeah," Parker says, mouth full of cracker. "But she's *really* good at jump rope so she pretty much always gets what she wants."

"No talking with food in your mouth," I remind her for at least the two-thousandth time in her life. "It's a choking hazard. Do you want the Heimlich today?"

She shakes her head solemnly before swallowing and showing me her peanut buttery tongue.

"Gross," I say. "But very thorough. Please continue."

"*Basically,*" she says, waving the next cracker in the air. "If I don't learn how to do, like, twenty skips with no tripping by tomorrow it's the *Madison* show. *Again.*"

"And we all know it's the *Parker* show around here, right?" I tease.

"Right," she says without irony. "But the Parker show is *not* about jump-roping."

I think hard about how to help. I'm not much of a rope jumper, and even if I was, Parker's legs are pretty short—not to mention she absolutely will not wear any shoes besides rain boots. The chances of getting her in fighting shape to square off with Madison tomorrow are very slim.

But then I think about my own situation. Kings, with all the jump rope skills in the world, and Joyce's with nothing but its reputation and a dream.

"Okay," I say as she finishes the last of the crackers. "What *is* the Parker show about?"

"Drawing rainbows and unicorns and baby animals and everyone being best friends even if they don't have the right clothes to go in the clubhouse," she answers, promptly, and in one breath.

"Best show ever," I say with a smile. "And it sounds like no one else really likes Madison's way of doing things either, right?"

Parker sighs. "She is beautiful, but she is *not* beloved," she says.

I stifle a laugh. "So what if, instead of letting Madison bully you into doing the thing *she's* best at, you get everyone involved? Have a vote about the clubhouse instead of letting her push you all around."

She chews on this harder than the peanut butter crackers.

"The thing is," she says. "Madison always has the *best* birthday parties. Her dad has a *pool* so everyone goes swimming and if she doesn't like you, you don't get invited. So what if everyone's too scared of getting disinvited to change her rules?"

It's a solid question, and I'm suddenly devoutly thankful I'm not enmeshed in the complex world of first grade recess politics. Parker waits patiently for me to respond, that hopeful little face turned up to mine with total confidence that I will be able to solve this problem—and any other she might be able to throw at me.

"Let me think on that one," I say.

She goes off to play paper dolls, and I sit down with my business plan, surprised to find inspiration still close to the surface even after the relative chaos of the day.

By the time Inez arrives after closing, the kitchen table is invisible again—this time under a pile of papers. Some of them are Parker's drawings, which she did to keep me company until she went to bed, but the grand majority are ideas. And I think I have a pile of mostly usable ones to finish the plans.

"Honey, I'm home!" she calls in her usual fashion. She breezes into the dining room carrying a six-pack from the walk-in and a mixing bowl full of Tater Tots—the only Joyce's food I'll eat. "I'd ask how the plans are coming, but I'm afraid you're abandoning me for a career as an artist."

Inez sets down the Tots and picks up a scrap of paper on which I tried (and obviously failed) to draw a carousel for Parker. She raises an eyebrow.

"It's a horse," I say with unearned confidence.

"Really." It's not a question. We both bust up laughing, and for a minute everything feels delightfully normal.

"So, I think I have it," I say when the laughter has subsided and half the Tater Tots are gone. "And it's perfect. Real stage for live music, kitchen upgrades, new floors and windows, even some marketing ideas that will expand our business past daytime tall cans and karaoke."

Inez is leaning back in the chair across from me, eyes half closed in post-shift, half-a-beer sleepiness. "Okay," she says. "It sounds great. So why do you look like someone kicked your puppy?"

Instead of answering out loud, which would make it too real, I slide a piece of paper with a series of numbers on it across the table. There's one circled at the bottom. A big, scary one.

When she sees it, Inez whistles. "That's the cost?"

I nod.

"And you think it's all totally necessary?"

"I've been over it a thousand times," I say, rubbing my eyes. "If we want to compete with a place like Kings, this is the bare minimum we can get away with."

For a long minute, there's silence. Inez sips her beer. I eat a few more tater tots. I had kind of hoped she'd tell me it was no big deal. That George and Linda would agree no problem. But if even Inez is worried, there's a reason to worry.

I try to envision my life without Joyce's and come up blank. It's the reason I moved here with a barely one-year-old and no support system. I googled *restaurant jobs with good health insurance* within two hundred miles of Portland and Joyce's was one of a handful of places that came up.

George interviewed me on the phone because I couldn't afford the bus ticket unless it was a sure thing. It seemed too good to be true—a living wage, benefits starting immediately, free use of one of the duplex units in the back. It wasn't just a chance to start over away from Parker's dad and the party scene I'd been part of since I dropped out of high school. It was a chance to save money, to find a community. To build an actual future for myself and the baby I could still hardly believe I had.

But none of that stands out as the first reason I can't imagine my life without Joyce's.

Across the table, Inez sits up suddenly, setting down her empty beer can. "It's gonna be fine," she declares.

Despite the dire circumstances, I smile. "Getting a psychic download?" I ask.

She ignores this. "George and Linda are old white business owners with a rental property, who take three cruises a year," she explains. "If they don't have the money in the bank they'll get a loan. That's what these people do. This is going to happen, Cash. We're gonna build the bar of your dreams and run that handsome scumbag out of town and everything is going to be fine."

This is the confidence I was hoping for, and even though I know she can't possibly be sure, it comforts me. It was the first thing I loved about Inez—the way she made the impossible seem not only possible, but like a foregone conclusion.

"What would I do without you?" I ask, aware this isn't the first time I've asked her this question in the past week.

"You'd figure it out," she says, waving a hand. But she doesn't break eye contact, and I don't laugh.

"No," I say. "I really don't think I would."

There's a charged pause that I attribute entirely to my dreams scrambling my brain, and I shake myself mentally.

"Wow, I'm exhausted," I say, slightly too loud.

Inez stands up. "Yeah, I should get out of your hair."

It's after midnight, and she looks tired, too. "Stay," I say. "You shouldn't be driving so late, you know your night vision is crap."

"Hey!" she says, swatting my arm. "I can see fine!"

"You could if you wore the glasses they prescribed you for astigmatism," I agree.

"The ones that make me look like an owl who stuck its tongue in the toaster? Pass."

"You'll make a very beautiful roadside corpse," I say. "And then where will we be?"

There's a brief pause, and then Inez throws up her hands. "You know I was gonna stay anyway, there was no need to bring my astigmatism into this."

Inez has stayed here countless times over the past two years. Late bar shifts, nights out, disastrous dates nearby, any and all of them have ended with her on the couch. She even has one of my T-shirts for her express pajama purposes and a toothbrush in the cabinet above the bathroom sink.

But for reasons I'm all too aware of, it feels different heading up the stairs together tonight.

She goes straight for the T-shirt drawer once we're in my room, pulling out the oldest and softest of my Joyce's shirts and promptly taking off her own over her head, revealing a black bra not dissimilar from the bikini my subconscious conjured during its absurd— but *totally normal*, according to the internet—car-washing dream.

The jeans follow, and I know this is par for the course, but it feels voyeuristic in a way it never did before. Not because the sight of Inez in her underwear has changed, but because she doesn't know about the dreams, and maybe if she did she'd choose to get undressed somewhere else.

This whole friendly intimacy thing we have going is based on the inalienable truth that we have a completely platonic relationship—which we *do*, I remind myself—but the dreams make it feel less safe than it used to. I'm suddenly afraid I'm not being fair to her, but I also absolutely cannot tell her, so I'm frozen.

"You good?" she asks, standing in the middle of my bedroom floor in her underwear as I look studiously at the carpet.

"Y-yeah," I say. "I'm just gonna grab a shower actually."

"Cool," Inez says, unhooking the bra deftly behind her.

"Be right out," I say hurriedly, and dash for the hallway before anything else can be revealed.

Under the punishing spray of the extra-hot shower, I loosen up physically and mentally. I'm being totally ridiculous, and I know that. Inez and I are best friends. Nothing has changed because my subconscious is suddenly on a cliché '80s-music-video-fantasy bender.

Telling her about the dreams would be ridiculous, because they don't change anything. When I look at her in real life, without the lens of the dream world, I still feel exactly like I used to.

Feeling better, I turn off the water, towel off, and make my way into the bedroom to get dressed. Inez must already be downstairs, so I make my way down in my shirt and boxers to find her snuggled under the blanket she always uses, looking half asleep already.

"Sorry," I say.

"For showering?" she asks, smirking. "Please, I should be thanking you."

"Ha ha," I say from the base of the stairs. "All right, you know where everything is, I'm gonna pass out. Apologies in advance for the noise we're gonna make getting ready for school in the morning."

"First, I'm used to it," she replies. "Second, I have three room-mates, four dogs, six chickens, and a goat. Not to mention the don-keys. You know I can sleep through anything."

"Fair point," I concede, laughing. "Okay well, goodnight."

"Night!" Inez calls from under the blanket.

My shower pep talk seems to have done me some good, because I don't bother googling anything before going to sleep. No one is responsible for their dreams. They're just the random misfiring of unconscious brain cells. And I'm sure this particular trend is al-ready over . . .

In the earliest hours of the morning I wake to my door creaking open, light from the hallway falling across the floor. It must be Inez, the footsteps are far too quiet to be Parker's.

"You okay?" I ask groggily, sitting up in bed. "What time is it?"

She doesn't answer, just pads silently across the floor toward the bed. She's wearing my T-shirt still, her long legs bare, her curls hanging down her back. Her eyes are wide, reflecting the moonlight coming in through the window. She looks determined, and she doesn't stop when she reaches the edge of the bed.

"Inez," I say. "What—"

But the rest of the question sticks in my throat as she lifts the covers and slides beneath them. I know I should stop her. That I *just* told myself this was a dream-only phenomenon, but the smooth skin of her legs against mine feels so good.

"Cash," she whispers. "I want you."

There are a hundred reasons why this can never happen, but my mind fills with static when I try to access them. There's only the pounding of my pulse everywhere. The electricity when she moves closer, her hands grazing the skin of my exposed thigh.

"*Fuck*," I hear myself moan. "We can't."

"Why not? Because you're straight? It doesn't mean you can't be curious . . ."

She's looking up at me through long lashes. I know she won't make a move unless I say it's okay. I have all the power in this situation, so why do I feel so helpless?

The charge from earlier tonight is back, magnified by a thousand. I can feel the pounding traveling lower, from my throat to my chest to my belly, gathering at my center until I'm slick and throbbing and needy.

I'm kissing her before I can stop myself, giving over to the sensations now overpowering my conscious mind. I can tell by the greedy way she runs her hands over my skin that she's just as far gone as I am. She kisses my neck, her hands drifting to the waistband of my boxers, every inch of my skin is on fire where she trails her fingers.

"Please," I gasp when she stops at the waistband. My head is tilted back, my entire body tight as a guitar string, desperate to be plucked by her . . .

7

I WAKE UP gasping. Disoriented. The room is bathed in sunlight and Inez is nowhere to be seen.

It takes me several minutes to calm my heart rate. To separate the dream from reality.

Inez was never here, I tell myself. *She slept downstairs on the couch.*

My mind understands faster than my body, which is still half in that moonlit reality where my *female* best friend's hand is sliding into my waistband and I'm absolutely dying for her to touch me.

Unfortunately, the feelings the dream conjured have had some very real consequences. I shift beneath my blankets, feeling how wet and sensitive I still am. Before I can think it through, my hands are drifting down, knowing there's only one thing that can release this awful tension.

With a full-time job and a first-grader, self-pleasure is a luxury I can rarely afford, but everything is quiet, and my fingers are nearly there, and I know I won't take long with how incredibly turned on I am, and—

Wait, I interrupt myself. *Why is it quiet? What* time *is it?*

I pull my hand ruthlessly out of my boxers and scramble for the phone on my bedside table. "That can't be right," I say out loud. It's almost nine. Parker has never slept this late in her life, we're already late for school.

Jumping out of bed, I ignore the disappointed protests of my unsatisfied libido, throwing on my clothes at hyperspeed and tearing out into the hallway.

"Parker!" I call as I approach her room. "We're late, pal, I'm sorry. You gotta get ready pronto, okay?"

No answer. It's not like her to sleep past the crack of dawn, but her room is empty. Is she already downstairs? I have several consecutive visions of her plugging things in, or deciding today is the day she walks to school on her own. *How* could I have let myself sleep this late?

When I reach the living room, the couch is empty, too. The throw blanket folded over the arm. Why the hell wouldn't Inez have woken me up?

I'm about to truly lose it when I notice the note folded on the coffee table.

DON'T PANIC, it says in block letters. READ ME.

Feeling totally out of step, I pick it up and unfold it.

Don't be mad, it reads. Parker got to school on time with an amazing lunch, and we had a great morning. We were both happy you got a little extra sleep. Text me after you talk to G+L and I'll see you tonight for karaoke. Xo, Inez

The panic slowly begins to release its grip. Parker is at school. Inez is gone. I have an hour until I need to be at work. Everything is okay.

I'm not proud to admit that the first thought I have is returning to bed and finishing what I almost started up there. But I'm fully awake now, and dressed, and this note is reminding me of all the reasons why it would be *insane* to go to bed and get myself off thinking about a woman—but especially this woman.

Instead, I take another shower. This one is ice-cold, and it helps me return to my senses. I can't deny that three dreams in three nights is tough to dismiss—but when I really think about Inez, about our friendship, about our life, I don't want anything to change. That should be enough to get me through until my sub-conscious develops a new, less inconvenient fixation, right?

All I can do is push forward. Focus on the business. One catas-trophe at a time.

To that end, I read back over my business plan one last time, steeling myself to call George and Linda. They're in Alaska visit-ing their son for the next month, but they're usually good about answering calls.

When I feel ready—or as ready as I'm going to be—I sit down with a cup of tea amid the papers and drawings and take a deep breath. Inez is counting on me, I tell myself. And so is Parker.

George Waylon answers on the second ring. "Cassandra! How's our favorite second-in-command?"

I roll my eyes at the use of my given name for the second time in two days. No one under the age of sixty has dared to call me Cassandra since I was twelve. "It's Cash, George, and I'm doing well. How's Alaska?"

"Oh, it's great, Cash, thanks for asking. Listen, is everything okay at the bar? You don't call too often so you've got me wor-ried."

A deep breath. A reminder of what's at stake. "Well, George, that's why I'm calling. Everything's fine for the moment, but I got some unsettling news recently." I launch into my spiel about Kings. The one I practiced three times before I called. The one that makes it sound like Sauron is installing a franchise of his all-seeing-eye in downtown Ridley Falls.

"Oh, shoot, well that's a shame to hear," George says. "We always liked that Ridley Falls has that small-town feel."

"Right," I say. "That's kind of what I was hoping to talk to you about. See, if Joyce's can't upgrade a bit, add a new stage for live music, maybe a food menu, I don't know if we're going to be able to compete with a place like Kings."

George is silent, so I press on.

"I've run the numbers, and with a Kings open in city limits I think we've got six months before we're no longer turning a profit. And you know what a tight margin it is, even now."

"I hear you, Cash," he says. But I hear him, too. This is the same tone I've been met with anytime I've asked for a fix involving money. "But the stuff you're talking about, that's big money. Kitchen upgrades, renovations, new staff . . ."

Hearing the defeat in his tone, I cut in. "Listen, George, we can get it done for way less than any contractor will quote you. Some of it I can do myself, so we'll only need materials, and I know I can get some help from friends around town."

"What's the number, kiddo?" he asks when I pause for breath.

"It's twenty thousand." The words fall like a lead balloon. "But it's twenty thousand for forty thousand's worth of work, George. And it's an investment that will absolutely pay off in time, especially when the alternative is going under."

The resulting pause only sinks my hopes further. While I wait what feels like an eternity for him to speak, I'm forced to acknowledge that we might actually be done for. That Joyce's will be gone.

"I'm really sorry, Cash," George says finally. "But we couldn't even get close to that much. And we love the place, of course, but we'll just have to see if it sinks or swims with a little competition."

You don't understand anything, I think hollowly. *How can you love a place you won't save?*

"I know it's a lot of money," I say feebly. "But I thought . . . maybe a loan . . . ?"

"No." George's voice is firm this time, and there's no pause to precede it. "We can't go into debt over this. Everyone knows the restaurant industry is fickle, sweetheart, we'll just do the best we can with what we have. Now, if that's all—"

"—Wait." I know I'm pushing my luck. That the best option is to hang up, strategize, and try again another time. But I can't take the thought of the place Inez and I built together going under because of some idiot like Chase or some skeezy franchise, so instead of that imminently reasonable course of action, I say something very stupid: "What if you didn't have to pay for it? What if I could get the money myself?"

"Now, how the hell are you gonna do that?" George asks, and I know he's getting impatient. The worst part is, I don't have an answer. Not yet anyway.

"I'm not sure," I admit. "But if I can figure out a way . . . will you let me make the improvements?"

There's muffled conversation on the other end, and I know George is talking to Linda, his wife. This can't be bad news for me, Linda loves Parker like the grandmother she never had. Maybe she can convince George that Joyce's is worth saving.

"Cash, you there?" George asks.

"Still here."

"Hi, honey," Linda says, tinny like she's on speaker phone.

"Hey, Linda."

"So listen," Linda says. "We know how much you've put into Joyce's, and I'm sure the idea of losing it is just as heartbreaking for you as it is for us. We can put five thousand toward the renovations, but that's the best we can do, honey. If you can raise the rest, we're happy to sign off on changes, but I want you to think about this. It's just a bar. I'm sure you could get a job at that new one, or anywhere else you wanted. You know we'd give you an amazing reference."

I wish so much in that moment that I were better with words. That I could explain what Joyce's means to me beyond just a job and a free apartment. This is Parker's home. It's a place for community. It's a place that feels like mine, even though this conversation is reminding me painfully just how little right I have to that claim.

"I have thought about it," I say, lying through my teeth. "Five thousand is a great start, Linda, thank you. I'll be in touch soon with details about the rest."

"Okay, Cash," Linda says, and I can hear the pity oozing from her tone. She doesn't believe I can do this. Not for a second. "Bye now."

"Goodbye."

Thursday is the one day a week I don't get to leave early to pick up Parker. It'll be all-hands-on-deck after three as we brace for our busiest night. But in the morning it's just me.

There's no time to think about the absurd idea I pitched George and Linda today with karaoke on the horizon, which is a blessing. Fifteen thousand dollars? I might as well have promised them I could fly to the moon with wings made of Joyce's napkins and little plastic cocktail swords.

My phone buzzes a few minutes before opening, just as I'm finishing the garnish trays. It's Inez, of course. How did it go?

I'm still struggling with how to respond when Charlie and Mo arrive right at eleven. On a Thursday, they're either getting their games in before the rush or staking out their table for the festivities. Today it seems to be the latter. This morning's featured argument is about who sang "Always on My Mind" better, Willie Nelson or Elvis.

"Willie did it first!" Mo exclaims over darts and High Life. "It's better suited to his register!"

"The King never met a song he couldn't improve," Charlie insists. "He was once in a lifetime!"

I take the welcome distraction from this unanswerable text, grabbing a broom to sweep under the pool table. "How about you geezers have a sing-off tonight? Mo sings Willie, Charlie sings Elvis and we'll let the crowd decide."

"You're on, little missy," Charlie's saying, pointing at me with a dart.

"Who are you calling *geezer*?" Mo complains from beneath his fishing hat.

A few more people trickle in throughout the early afternoon. It's already three when I realize I never texted Inez back. Probably for the best; aren't you supposed to deliver extremely unhinged news in person, anyway?

When Eduardo (our backup bartender) arrives, I take my lunch break to spend a precious few minutes with Parker at home—who is coloring at the coffee table while her fifteen-year-old babysitter scrolls on her phone on the couch.

"Hey, y'all," I say as Juliana guiltily stows the phone. "Everything going good?"

"Mama!" Parker screeches, leaping up and running for me with her stuffed snake trailing behind her.

I catch her with an *oof*, grateful but perplexed by this display of affection. Parker has taken to acting very nonchalant about my comings and goings, which I'm told is a sign of healthy attachment, but still, I don't mind the validation.

"What's up, pal?" I ask as she pulls back, giving me a rare kiss on the cheek. "Good day?"

"Mama, you won't believe it!" she says earnestly.

"Believe what?"

"We had a vote, and everyone agreed that Madison can't *gatekeep* the clubhouse anymore!"

I really want to ask where she learned the word *gatekeep*, but there's no time. "How'd you pull that off?" I ask.

"Easy," Parker says with a shrug. "I told them all my birthday party is gonna be two hundred times better than Madison's. That we're gonna have a stage, and ice cream, and even donkeys."

"Parker," I say carefully. "Why would you tell everyone that?"

"Because it's true! Your work has a stage, Auntie Inez has donkeys, and every party has ice cream."

The confidence with which she says all this reminds me too much of my own bluff with George and Linda earlier to make me truly angry. Instead I kneel down and put my hands on her shoulders.

"Listen, pal," I say. "That was a big promise to make without knowing for sure. So big that it was actually closer to a lie than a promise, does that make sense?"

"So, we can't have the party," Parker says, defeated.

"I'm not saying that, necessarily, but I am saying you need to check with the adults that make these things happen before you go promising kids donkeys and ice cream just to get your way, okay?"

"'Kay," Parker says, the wind let out of her sails a little.

"I know it can feel good to make a big promise," I say, too aware of the ticking clock on this very important lesson. "But remember that people judge us more by our actions than our words, so make sure they match up, got it?"

"Got it." But she's got a gleam in her eye again. "If I make the stage myself out of boxes and ask Auntie Inez about the donkeys maybe could we—"

I hold up a hand. "For now I want you to think about matching up your words and actions," I tell her. "We can talk about the party once you understand that part."

She nods, hugging me again. "Okay. But I do understand."

"I know. Now be good for Juliana and I'll see you in the morning."

Once my time with Parker is over, I remind Juliana that the phone is for emergencies only while she's on the clock and then it's time for me to head back to the bar. From the back door, I can tell the lot is already filling up.

Inside, there are a few folks milling around—most of them are Thursday regulars who greet me by name. They're here to claim tables before the festivities start. I spot Larry Cross (the town's only Lyft driver) in his tie-dye Grateful Dead best, Mrs. Blair from Stitch-n-Bitch, Sasha from Badger's, Ginny and Brad from Ponderosa's, and a handful of the kids from the patio the night of my "date" with Chase.

Inez is here now, and I'm slightly relieved we won't be alone tonight. If for no other reason than the fact that keeping this huge secret from her is getting weirder and weirder. I try to remember the last time I had a problem I didn't tell her about and draw a blank. Although, to be fair, none of my other problems have involved involuntary fantasies of her wearing very little clothing.

I can tell she wants to ask about George and Linda, but it's time for the pre-karaoke huddle, so I pull Eduardo in, too.

"Remember," I tell them, "upsell to more expensive liquor when you can but *never to our regulars.* Business owners and community bigmouths get one of their drinks comped whenever you think it'll inspire loyalty. Above all, *no one* drinks and drives. You know who to watch out for. Larry's on the clock, and I can drive a few people home at closing time, but mostly just keep an eye out and don't overserve, okay? Making more money isn't worth anyone getting hurt."

Eduardo nods. He's not much for talking. George and Linda hired him as a handyman ten years ago, but shortly after I became manager he approached me one day and said he'd always wanted to be behind the bar. He said he never felt right asking Chase or the bosses, but with *gente* in charge he felt more comfortable.

It was one of those heartwarming moments every mixed kid carries around in their back pocket. People don't usually clock me as Mexican—my white dad's genes sort of overpowered the color palette—but that day Eduardo really saw me, and I was all too happy to return the favor.

"Aye-aye, Captain," Inez says, putting her hand in. I laugh and put mine in, too. Hers is warm to the touch and soft beneath my calloused fingertips. After a little cajoling, Eduardo joins us.

"Joyce's on three," I say, as the door opens and more karaoke hopefuls spill in. "One . . . two . . . three . . . *Joyce's!*"

The folks at the bar overhear and cheer. Next to an empty bar with all its potential, this is my favorite version of Joyce's. Standing room only, these four walls containing the kind of community joy that only a tiny speaker and a karaoke microphone can engender.

We're moving nonstop until 6:45. Serving drinks and fries, making small talk with the regulars, introducing ourselves to the few folks we don't recognize. Inez catches me behind the bar after a while, bumping my shoulder with hers.

"You've been elusive," she says as I pour a microbrew for a new guy in a flannel shirt and ironic trucker hat. "How did it go today?"

"Hey, thanks so much for taking Parker in this morning."

"No problem," she says. "But George and Linda? What did they say?"

"It's . . . kind of a long story," I reply, topping off the pint glass with a regulation inch of creamy white foam. "I'll tell you after."

"Got it," she says, unbothered. She trusts me, I realize, and I feel worse than ever.

People judge you by your actions more than your promises. Ugh. If only I could parent myself along with my six-year-old.

A few minutes later, I'm scooping ice in the back when Inez calls out: "I need a bucket of Coors Light!"

I look up with interest. No one ever orders a bucket. And Coors Light? This is a Miller High Life town. I find Inez at the end of the bar before I find the guys who ordered. Her eyebrows have disappeared into her fringe, and she's looking at me like she's trying to burn words into my brain telepathically.

As casually as I can manage, I sweep the group in front of her looking for the culprits. It takes me a while to find them over the hair of Donna Mae (of Donna Mae's Beauty Salon), but when I do I can't look away.

Standing at the front of a knot of men in suits is Chase, wearing a blazer and a smirk. He's already looking at me but looks away when I catch him. The guys he's with can only be members of Kings corporate—a bunch of smarmy, overdressed, over-gelled white guys laughing in that loud, pompous way that feels like sandpaper on my nerves.

"Bucket of Coors coming up," I call back to Inez, as if this is normal, and then I stomp back to the storeroom to fetch the bucket.

I'm just considering filling it with dirty mop water when the door eases open behind me. "I knew you'd have to come back here for the bucket."

The idea that he thinks he can use some seductive voice on me after everything he's done is infuriating. I want to throw the ice in his face.

"This area is for employees only," I say coldly.

"Oh, come on, make an exception for an old friend."

"I don't see a friend, I see a traitor," I say, spinning around to face him. I know there was a time when I saw something appealing in him, but now all I can see is the fifteen thousand dollars I have almost no hope of raising. The corporate franchise that's going to take over my business. "I can't believe you brought those guys here. I should have known that *let's work it out* text was bullshit."

"So you *did* get my text," he says pointedly. "Hard to tell without a response."

"Yeah, well, I've been a little busy trying to come up with ways to keep this place in business. Thanks for that."

"Look, the suits came up on their own," he says, his eyes locked on mine. "They wanted to scope out the town before the pitch and they obviously read about karaoke in the *Times* piece. There was no way I could have stopped them."

"Sure," I say. "Now if you'll excuse me, I have to serve *beer in a fucking bucket* to the people trying to destroy my bar."

And I push past him before he can say anything else.

8

CHASE DOESN'T APPROACH again as I get set up. I take some comfort in the methodical routine of it all. Pulling down the screen, rolling out the little stack of speakers, plugging in and checking the mic. But even this usually calming ritual is punctuated by spikes of anxiety.

How many more times will I plug in this machine?

Will someone else buy the bar? Turn it into something terrible?

Can I stay in Ridley Falls? Work somewhere else?

Joyce's is fully packed now, and once the screen is in sight you can feel the atmosphere shift. I let myself give in to it completely, banishing my what-ifs for the moment. I'm generally an introvert—happier alone or with the two people I like than in a crowd—but there's something about this kind of electricity. It gets in your system.

It's been like this ever since Max Ryan performed here a few years back. Since Sammy Espinoza opened Verdad Records with an office in Ridley Falls. Since the two of them broke ground on their recording studio/retreat for Northwestern musicians looking for a little peace and quiet.

Karaoke was always silly, a drunken good time, but now there's some sparkle to performing at Joyce's. The idea that there could be *industry people* in the crowd. That everyone who steps up on that cardboard square of a stage is just minutes from being discovered.

The truth is, most of our regulars don't have what it takes to sing the national anthem at a minor league baseball game, let alone sign a recording deal. But there's something about hope. About a fantasy.

"Good evening, Joyce's," I say into the mic when the light-up Budweiser clock strikes seven on the dot. "How are we all doing tonight?"

Everyone cheers. From behind the bar, Inez flips on the light over the performance area. She always makes fun of me for the "sultry" voice I use when I'm at the mic. The leather jacket I put on from my punk rock days. And maybe she's right. Maybe it's silly. But it's important to me, to have a sort of persona when I'm up here. Something I can shrug off when it's time to stop being perceived.

"Sign-up sheet is officially open," I say, holding up the clipboard. "Please form an orderly line, and anyone who spills a drink on my shoes automatically gets bumped to the bottom."

The stampede is immediate, but mostly well-mannered. Despite my easy listening voice, I have a reputation for being ruthless about sending folks to the back of the line. It comes effortlessly. Managing a crowd of fifty tipsy adults is about equal in difficulty to managing one stubborn six-year-old, I've found.

Most people don't need the songbook. They know what's on offer and they practice all week. In a matter of minutes the list is twenty-five songs long, and it's time to kick things off.

"Remember, y'all, the list does not carry over to next week, so if we don't get to you before closing time the only solution is to get here earlier next time. Our first performance will be"—I peer over at the list, which is still being swarmed—"Bonnie, singing Dolly Parton's 'Jolene.'"

There's a respectable amount of early evening applause for Bonnie as she takes the stage. She looks young and sweet, wearing the exact kind of sundress I couldn't picture myself in when I was leaving for the world's worst date. She winks to a guy at a nearby table as the opening notes of "Jolene" ring out through the room.

She's not bad, actually. She doesn't have Dolly's gravitas, of course, but she hits all the notes, which is a mercy. The song is short enough that I don't have time to stew, which is another one.

"Next up are Jason, Dylan, and Stew singing NSYNC's 'Bye Bye Bye,'" I say when Bonnie has finished up. The twentysomethings from Badger's stumble forward, already cracking up. They reek like weed and they've clearly been pregaming. I make a note to tell Inez not to let them drive home as they launch into a ridiculous rendition of the boy band classic.

The first hour flies by. I keep an eye on the bar and make frequent reminders to tip generously, as if somehow I might count the sticky ones and fives and find they add up to fifteen thousand. Chase and his sleazy friends stick to their corner. I avoid looking at them. Everything is going smoothly until around eight-thirty when several things happen in quick succession.

Honestly, the first one shouldn't surprise me. It happens almost every week. Inez stands up on a stool behind the bar and shouts: "Hey, Cash! Why don't you sing us one?"

The crowd, used to this intrusion, takes up the chant with very little prompting. *"Cash! Cash! Cash! Cash!"*

"You know, one of these days I'm gonna make *you* get up here," I say into the mic, rolling my eyes across the room at Inez. "But sure, okay, I'll sing one for you."

They all cheer, and I pretend not to be flattered. I plug in Melissa Etheridge's "I'm the Only One"—one of the few songs in our catalogue that's in my register, since this crowd isn't much for the shouting/screaming/growling that characterized the band I fronted as a teenager.

I try not to think too much about Teen Cash and what she'd make of tonight's song choice as I step onto the cardboard stage. Inez catcalls from behind the bar. The opening begins, and I close my eyes, settling into the moment.

Whenever I sing in front of a crowd it brings it all back. The house shows and tiny dive bars, the endless Pabst Blue Ribbons and packs of cigarettes. The "found family" that evaporated when I had to clean myself up. Become a parent.

I'm belting my way through the second chorus when the next domino falls. The door opens to my left, and I can tell who it is by the way every head in the place turns to look. It's a credit to the crowd that they rejoin me for the end of the song, clapping and whistling like there's not a true celebrity in our midst. But when I step off the cardboard I can see them making their way toward the bar.

Max Ryan, a former rock sensation currently enjoying a hell of a comeback. Beside him, his very pregnant wife, Sammy, and her two best friends. One of them I recognize from Stitch-n-Bitch—Brook, who made the killer croissant.

Normally, I'd be thrilled to have our town's most notorious couple in the house, but this isn't a normal night at Joyce's. My hackles are immediately up as I look to the corner Chase and his corporate entourage have been occupying.

Sure enough, they're all on their feet, making their way toward the bar with greedy expressions on their weasely little faces. Did they invite Max and Sammy here? Is this some horrible attempt to get them on board for the Kings franchise?

If so, it'll probably work, I tell myself, aware of how long I've been quiet at the mic. I'm usually not one for impulsive moves—especially not the kind that require public speaking—but suddenly I'm remembering a key line from Chase's spiel in his car the other night. *I'm here to gauge community support.*

All his money guys are here tonight, if the price of their suits is any indication. Maybe I can't come up with fifteen thousand dollars—yet—but if I play my cards right I can show these guys exactly what the community thinks of places like Kings.

Chase is sticking out his hand to shake Max's as I click the mic back on. "Thanks for the love, y'all," I say in my stage voice. "It's so great to see you all here tonight. Joyce's isn't a fancy place, you all know that. Not like one of those personality-less slickster bars you see up in *Seattle,* where everything's perfect and the drinks are twenty dollars and . . . blue for some reason."

Boos and laughs from the crowd tell me I'm on the right track. The money guys are certainly looking around. The loudest voices are coming from Mo and Charlie's table, and I remind myself to comp all their beers tomorrow.

Whatever small talk Chase and Max Ryan are exchanging grinds to a halt as the latter turns to look at me curiously.

"I like to think this is a place to have a great drink and listen to some local talent," I continue, "but it's also a place that values this community. A place for us all to gather. A place that's more about neighbors and its friends than just making a buck."

More cheers. Someone jumps up and sticks what looks like a twenty-dollar bill in the tip pitcher right under Chase's nose.

"Now I know y'all see our most notorious neighbor, Max Ryan, in the house tonight," I say, to more whistles and cheers. "He made his first public performance in almost a decade right here on our humble little cardboard stage, did you guys know that?"

The crowd goes wild. Max's heart-wrenching cover of "Wonderwall," right where I'm standing now, is the stuff of Ridley Falls legend. The shaky phone video someone made that night had almost two million views on YouTube last I checked.

Max waves as everyone cheers, looking how he's looked every time I've ever seen him—grateful, a little sheepish, and absurdly handsome. Convinced I've reminded him what he owes to Joyce's, I move on to phase two.

"Max, I'm willing to put everyone's next drink on my personal tab if I can get you to come up here and sing us a song. What do you say?"

There's a long moment during which the crowd puts the pressure on, cheering and chanting. I can see Max whispering to his group. I almost feel bad for putting him on the spot, but if he comes up here now it'll make a powerful statement to Chase's corporate cronies about what it means to have a business in Ridley Falls—and what it means to destroy one.

I swear I don't even breathe until Max flashes his famous grin in my direction, and the crowd parts for him to make his way to the stage. My heart is rioting in relief, and I hope the mic isn't too sweaty when I pass it to him.

"Thank you," I say, low enough that only he can hear. "You have no idea how much this means."

"Anything for Ridley Falls," Max says, then he takes the mic and turns toward the now-feral crowd.

As I step back out of the light, my heart is full. I still have no idea where we're gonna get the money we need for improvements, but suddenly I don't feel alone in it anymore.

The party doesn't die down until well after midnight. I text Juliana around ten to let her know I'll be late. She lives in the next unit over so she usually crashes on the couch or Parker's bottom bunk and heads home in the morning before school.

I always feel bad keeping her up so late, but her mom says she keeps vampire hours anyway. At least this way she makes a little money for her college fund.

Larry Cross shuttles home the eight or so people who've over-imbibed without a transportation plan, one at a time. When he takes the last straggler he squeezes my shoulder. "Nice job out there, kid," he says. "I've heard the rumors about the franchise. Maeve and I don't want a place like that within fifty miles of here."

"Thanks, Larry," I say. "We're gonna do whatever we can."

When he's gone it's just Inez and me left. The place is an absolute wreck, but we have a tradition. Leave the mess, come in early the next day and clean, with black coffee, donuts, and loud metal.

I'm about to flop into a chair and exclaim that we did it when I see her looking at me strangely. Like I'm missing something important.

"What's up?" I say, already anxious.

"Chase is waiting for you by the door," she says under her breath.

My eyes dart surreptitiously toward the door where Chase is indeed stalling. There's part of me that wants to kick him out of here without a spare word. But there's a bigger part that wants to rub tonight's victory in his face.

"Can I help you?" I call from behind the bar.

"Do you want me to go?" Inez whispers.

"Hell no," I tell her, and she smiles.

Chase stalks over, looking furious. "You know, you really fucked me tonight," he says, unbothered by Inez's presence. "That whole speech in front of my boss and our investors? They're thinking about pulling out now because they don't want to deal with the *hassle* of the locals resisting."

"Gee," I say, not hiding my delight at the prospect. "What a shame for all of us."

"You're so smug," he says. "Kings wouldn't be *bad* for Ridley Falls, Cash. It wouldn't even have to mean the end of Joyce's if we worked together. They have totally different energies. Kings is upscale. Specialty cocktails and headliners they can actually afford. No one's coming for your little karaoke night."

"Aww," I say, stepping forward, leaning across the bar. "I bet you say that to all the *resistant locals* trying to screw up your fancy deal."

He's frustrated. Face flushed. "So you're not gonna back down?"

"Let me be perfectly clear," I say, not dropping his gaze. "There will be a Kings in Ridley Falls over my dead body. I will never compromise with you. If you choose to keep going down this road you will have to fight me at every turn."

Chase scowls. "You're not making this go away with some hokey speech and a karaoke performance."

"Great, I'll come up with something better," I say. "Now get the fuck out of my bar."

"You know," he says, backing toward the door. "You were more fun before you became a dyke. What a waste."

"You want to say that again?" Inez shouts, planting her hands like she's about to jump over the bar. I put a hand on her arm as he walks away chuckling.

"Not worth it," I say, but Chase's words are burrowing somewhere deep. *Before you became a dyke.* Does Chase think I'm a lesbian? Do *other* people think that?

"He's such a piece of shit," Inez spits, already dismissing him and what he said. I know this isn't the first time she's dealt with shitty, small-town attitudes around queerness, but it's the first time *I* have. Directed at me at least.

"Yeah," I say, my heart still pounding in my ears. Fear? Anger? I don't even know anymore. "He's the worst."

Now that we're officially closed, Inez pours herself a drink. "God, *please* tell me George and Linda said yes so we can put that little asshole on the next bus out of here."

I'd been planning to tell her as soon as everyone left, but suddenly I'm thinking about how this looks instead. Inez and me, drinking in the bar after hours. And all the other stuff, too. Her sleeping on my couch. Changing and brushing our teeth together.

I think about last year when a kid in Parker's class was bullied for having two dads. The principal had to get involved, talk to both the families.

"Uh, can we talk about this tomorrow?" I ask, suddenly nauseated. "I should get home. It's already late for Juliana."

"Isn't she sleeping?" Inez asks, puzzled, drink frozen halfway to her mouth.

"Yeah, but Parker's been having nightmares," I lie, the guilt adding to the nausea. "I should be there just in case."

"Aw, poor peanut," Inez says with a look of genuine sympathy. She doesn't doubt my lie for a minute, and why should she? I never lied to her before this week. "Yeah, get out of here, I'll lock up and see you tomorrow for donuts yeah?"

"Yeah, thanks," I say, and before she can try to hug me I head for the back door like my boots are on fire.

9

FOR THE FIRST time in three days, I don't dream. When I wake up, I tell myself it's a good thing. That last night's reality check must have served as an off switch for my misbehaving subconscious. But I don't feel the relief I expected to. Instead I feel ashamed.

I know that Inez has faced struggles being openly queer in Ridley Falls. When I convinced George and Linda to hire her it was because she'd lost her job at the assisted living facility after bringing her then-girlfriend to the Christmas party. They'd come up with some other reason, of course, but it was clear what their problem was.

We didn't know each other as well back then, but I remember telling her in no uncertain terms how wrong that was. That she was right to stick up for herself. To *be* herself as loudly as she wanted to be no matter where she was.

And then last night, *one* person thinks I'm queer and I panic. Worrying about what people will say, what they'll think of my friendship with Inez. I feel like a coward for leaving. Undeserving of her confidence in me.

But it's different, I tell myself after Parker is at school. If I were queer myself it would be worth it. I just don't want Parker to suffer because people have made a mistaken assumption about me. Is there something so wrong with that?

At the bar, Inez is arriving at the same time I am. I'm coming from Ponderosa's, where Ginny complimented me on last night's speech and told me she and Brad were *vehemently* opposed to a Kings franchise in the area.

"I know it seems hypocritical, since we came from Seattle and all. But we came here to make Ridley Falls our home, and we don't want anything ruining that."

Despite the tangle in my mind, I feel as bolstered by this as I did by Larry Cross's similar sentiment last night. But does it matter that none of us want this if we don't have the power to stop it?

Inez hops out of Gladys's car in front of the bar—the quintessential old-lady Buick—and waves at me as I pull the Jeep into the next spot.

"Bye, Gladys! Good luck today!" she calls before turning to me.

"Is the Bug not running?" I ask, taking one of Inez's bags so she can wrangle the donut box.

"No, I let Mars borrow it. And Gladys was coming this way anyway because she has a *date,*" Inez replies, waggling her eyebrows. "Some woman she met in the waiting room at physical therapy. A hip injury and a knee injury. Match made in heaven."

"I hope they're not going rock climbing," I tease. But now I'm thinking about Gladys. How much harder it must have been for her and her late wife fifty years ago . . .

"You okay?" Inez asks as we get settled inside, flipping the lights on to expose last night's mess in full.

"Fine," I say, grabbing a dish bin from the back to collect all the glassware left on the tables. Inez has a trash bag, tossing in napkins and receipts.

"Parker didn't have any nightmares?"

My conscience finally draws the line. I drop the dish bin on the nearest table and turn to face her. "Parker isn't having nightmares," I say. "I lied to you."

She doesn't look angry, just confused. "Why?" she asks.

My face is heating up, I can feel it, but I have to get this out. "Because of what Chase said about us. Just . . . do you think people think that? That we're dating?"

She laughs, an explosive firecracker of a sound, then she covers her mouth when she realizes I'm being serious. "Oh, I'm sorry. For real?"

"Yes, for real," I say. "I know this is ridiculous, I just don't know anymore. We spend so much time together, and people know you're a lesbian, and it's not like I'm parading around with a bunch of guys all the time so . . ."

Inez drops the trash bag and sits backward on a chair, examining me. "Would it bother you if people thought that?" she asks.

"I guess it would bother me as much as anyone thinking something about me that isn't true. Or you, for that matter."

"Okay." Inez looks thoughtful, like she's choosing her next words carefully. "But it wouldn't *specifically* bother you if people thought you were queer."

This feels like a trap, which tells me I'm activated, because Inez would never try to trap me. "I don't know," I say, repeating my earlier thoughts out loud. "It wouldn't bother me if it were true, but you know it's not easy in a town like this. Kids get bullied, people act differently. And I could handle it if it were who I really was, but if it's a mistake it just seems like a lot to put Parker through, or myself through."

I'm afraid I've mortally offended Inez by daring to discourse on the small-town queer experience, but eventually she nods. "That all makes sense," she says. "Listen, I don't think there's much chance that anyone but some jealous dickbag with a chip on his shoulder would assume we were dating. Even most overt lesbian couples are seen as 'just friends' by most of the general public. Thanks, compulsory heterosexuality."

I don't admit I'm relieved, but I am. "I don't know what that is, but you sound very smart and worldly when you say it."

She laughs, picking up the trash bag again and tossing a clump of napkins into it. "Basically it's the idea that society is so geared toward heterosexual relationships that lots of people get and stay on that track without really considering if it's right for them—but it also has to do with people seeing heterosexuality as the default to such an extent that they don't see queerness even if it's right in front of their faces."

I nod, getting back to clearing glasses. It makes sense, of course, but it's the first part I'm stuck on. The idea that someone could live their life as straight just because it's what's expected of them by everyone—even themselves.

"Have you ever had a sex dream about a man?" I blurt out after at least ten minutes of quiet cleaning.

This time when Inez busts up laughing, I laugh, too. "Where the hell is that coming from?" she asks.

"Just answer the question." I know my face must be the color of an overripe tomato right now, but I find I need more personal confirmation than just the general denizens of the internet.

"Of course!" she says. "I mean, I can't speak to the accuracy since I've never actually *had* sex with a man, but yeah, obviously. I've had sex dreams about all kinds of people. Now I expect you to tell me where the hell that question came from."

"I *may* have had a slightly spicy dream about another woman," I say in a rush. "And it's not a big deal, but I just wanted to make sure that, like . . ."

"That having a sex dream about a woman didn't mean you were secretly gay?" Inez asks, and I can tell she's doing her absolute best not to laugh.

"Yes!" I reply, feeling a hundred times lighter just for having gotten this part of it off my chest. "I don't know! It's not something people talk about!"

"Look," Inez says, stepping closer, unaware that in discussing this mystery dream she's also discussing herself. "There's a simple truth about sexuality and gender and all that stuff that will probably help with the panic."

I gesture for her to continue.

"You are whoever you say you are. You are whatever you *feel* like you are. If you say you're straight, you're straight. It doesn't matter if you have spicy lady dreams, or if someone makes an assumption about you. You're the one who gets to decide who and what you are. No one else."

It *is* simple, but for some reason it gets into my head and calms me down in a way nothing else has managed to. How stupid of me to think that there could be some higher authority on my own identity than me.

"Thank you," I say, trying not to show how emotional this makes me. "That really helps."

"No problem," Inez replies with a grin. "I usually give that pep talk to people feeling impostor syndrome about their queerness and *worrying* they might be straight—but hey, it still applies."

I laugh. Inez gets the donuts out. We each eat three before she speaks again.

"Listen, while you're already confessing?" she asks.

Full of sugar and relief, I gesture for her to continue.

"What's going on with George and Linda? You were giving me the run around all night and then you practically bolted out of here after closing."

I sigh, almost wishing we could return to the sex dreams portion of the conversation (but not really). "Right. About that."

"They said no, didn't they?" she asks.

"Not exactly."

Inez visibly perks up, waiting for me to continue.

"Okay, don't get excited. They definitely did say no at first. And . . . then again when I asked about the loan. And then I was so horrified by the thought of losing this place that I may have done something pretty stupid."

"Oh no," Inez says, covering her face with her hands. "How stupid?"

"Basically I told them I could get the money myself," I say with a grimace. This is the first time I've said it out loud, and it sounds worse than I expected.

"You told them you could get ahold of *twenty thousand dollars* on your own?" Inez asks.

"Well, the silver lining is that Linda offered to put in five out of what I can only assume was sheer pity, so it's only fifteen thousand now!" I try to sound optimistic and land somewhere between sarcastic and delusional.

Inez gets back up, grabbing a rag to start wiping down the tables. But I can tell she's thinking hard because there's a wrinkle between her eyebrows.

"Just say it," I demand after the silence has stretched too long. "It was a terrible, stupid thing to do and I'm doomed to fail and we should just accept that Joyce's is toast and try to enjoy the death rattle."

Infuriatingly, Inez wipes down every last table before she answers. "It was a little impulsive," she admits. "But fifteen thousand isn't a totally insurmountable number, right? I mean, maybe there's a way we can pull this off."

"I have about five thousand in savings—" I begin, but Inez cuts me off.

"That money is for you and Parker," she says. "I'm sure we can do better."

Just hearing her say *we* is enough to lift the rest of the immeasurable burden I came in here with this morning.

It's a slow Friday—there's one of those concerts on the lawn just outside town and we're dead by eight. We toss around some ideas—selling organs on the black market, robbing a bank, finding a rich old person and marrying them for the insurance money—but as most of them are felonies they don't exactly stick.

"We'll think of something," Inez says bracingly as we're closing up.

"Something legal," I clarify.

Inez smirks. "No promises. But if we go down I'll take the heat. You have Parker to think about."

We laugh, stepping out into the darkness, lit by the streetlamps on the highway. "Come over?" I say. "The rest of that six-pack you brought is still in the fridge."

She smiles. "Thanks, but I have a date."

Inez has gone on thousands of dates over the course of our friendship, so there's absolutely no reason for my voice to be high and awkward when I say, "Oh! Yeah, Friday night! Well, have fun."

"Why are you being weird?" she asks, eyebrow raised.

"I'm not," I promise her. "I'm just exhausted, and I have a fifteen-thousand-dollar problem to solve. But we can talk about it another time, seriously. I should get some sleep anyway."

"If you're sure," Inez says, checking her phone. "Because you know I'd cancel if you needed me."

For one stupid second I think about asking her to. But then I realize how ridiculous it sounds and laugh. "Seriously, go. But if she's rich you gotta try to get her as an investor."

"Deal," she says, as a car that is not Gladys's Buick pulls into the lot. I can barely see who's driving the doorless Bronco—short hair, button-down shirt—but Inez's smile is dazzling as she hops in the front seat and waves.

I stand in the parking lot until the taillights disappear, then go inside without letting myself wonder why.

10

INEZ HAS SATURDAYS off, so we don't see each other at work. She also doesn't text in the morning to complain about the date, which means she must still be on it. Or sleeping it off.

For my part, I got to tuck Parker into bed and slept dreamlessly again. No erotic fantasies, but also no clairvoyant solutions to my five-digit problem.

I take Parker to breakfast at Sassy's before I drop her with Juliana and head to the bar. The owner, Claudette Perkins, is behind the grill as always. She looks at least two hundred years old, but for all that seems fully in possession of all her faculties.

"I haven't made it over to Joyce's since Joyce herself passed," she says after industry pleasantries have been exchanged. "You still have that old jukebox?"

I nod. Joyce died sometime in the 1980s, but I'm pretty sure it's the same one.

"Good girl," Claudette says. "History's important, you know. And honey we're all just incensed about that new franchise."

"How did you hear about that already?" I ask. "Gossip train's sure fast around here."

"Wasn't gossip this time," Claudette croaks. "Chase came by yesterday and handed out a stack of these. Asked me to hand them out to the customers if you can believe it."

I do my very best to keep my face impassive as I reach out and take one of the little flyers. It reads, in bold letters: GOOD FOR ONE FREE APPETIZER AT KINGS—COMING SOON TO RIDLEY FALLS. In the bottom corner is the Kings logo. A black-and-blue thing that looks like a sports car a balding middle-aged white guy would drive.

"Seems a little tacky to be giving away free food before you even have a restaurant," Claudette says. "But what would I know? I've only been in business fifty-three years."

"He's unbelievable," I say as Parker colors in her kids' menu. "No one in town wants this, I'm telling you."

Claudette shrugs. "The business owners won't like it, but people don't really care about community politics as long as they've got somewhere cheap to eat and drink. Sorry, sugar, I know this can't be good for your place."

"We'll figure something out," I assure her, thinking of Inez's and my aborted list of criminal solutions from last night. "Don't worry about us."

I do my best to enjoy my breakfast with Parker, but my appetite is mostly gone. I can't stop looking at the stupid coupon. COMING SOON TO RIDLEY FALLS.

Not if I can help it.

I text Inez from the bar that afternoon, a picture of the coupon and nothing else.

She replies in seconds: THAT SNAKE!

We have to do something, I reply. At this point I'm cool with misdemeanors.

She's already typing before I send my second message: Busy

the rest of the day, but come by the farm tomorrow? I could use some handy help, and we can brainstorm ways to skewer him.

Immediately, I feel the wind leave my sails. I'd been imagining one of those days where we text rapid fire until the problem is solved. Or where she shows up at lunch just to hang out.

Busy the rest of the day, I think. And then I'm picturing the girl from last night in the Bronco. It's almost two in the afternoon. Inez has had some marathon first dates before, but this would probably be a record . . .

It's none of my business, of course, but suddenly I'm imagining the two of them getting serious. Moving in together. It's always been in the back of my mind, that someday Inez would have someone in her life who was more important than me. It's just that now would be really bad timing for all that.

Sounds good, I say. See you around eleven?

She hits the thumbs-up react, and then she's gone.

Early Sunday morning, one of Parker's neighborhood kid friends knocks on the door, so she's distracted playing cars in the back while I get ready to head to Inez's.

When I've got my toolbox organized and I'm dressed in jeans with the hammer loop and my hardware store hat, I call her back inside.

"Mom?" she calls, opening the sliding glass door, face smudged with dirt. "What's a heathen?"

"Where did you hear that?" I ask her, grabbing a paper towel to wipe her face.

"Isabella P.," Parker replies, referencing the girl she was just outside with. "I told her we were going to the farm today and she says that her mom says the farm is a gathering place for heathens."

Gritting my teeth as I comb her hair, I make a mental note to ask Jaz—Inez's witchiest roommate—to put a hex on Isabella P.'s mother for making me have this conversation before coffee. Among other things.

"In this case," I say, "*heathen* is a word someone ignorant uses to describe people who have made different lifestyle choices than they have."

Parker chews on this for a minute. "What kind of choices? Like how I like peanut butter sandwiches and you like cheese?"

"Not exactly," I admit, although I wish I could leave it there. "You know how a lot of your classmates have a mom and a dad who are a man and a woman?"

"Uh-huh," Parker says. "But I just have a mom."

"Right. But some people have two moms or two dads, or parents who use different words for their genders."

Parker nods. None of this is news to her. She still looks politely puzzled about why Isabella P.'s mom is upset.

"Well, there are some people who think everyone should be the gender that got picked for them when they were a baby. And some people who think it's bad for anyone but a man and a woman who were born men and women to fall in love."

"That's stupid," Parker declares. "Love is fun. It's good for everyone."

"You're absolutely right," I say, tying off her second braid with a blue sparkly hair tie. "But people like Isabella P.'s mom are scared and closed-minded and they want to save all the good stuff for people who are just like them."

"Boo," Parker says, sticking out her tongue and turning around to face me in her tractors-and-trucks pajamas. "But what does it have to do with the farm?"

I pinch the bridge of my nose. "Inez and her friends who live at the farm are all people who present or love differently than the way Isabella P.'s mom thinks is right," I say, hoping I'm not butchering this. "And because she's scared and judgmental about that she's telling Isabella it's bad."

"Man," Parker says in a long-suffering tone. "Isabella P. might never get to see baby donkeys then. I hope she tells her mom that's dumb and everyone can be who they want and love who they want and they both get to see the donkeys someday."

"I hope so, too," I say, reaching out and pinching her nose. "And on that note, we need to go see those donkeys ourselves."

We're halfway to the farm, and I'm congratulating myself on navigating that conversation well, when Parker pipes up again from the backseat.

"Hey, Mama?" she asks. "What kind of people do you love? Boys or girls or people who use different words?"

I shouldn't be surprised by this, but I am totally unprepared. I think back to my conversation with Inez at the bar. *You are whoever you say you are.*

"I'm like you," I say, wondering if I can dodge for just a little longer. "I think everyone should fall in love with whoever they want as long as that person is kind and respectful and loves them back."

"But what about *you*?" Parker asks. "I've never even seen you *kiss*. Even Anna kisses in *Frozen* and she's a *teenager*."

I open my mouth to say I like boys—or men. But what comes out is something entirely different. "I guess you'll find out if I ever find someone to fall in love with."

"I hope you do," Parker says a little dreamily, as she stares out the car window. "And I hope they like me."

"I could never love anyone who didn't like you," I promise her. "Now let's listen to some music, okay?"

I turn up the radio—that song is on again, the one Parker knows all the words to, and I welcome the distraction from more questions.

It doesn't work so well on me, though. I'm thinking about what Parker said. About hoping I fall in love someday. Of course she hopes that. She's a Disney princess–movie fanatic. Love to her is a fairy tale because she's never seen it up close. How messy it can be. How lost people can get.

I'll never tell her that the reason I've never let anyone get close in all these years is because I've never met a man I could trust with her heart. Her future. I think of my own parents, who didn't even break up, just quietly resented each other and made it everyone's problem. Whose expectations for me were so rigid and all-consuming that I left home the moment I could and never looked back.

Most of my friends growing up had seen messy divorces. Some of them violence. All of us were screwed up by it in our own ways.

I tell myself it'll be better for Parker this way. That she'll get to fall in love with a clean slate when it's her turn. What's another twelve years of emotional celibacy if that's the reward?

Even with a six-year-old girl singing at the top of her lungs in the backseat, driving onto Inez's farm feels like exhaling.

The fence along the front pasture is painted with a sun and trees and clouds. The grass is knee-high and vivid green after the long, rainy winter. We turn up the drive and a little herd of mini donkeys approach, joyfully chasing the car to the delight of my passenger.

There's a willow tree in front of the house—which was painted bright yellow last year, with pristine white trim. Underneath it a few chickens get reluctantly to their feet, clucking in a way that sounds just like Granny O'Connor's judgmental muttering.

I get out of the car and help Parker out of her booster seat. She's been here at least twice a month for years, but it never seems to get old.

"Hello, chickens!" Parker calls. "Hello, ducks! Hello, little shed that looks like a rainbow! Hello, baby donkeys!"

I can't help but share her enthusiasm, though I've been here even more often than Parker has. The farm looks like the place every kid dreams of living when they grow up. Before they get older and settle for neutral tones and HOA-approved lawns with no weeds. There are wildflowers everywhere. A riot of colors and textures. Every wall and fence has been either mosaicked, muraled, or rainbowed.

A hundred wind chimes hang from the willow tree, and they all go off at once when a breeze blows through.

Inez walks out onto the deep porch then. She's wearing a floaty yellow dress that almost matches the house. Her skin glows against it and she smiles, waving at us.

"Auntie Inez, you look like a real princess!" Parker shouts, running across the grass to greet her. Inez hoists her up into her arms and carries her back toward me as I dig out my toolbox.

I grab it and the gloves I brought out of the back of the Jeep. "Morning!" I call. "I hear you need your donkeys tuned up."

Parker breaks into giggles as I brandish a wrench.

"Yup," Inez says, setting Parker back down on the ground, adjusting the dress until it's floating around her again. "Loosen the ears and tighten the tails if you don't mind."

"Done and done," I say, turning toward their pasture with a smirk.

"Noooo!" Parker cries. "You can't use *tools* on a *donkey*."

I turn back to Inez, shrugging. "You heard the expert."

Parker loses interest in the joke a second later when she remembers the existence of the tire swing. "I'm gonna go swing!" She's already running. "Oh, is it okay?" she asks as an afterthought, looking at Inez and me.

"Not too high," I say when Inez nods. "And stay where we can see you." It's starting to dawn on me how difficult it's going to be to get anything done with her running around underfoot, but before I even finish the thought, Gladys comes out onto the porch in work pants and a fleece vest.

"Morning, Gladys," Inez says, hugging her. "Cash is here to be handy."

She beams at me. "I hope you brought that little girl of yours."

"Headed for the tire swing," I confirm.

"I'd be happy to watch her while you two work if you'd like," Gladys offers. She's the newest member of the farm, but she's already earning lots of points with me.

Relief surges through me. "You mean it?" I ask.

"There's a leaky faucet in my shower," she says with a wink. "Maybe you hear it dripping on your way by and give it a tinker."

"You got it," I say, and Gladys makes her way toward the swing, leaving Inez and me alone.

"Okay," she says, clapping her hands. "We should get started. Fixing *and* brainstorming."

I hold up the toolbox. "Your wish is my command."

"Let's start inside before Gladys loses her stamina," Inez says, looping her arm through mine and leading me in through the big farmhouse door.

The inside of the house is just as eclectic and charming as the outside. A mix of antique furniture that probably belongs to Granny O'Connor, bookcases, bright rugs, all manner of knick-knacks and tchotchkes. It's cluttered, but the cozy kind. The kind that makes you feel like you're at home.

In front of the TV with a bowl of cereal, Mars is watching what appears to be a reality show. They mute it as we walk in, smiling sheepishly. "What's up, Cash? You caught me at my guilty pleasure."

"No worries," I say, reaching out to bump fists when they offer. "What is this anyway?" On the screen, the now voiceless people leer, scream, and cry by turns.

"It's called *Are You the One?*," Mars says with a laugh. "It's a matchmaking reality show where everyone is paired up by compatibility experts but no one knows who their match is. This season everyone's bi so it's a total free-for-all. Everyone's a mess."

"Oh god, I love this season," Inez says, leaning on the back of the couch, her hair spilling over her shoulders. "Is this the episode where Kai and Remy—oh, yep, there they go."

I turn back to the TV just in time for two of the cast members to disappear into a dark room. A black-and-white camera shows the blankets moving unmistakably. My cheeks heat up.

"Hey, I wanted to say thanks for the clothes loan the other night," I say to distract from the screen. "The date was a dud but I gotta get one of those shark shirts."

"Wildfang," Mars says. "Another guilty pleasure. They're expensive and it's way more eco-conscious to buy secondhand, but damn do they know how to make a gay shirt."

I laugh again, holding up the wrench. "All right well, leaky shower calls. You got anything you want me to fix? I have tools."

Mars's shoulders sag in relief. "Oh damn, really? This is great because I'm a completely aesthetic masc. I needed a YouTube video to put together a shelf from IKEA and I'm honestly surprised I lived to tell the tale."

"Whatever you've got," I say.

Mars adds a broken door hinge and a stuck bedroom window to my list before taking off for work. As soon as they're gone Inez turns off the TV—which she wants mounted on the wall. My first project.

Now that we're alone again, I expect Inez to launch into a hundred-idea-long list she's come up with since we saw each other last. But she doesn't say anything as I screw in drywall mounts, or even as I level out the TV.

"Okay, I'm holding up my end of the bargain here," I say, waggling the screwdriver at her. "And I was promised brainstorming of the misdemeanor and below variety."

"Oh, right!" Inez says. "I'm so sorry, I haven't had much time to think of ideas."

I'm not sure why, but this hurts. That while I've done nothing but try to think of ways to save our business, Inez has been so busy on a thirty-six-hour date she hasn't even thought about it.

"Must have been some date," I say, trying to make it sound teasing, but hurt flashes on Inez's face, too.

"What does that mean?"

"Nothing," I say quickly, feeling guilty. "I just know you had that date, and yesterday you were busy all day so I thought . . ."

The look she levels at me is unfathomable. Equal parts pissed and self-righteous and some secret third thing I can't identify. "Not that I owe you an explanation, but the date was like an hour long and all she talked about was her truck. I do have a life, you know?"

All of a sudden, my irritation vanishes like it was never there. "No, of course. Look, let me take it back? Please? I'm so stressed about Joyce's and these stupid coupons and I just said something dumb. You don't have to spend every waking second of your life thinking about this, it was a shitty thing to insinuate."

For a moment, the unfathomable look persists, but then the familiar smirk breaks through. "Apology accepted," she says. "And I'm sorry I haven't had more time. But I'm ready to brainstorm, seriously. Where did we land on stealing a car and selling it to a chop shop?"

I laugh. "Unless it's a Ferrari I don't think that's gonna work. And I'm pretty sure no one in Ridley Falls has one of those."

As we move through the projects on the indoor list, we start floating ideas that aren't jokes. We find out with a quick Google search that I'm not likely to qualify for a loan big enough for the project. We briefly discuss taking on investors, but that seems overly complicated considering we don't own the business, and everyone we know is struggling nearly as much as we are.

A town-wide garage sale gets us to lunchtime, but we abandon it when we realize how much work organizing it would be, and how high the probability is that we don't get close to the amount we need.

"But something community wide isn't a bad idea!" Inez says, leading me into the kitchen.

Jaz—Inez's third roommate, a gorgeous, dark-skinned trans

woman—is already in there in a silk robe and headwrap. She watches us as she makes tea, finally laughing as I try to cut a PB&J into cute little triangles.

"Listen," she says, taking the butter knife gently out of my hand. "You reinforce my grape trellis out there and I'll turn this mess into something fabulous," she promises.

"You're on," I say, giving her a high five. Her robe falls open a little to reveal a lacy tank top that says GOD IS TRANS across the front. I think of Isabella P.'s mom calling these people heathens as she teaches her own child bigotry.

In that moment, I realize I'd rather be mistaken for this kind of heathen than her kind.

Inez stays behind to be Jasmina's sous chef, and I head outside to find Parker and Gladys feeding carrots to the donkeys through the fence. The humans are flush-faced and giggling and the donkeys are adorably fuzzy, clearly delighted by the snacks.

"Mom!" Parker calls when she sees me. "Gladys is so cool! Look what she taught me!" Proudly, Parker puts a carrot piece on her palm and holds it out perfectly flat. She giggles wildly as the closest donkey nibbles at it, its soft lips tickling her palm.

"Nice," I say, bending over the fence to scratch the tiny beast's fuzzy ears.

"Gladys says if you don't keep your palm flat the donkeys might think your *fingers* are a *carrot* and crunch them right off," Parker continues, now the foremost authority on donkey-feeding.

"Gladys is very wise," I say, winking as I turn to address her quietly: "Has she totally worn you out yet?"

"Not at all!" Gladys assures me. "She's making me feel young again! We're going to go dig holes in one of the empty garden beds next. We might even find *worms*." She wiggles her fingers at Parker, who shrieks delightedly.

She's just telling me she saw a *witch's* house, which I interpret to mean they made it over to Granny O'Connor's carriage house, when Inez and Jasmina—now wearing a neon blue bodycon dress—come out of the house carrying a truly gorgeous kid-friendly charcuterie board.

We all have lunch together at a sky-blue picnic table under the willow tree. Parker chatters through most of it and Inez sits beside me, our elbows bumping companionably as we eat.

"I wish *we* lived here," Parker sighs as she finishes a cracker with cheese. "This is the best place in the entire world."

11

AFTER LUNCH, JASMINA disappears inside to get ready for a drag night in the next county over. Gladys promises another hour or two with Parker won't kill her, and Inez and I start on outdoor chores with a promise to think of a legitimate plan for raising money before I leave for the day.

As I rewrap a section of the donkeys' fence, we debate the merits of some kind of bake sale—ultimately abandoning that plan when we realize we'd have to sell 7,500 two-dollar brownies to reach our goal, which is officially more brownies than there are people in Ridley Falls.

"If we're doing an event of some kind, we have to consider what we want to say as a business," Inez points out. "Bake sale and garage sale are both cute ideas, but they don't really scream *Joyce's* to me."

"Okay," I say, holding a post steady as quick-dry cement does its thing. "Well, we're known for karaoke. And cheap beer. Is there anything there?"

Inez laughs, then reaches forward to wipe something off my cheek. I feel my face flush, and for the first time all day I'm thinking about the dreams again. About Parker asking me what kind of people I love.

"A recipe for disaster," I answer myself, a beat too late.

"But we could do something karaoke-themed," Inez replies. "I'm just not sure how we get fifteen thousand dollars from that."

The fence post is secure, and we make our way toward the greenhouse slowly. Meandering. Letting the sun warm our shoulders. This is my favorite season, I think, as the breeze blows the smell of Inez's chamomile-and-rose shampoo across my face. Late spring. Nearly summer. When everything is being reborn.

"We need the whole community involved," I say, holding the greenhouse door open for Inez. "Not just the beer-and-karaoke crowd."

"Okay, so let's expand," Inez says, stepping inside. The greenhouse is small, built from salvaged windows of different shapes, sizes, and materials. Like a window quilt full of seedlings. It's wide enough for us to walk down the center together, but just barely.

"If we get our way there'll be a real stage for live music," Inez goes on, reaching out to stroke the leaves of a tiny plant. "So what about something music-themed?"

This has merit. I can feel the perfect idea tantalizingly out of reach. Music, community, something people of all ages can get behind. I try to think of an event that could raise money for a seedy karaoke bar, but that Parker would also enjoy.

And then I remember Thursday night. The party Parker planned to outclass Madison's birthday. A stage and donkeys and ice cream. I can't help it, I start to laugh.

"What is it?" Inez is facing me across the greenhouse, just a few feet of space between us. The toes of our shoes are nearly touching in the center.

"Would you believe me if I said Parker has already solved our problem?" I ask her.

Inez's eyes twinkle. "Of course I would. Parker is much smarter than either of us. What did her little genius brain conjure this time?"

"A party," I say. "With live music and food and games and donkeys. She pulled it out of thin air to impress her classmates the other day and I lectured her about lying, but . . . it's actually kind of perfect."

"Oh my god," Inez breathes. "A one-day festival. We could get local businesses to donate prizes for a silent auction, do a raffle—"

"—We could ask one of the Verdad Records bands to headline," I chime in excitedly.

"Sell tickets with all the proceeds going to Joyce's renovations," Inez says dreamily. "A little petting zoo for the kids. Beer and wine by the cup."

"Could we do it here?" I ask, imagining the booths, the stage, the music drifting across the fields.

"Of course we can."

It's warm as she smiles at me. There's a stained-glass panel in the greenhouse ceiling that casts colorful dancing lights on the ground. On our shoes. On the front of her dress. The chamomile-and-roses scent is stronger in here.

"This is it," I say, feeling giddy and reckless in my optimism. "This is how we're going to save Joyce's."

"I think you're right," Inez says. She hasn't dropped my gaze. Neither of us has moved, but she feels closer than she did a second ago, leaning against the shelf of hopeful little sprouts.

I'm a little dizzy all of a sudden, struck by a sense of déjà vu. But we've never stood in this greenhouse together before, I know that. I've never seen this light dancing across her skin, reflected in her eyes. Never seen her smile precisely like this.

It takes me a moment to realize that what I'm remembering is the feeling of dreaming. Inez leaning across the bar top, pressing against me in her bikini, sliding into my bed in the middle of the night. What's familiar is the way her beauty, which is obvious to anyone, feels personal to me. The way it heats up in my veins. Gathers in places it has no business gathering.

"I love it when you're like this," Inez says quietly.

"Like what?" I ask.

"Happy," she says, smiling a little helplessly. "Confident. I swear, Cash, sometimes I think you can do anything."

I know I'm not dreaming, but it's hard to tell the difference now. The glow of her, the yearning, the static across my skin . . . those things I've ascribed to only dreams are here with me waking and I feel too fragile all of a sudden to hold them inside.

When I move forward, I expect her to stop me. I expect to stop myself. But she doesn't. I don't. I'm halfway to her. Three quarters of the way. Moving like cold honey in case one of us comes to our senses before I reach her.

Our mouths meet in a shower of sunlight. There are no Google search terms in my mind when I kiss her. I don't wonder what the irresistible warmth and softness of her lips means for the labels I've chosen. I only know that the version of me that's kissing Inez is the most me I've ever been.

We move together instinctively until our legs are tangled—my jeans with the hammer loop, her yellow dress—arms going around each other like we've done this a thousand times.

She parts her lips, gasping just a little when I follow suit, the kiss deepening quickly. I can feel the questions building along with the pounding in my veins. I know I will pay for this moment, but right now no price seems too high.

When the doorknob rattles, when Parker's voice rings out, I half expect to wake gasping in my bed. But I don't. Instead my whole body goes cold as I spring away from Inez, straighten my shirt and wipe my mouth. There's barely time to turn to the loose windowpane before Parker charges in, bringing reality with her.

"Mom, you *gotta* see this, there's a pond over there and it has *tadpoles*!" She's holding out her grubby little hand. The sight of it, the dirt in the creases, reminds me that there's more at stake here than my fracturing sense of identity. There's Parker. Parker, who loves Inez, and whose heart I could never risk no matter how confused I feel.

Oh no, oh no oh no . . .

"Tadpoles!" I say, my voice cracking unnaturally. "That's awesome! That'll have to be the last thing though, okay? It's getting close to dinnertime."

Fuck fuck fuck fuck . . .

"Aw, but Mom!" Parker begins, and I follow her out. Not daring to look back.

12

PARKER EATS HALF a cheese stick and falls asleep at the table at five-thirty. I'm able to keep the events of the day indistinct by focusing on her until then, but as I carry her to bed I feel the fog starting to clear.

The house is so quiet once she's asleep. I was counting on at least three more hours of mind-numbing logistical parenting tasks and questions about donkeys to keep me distracted, but now there's nothing.

I seize on to the tedium of household tasks instead, determined to keep this at bay for as long as possible. The house is a mess, thank god. The laundry Inez did on sleepover night is mostly dirty again. I start a load. Cram tonight's dishes in the dishwasher before starting that, too. Open the mail and sort it into junk and bills. I look at the clock in the kitchen, sure it's been at least two hours by now.

It's been twenty-nine minutes.

Straightening up the living room, vacuuming under the couch cushions and shaking out and folding the throw blankets makes it an even hour. Why is it, I wonder, that when I have no free time these tasks seem to swallow a whole day, but when I desperately need them to distract me they're effortless?

The reality of what happened today is pressing in from all sides. The pressure tells me there aren't enough menial tasks in the world to keep it at bay. So I have to deal with it. And that's that.

I sit down on the couch, facing an empty chair. I feel absurdly like I'm about to interview myself. *What the hell were you thinking?* is the first question on the list.

Examining the kiss from a distance of a few hours, it feels just as surreal as my dreams did. Like someone else was at the controls, piloting my body like a spaceship into an unfamiliar atmosphere.

Here, in my living room, I don't have the overpowering urge to drive back to the farm and pick up where we left off. When I think about Inez I still mostly feel the same. She's my best friend. She's funny and interesting and smart and silly and I'm endlessly grateful for her presence in my life.

But that feeling that flared to life in the greenhouse and made me kiss her, the feeling all my dreams about her were saturated with, feels like a mirage that immediately faded when I looked away.

This realization feels like an immense relief, even if it leaves complications in its wake. I think back to what the internet said after the dreams started—to what Inez herself said when I brought it up to her. *You are whoever you say you are.* I know I'm straight. I always have been. I've rebelled against almost every social convention there is, there would have been no reason to skip being queer if I was, right?

So that leaves the obvious explanation: I'm a straight girl who had some very risqué dreams about kissing a woman I'm close to, and in the heat of an emotional moment my curiosity got the better of me. It'll end up being part of our friendship lore. *Remember the time you kissed me?* We'll laugh about it for years to come.

And anyway, we have more important things to think about now. Like how we're going to pull off an entire daylong music festival before Chase presents his plan for Kings to the Seattle investors.

We'll talk about it tomorrow, I tell myself, heading upstairs to bed. I'll finally have to come clean about the dreams, which will be embarrassing, but she'll tease me and eventually things will go back to normal. That's all I want. Normal.

When I sleep, we're back in the greenhouse, and this time no one interrupts. The sun is warm as we map each other's bodies with fingers and lips and tongues and teeth. Inez smiles against my skin. "*I never knew it could be like this.*" I drop my head back in helpless surrender. "*Neither did I.*"

It requires real effort to fold up the dream this time. The edges are a little sharper when I put it away. It'll be better after we see each other, I tell myself. It'll all go back to the way it was.

I text her on my way to drop Parker off at school. Can we talk?

Part of me is afraid she might not answer. That she might be angry, or horrified, or some other terrible thing I haven't imagined yet that will make this all much harder.

My whole body sags in relief when her reply comes a minute later: Already on my way.

She knocks on my door just a few minutes after I get home. This is the first official sign that something is off. Inez never knocks. "Come in!" I call. I have a notebook open on the table in front of me in case she wants to pretend it never happened. Move immediately to party-planning. I wasn't sure what else to prepare for.

When she walks in she's carrying a drink holder with two cups of coffee and a giant croissant sandwich. There's a smile on her face that says I don't need to worry about half the horrible things I've imagined since yesterday.

It also makes the folded-up dream rattle a little behind its lock.

"Hi," she says. "Can I cut this in half?"

"You know where the knives are," I say. "Just promise you won't use one on me."

"Ha ha." She disappears into the kitchen and comes back with half a sandwich on a plate, which she hands me along with my coffee.

"Not sure I deserve this," I mumble.

"Oh, come on," she says. "Let's skip the self-pity and get it over with."

I take a fortifying gulp of the coffee and set the sandwich down beside it on the table. This doesn't seem like the kind of conversation you want to have with crumbs on your face.

"I'm sorry," I say when there's nothing left to arrange in front of me.

"For what?" she asks.

"I kissed you!" I blurt out. "And you're queer and I'm not and I have a really humiliating explanation for all of it, but first of all I just have to apologize. I'm an adult, and you're my best friend, and I shouldn't just be throwing caution to the wind with one of the most important relationships in my life."

There's a long pause. Inez is looking at me so intently it feels like she's trying to discover uncatalogued creatures in the depths. "Before I can decide whether I forgive you, I think I need to hear this humiliating backstory."

"I was afraid you'd say that," I groan, taking another drink of my coffee. "It's about what I told you the other day."

"The sex dream," she prompted.

"Yes. Only it wasn't one dream, it was several. And you were kind of . . . in them."

Her eyes go wide, and I know how hard she is to shock. "I was . . . having coffee with you after the sex?" she asks innocently. "I was a casual bystander?"

"You were *in* the dreams. With me. Like. Participating in the activities." My face is so hot it could rival the coffee. "And I know that's completely weird and ridiculous and I was determined to just leave them where they belonged in my subconscious, but then yesterday . . . the greenhouse was so pretty and we were so excited about the idea and you were saying nice things to me and I just thought—"

"—Why not?" Inez finishes for me.

"Exactly," I exhale. "Why not? Which, of course, there were a zillion reasons why not. All of which came crashing down rather abruptly right afterward. Hence the apology."

"So you had a few dreams, we had an emotional, runaway moment, and curiosity got the best of you?" she asks.

"Yes," I say. "And I'm sorry. Very, very sorry."

Another long, searching look, then Inez's face splits into an almost too-easy grin. "Cash, if I had to apologize every time I had a sex dream about someone I'd literally never do anything else. And as far as the kiss goes"—she shrugs—"It was fun. Sometimes kissing is just kissing. You'd know if you did it more."

The relief that crashes through me is so powerful it sends all the questions out of my head. Like who she's had sex dreams about, and if she's ever had one about me. "Thank you," I say. "Let's seriously put it behind us and get back to normal."

"Not so fast," Inez says, leaning forward with a no-nonsense expression. "You got to say your piece, now let me say mine."

"I'm all ears," I promise her.

"The other day you were all spun about these dreams making you queer," she says matter-of-factly. "And then yesterday you kissed me."

"Yes," I say, feeling the crawl-out-of-my-skin sensation that tells me I absolutely do not want to dig any further into this. But isn't it the least I can do to hear Inez out after she was so gracious before? I grit my teeth and let her go on.

"I meant what I said at Joyce's the other day," she continues. "You are whoever you say you are. You're the only one who gets to decide. But Cash, you can't use Parker to hide from yourself forever. If you're not queer that's completely okay, but I do think it's obvious that there's something you won't admit you want. And as your best friend, I think you owe it to yourself to figure out what that is."

Her words hit me somewhere deep. Somewhere that resonates. I've been so worried about what the dreams mean that I skipped the most obvious explanation: I'm an adult woman. A sexual being. Of course my subconscious is serving up erotic dreams about the person I spend the most time with, I've been starving it of one of its basic needs.

"I think you're right," I say. "Maybe not dating or having regular sex with anyone for the entirety of Parker's childhood wasn't the brilliant strategy I thought it was."

Inez looks relieved. "You're a person, not just a mom. You're not doing her any favors by using her as an excuse not to live your life."

"Noted," I say, suddenly ravenous. I reach for the sandwich and take a huge bite.

"Okay, now that we're through the after-school special," Inez says with a smirk. "I believe we had a truly fantastic idea before you interrupted us to try out one of your dream moves."

"I'm never gonna live this down, am I?" I mumble out of the corner of my very full mouth.

"Not in this lifetime," Inez confirms.

We spend the next hour before we have to open the bar going over everything we'd need to put an event together. Inez, who hosts skill shares and poetry readings at the farm fairly often, says for an event of that size we'd need a few months. But we can build buzz, let the community know we're fighting back against the intrusion. It feels so good to finally have a plan that I don't even care how long it'll take.

That is, until we get to the bar and find a flyer taped to the door.

"That son of a bitch," Inez says, reaching it first and tearing it off. I read it over her shoulder, feeling anger build at my core and radiate.

WANT A REAL MUSIC VENUE IN YOUR TOWN? JOIN US AT THIS MONTH'S CITY COUNCIL MEETING TO SUPPORT A KINGS FRANCHISE IN RIDLEY FALLS!

The date and time of the meeting are listed below. Three weeks away.

"Why do they need city council?" I ask, the anger making my mouth feel numb, my voice sound like it's coming from far away.

"I don't know," Inez says. "But this can't be good for us. Three weeks? We'll be dead before we even get to throw the party."

She hands me the flyer. I ball it up in my fist. "Not if we have the event sooner than we planned," I say. "We can't let them get away with this."

It's the first time I've ever been happy Joyce's is having a slow day. Inez and I use the time to make lists and plan and strategize. We're going to need permits, vendors, bands, a stage, raffle prizes. And all in less than three weeks.

"We can't do any of this alone," Inez says around midday, when the list (which I'm writing on receipt paper) is curling somewhere around my shoes. "The first thing is to start getting the other business owners on our side."

"Good point," I say, tearing off a new piece and taping it to the top of the list.

Next, I get out my phone, firing off a quick email to George and Linda making sure we have permission, but it's a foregone conclusion. As long as they don't have to pay for it, I know they won't say no.

"We already got a lot of support after karaoke last week. And the business owners might be willing to donate prizes for the raffle and the auction, too, so it's a two-birds-one-stone situation if we can do it right."

"We're not gonna have much money," Inez says, chewing on her fingernail worriedly.

"I've never let it stop me before," I assure her with a grin.

During my break, when I'm waiting for Parker outside the school, I decide there's another item I can cross off my to-do list. I can't imagine I'll have much time for untangling the realizations Inez helped me make this morning, about seeing myself as a person and not just a mom and a business manager, but I can at least make some sort of move in the right direction.

To that end, I get online on my phone and order a new vibrator. One with some kind of orgasm-guaranteed-or-your-money-back seal and ten thousand five-star ratings. I pay extra for overnight shipping.

When I get back to the bar, Inez is looking triumphant, and she has her own piece of receipt paper. "Okay," she says without preamble. "I called Cindy, remember that girl I went out with a few times who works at City Hall?"

"How could I forget?" I ask, although I totally have forgotten every identifying detail about Cindy. Truth be told, I've always found stories about Inez's dating life hard to hear. I'm always worrying that one of them will be *the* one, and the stories will turn to distance between us, and eventually there will be someone more important in her life than me or Parker. I know it's selfish, but sometimes smiling and nodding is the best I can do.

"So, I asked her why Kings corporate would need to go before city council to open a franchise," Inez goes on, oblivious to my thoughts. "And she told me it's because the city has to approve all new parking lots. Kings could open without permission but they'd never be able to do what they're trying to do without a big lot. They're going to be making a presentation and the council will have a vote."

I can picture it now, those smarmy jerks up there talking about how Kings will be good for the Ridley Falls economy. About how an increase in tourism means growing to meet the need for upscale venues.

"We need to pack that city council chamber," I say.

"But to do that we need the town to support Joyce's over Kings," Inez reminds me.

I think about what Claudette Perkins said when I took Parker to breakfast at Sassy's on Saturday. That the business owners will likely oppose, but the people don't care about local politics as long as they have somewhere to get a cheap meal and a drink.

"The festival should be the day before the vote," I say. "We'll raise the money, show the town a great time, and then we'll ride the momentum to crush it at the meeting. Game over."

Inez smiles. "I love it when you get that *shatter the skulls of our enemies* look on your face," she says. "I'd follow you into battle any day, Captain."

It occurs to me that she said something very similar to me in the greenhouse before I lost my mind entirely and kissed her. This time, I make sure my feet stay firmly planted. But I can't deny that she gives much better compliments than any of the men I've been with. If only all straight guys could take lessons from a lesbian.

When I don't reply, Inez clears her throat. Is it my imagination or are her cheeks a little pink? "So, first step is getting the business owners on board. I've ranked them from smallest to biggest fish. I say we get some of the small ones this week, then we'll have some support when we go for the big ones."

She slides her receipt paper list across the bar. I'm careful not to let our hands touch as I take it from her. I have to stay focused.

On the top of the list are the people who have already offered support since karaoke night: Larry and his wife, Maeve, who owns Mystical Moments—the crystal shop downtown. Claudette. Ginny and Brad from Ponderosa's. In the middle there are a few of the food truck owners—José the breakfast burrito guy, Nok from the Thai food truck, and Amy from the grilled cheese place Parker loves.

Then there's the boys club. Roark from the hardware store—a gruff old guy who won't even put flyers in his window—Terry from the liquor store and Brandon from the corner store across from it who are always feuding, and Donald from the bait shop who's at least a hundred years old.

Finally, at the bottom in all caps, are our big fish. The ones we better not approach unless we're sure we can pull this off. Robin Knight from Badger's and her wife who runs the *Gazette,* and Sammy Espinoza of Verdad Records.

"Looks like we have our work cut out for us," I say to Inez, feeling exhausted just looking at the list. Most of these people can't even agree on whether there should be a new stoplight in town, let alone something as important as a new franchise.

"We'll get everyone we can on board before Sunday," Inez says, no doubt whatsoever in her voice.

"What's Sunday?" I ask absentmindedly. I'm already thinking about telling Terry and Brandon that the other is supporting Kings to get them both on board.

"Badger's monthly half-off appetizers for business owners night," Inez says, as if this should be obvious. "Everyone will be there. And you can bet Chase will, too. Which is why you and I have to get there early and schmooze."

Usually just the word *schmooze* would have me running for the hills, but I know she's right. If we want to save Joyce's I'll have to smile and bat my eyelashes and play nice with the best of them.

"Okay," I say. "I'll see if Parker has a friend she can sleep over with."

"*Okay?*" Inez replies, incredulous. "You're just giving in? To a night of drinking and chatting and *smiling?*"

I grimace. "Anything for Joyce's."

13

BY THE NEXT day, I've arranged a sleepover for Parker (Monday is an in-service day, thank god, and the kids have the day off), and made calls to Claudette and the Crosses, who are all on board for the festival and taking down Kings. George emailed back saying (predictably) that he's fine with the party as long as it's not going to cost them anything. And best of all, no dreams.

"I knew you were the right firebrand for the job," Claudette says in her two-packs-a-day voice. "I'll bring the big grill we used to use for the Elks' pancake breakfast. Burgers on me."

Larry and Maeve Cross talk together on speakerphone, which I'm starting to think is a couples-of-a-certain-age thing. Nonetheless they're very enthusiastic.

"Free rides to and from the farm in Larry's Car," Larry promises. "And I'll set up a table for tarot readings," Maeve adds.

"Thank you both so much," I say, overwhelmed by their generosity.

"We should be thanking you!" Maeve says. "We love this town. The last thing we want is to see it overrun by a bunch of corporate yuppies. You stick to your guns, sweetheart."

Better still, Inez shows up for work the next day practically vibrating with excitement. "I got Roark!" she says without preamble. "He's gonna donate the lumber we need to fix up the stage at the farm before the event and he even said he'd put up a flyer in his window!"

I'm utterly gobsmacked by this information. In all the years I've lived here, I've never even gotten more than a stiff nod from Roark—and I go to the hardware store relatively often for minor fixes around the bar.

"How the hell did you pull that off?" I ask.

"I think he's lonely," Inez says. "I just went in and talked to him. He's got an ex-wife who's bleeding him dry and a daughter off at college in the city. He hates Seattle, won't even visit her, so I took the opening! Told him about Kings and how they want to turn this place into some kind of hipster paradise. He was furious."

I shake my head in disbelief, picturing Inez waltzing into Roark's and chatting up the world's grumpiest man without entertaining the thought of failure. "You're amazing," I say, spreading my hands out helplessly.

She gives a little curtsy. "I know."

While Mo and Charlie drink their tall cans, the lists keep coming. I have to order more receipt paper just to keep up. Beyond the business owners, we need permits, a bigger stage and sound system at the farm, some easy-up tents for Claudette's burger grill and Maeve's tarot readings, and hopefully more.

I'm picturing more booths for food, games, maybe even some kind of down-with-Kings piñata for the kids. When I look at Inez her expression matches how I feel. That maybe we're really going to pull this off after all.

*   *   *

That night, as if to reward me for working closely with Inez without any more kissing or illicit fantasies, I arrive home to discover a discreet shipping box on my doorstep.

I stash it in my bedroom as I go through the evening routine with Parker.

To tell the truth, I've always been a little lax when it comes to self-pleasure. Is there anything more awkward than deciding on the mood ahead of time? Choosing the entertainment? Getting down to the totally unserious business of getting off when you don't even have someone else with whom to appreciate the absurdity of it all?

And that's before you consider porn, in all its heteronormative glory. I could never get into it. Was I supposed to picture myself as the sassy nurse? The woman with amnesia who forgot she ordered a pizza? It's all just too ridiculous.

Even if you can somehow manage all that, there's the single mom of it all. The child who seems to know when you've decided enough is enough and go for it. The way they always need a drink of water, or a snack, or help with their nightlight just when things are getting good.

All that to say, I haven't been very successful at making the moment feel right. Which honestly may be at least partially to blame for my wayward subconscious.

I think of Inez, the morning after the kiss. Telling me that there's something I won't admit that I want. Hopefully acknowledging myself as a sexual being will be enough to take the edge off and return my nights to their formerly restful state.

Parker has been solidly asleep for an hour when I finally lock myself in my bedroom and open the box. The thing is certainly complex, with buttons and speed control and vibration pattern options and a gadget that stimulates almost anything you could possibly want stimulated—as well as at least two things I didn't even know could be.

I dash to the bathroom to wash it thoroughly, and make it back to my room without incident. Next there's the instruction manual, which is longer than any book I've read this decade. Once I've learned how to operate all the bells and whistles it's time to take it for a ride.

You're doing this for a good reason, I tell myself as I turn off the lights, strip down to my T-shirt and slide into bed. *It's either the Pleasure Wand 5000 or making a total disaster of your life. And possibly never getting a good night's sleep again.*

With that in mind, I close my eyes. I try to reach for a fantasy that will get me in the right headspace, but nothing is immediately forthcoming. The instruction booklet didn't come with directions about this part.

Chase is ruined forever, I don't even try that. I think of actors I find attractive and I can see them, but I can't picture myself in the scene at all.

Frustrated (in more ways than one), I flick on the wand. It has so many possibilities maybe my unimaginative brain won't be an impediment. Maybe the sensations themselves will do the trick.

Seconds after making contact, I know my prediction was correct. This thing is absolutely engineered to function as advertised. Within seconds I feel myself warming up, muscles relaxing then tensing in all the right ways. My self-consciousness melts away as I start to surrender to the pulsating pattern.

Almost unbidden, an image appears in my head. My back is up against the bar at Joyce's, my head tilted back, jaw slack with pleasure. I don't even care who's pressed against me, the things they're doing to me feel too good to need justification.

I'm so close. The fingers of my free hand fist in my sheets. Everything coils to spring.

Finally, I think, as weeks' worth of tension pulses within me, on the brink of unspooling at last. My visualizing keeps pace, Joyce's growing hazy as I glance down to see the identity of my fantasy partner at last.

Grinning up at me with a wicked, almost feral expression, is Inez. Her hair is mussed, her lips parted slightly.

In the real world, everything in me screeches to a halt. The Pleasure Wand 5000 is flung unceremoniously toward the foot of the bed, still vibrating. My body is horribly confused, the fantasy having tipped me over the precipice just as I panicked. I'm stuck in this kind of horrible limbo between orgasm and non-orgasm and I don't know what to do besides scrub the heels of my hands across my eyes and attempt to erase the image still lingering in my mind.

It was worse than any dream. Worse even than the actual kiss we shared in the greenhouse. I think back to Chase and me in his car before he divulged his nefarious plot. The way Inez came to mind just as he was sliding his hand into the front of my jeans.

What if these dreams have permanently rewired my brain? I think desperately. What quicker way is there to ruin a friendship than to have the face of your platonic friend permanently hardwired to your orgasm circuits?

After a minute or two, the heightened sensation in my body fades, leaving total deflation in its wake. *There's something you won't admit you want*, I think again. But how can I ever figure out what that is if I can't get past this subconscious speed bump?

I get out of bed calmly, picking up the Pleasure Wand and clicking it off. I take it back to the bathroom, wash it off, and put it in the box, which I bury at the back of my closet. It's disappointing that it wasn't the solution to all my problems, but that doesn't mean I can stop trying to find one.

Once I'm under the covers again, I take out my phone, hesitating before I commit to typing anything into the search bar this time. *Can't stop sexually fantasizing about my best friend even though I'm straight* is probably the most accurate, but I feel like writing it out will make it feel too real.

I settle for *How to stop thinking about having sex with someone you can't have sex with*.

There is some really terrible advice that's clearly intended for extremely Christian teenagers—notably wearing a rubber band around your wrist and snapping it every time you think about sex in general—but amid all the nonsense there are two pieces of advice I would consider common-sense adjacent.

The first is meditation. According to this web page, intrusive thoughts come from assigning those thoughts value or fear in your mind. In order to stop fixating on the unwanted thought, you should learn to see all thoughts and emotions as leaves passing on a stream.

The second piece of advice is to start having sex with someone else.

I download a meditation app on my phone and listen to the first lesson, determined not to fall asleep at all if I can help it. I can still feel Inez's blissful smile waiting in the murky depths of my misbehaving subconscious.

Before I can sleep, I need to learn to let these thoughts pass. Leaves on a stream. I'll stick to the meditating, and pretty soon I'll be an empty vessel, thoughts just drifting by, no pesky illusions or human desires to derail me from my goal of oneness with the universe.

Or at least a functional friendship and a great fundraiser.

14

THE NEXT MORNING I'm more determined than ever to make my to-do list my sole focus. Every time the memory of last night threatens to make my face hot, I watch it drift by. A leaf on a stream. Already a memory.

I didn't sleep at all. I've listened to fourteen meditation mini podcasts and done five guided meditations. I feel like an ethereal being, unmoored from the suffering of fixation and desire. But even ethereal, untethered beings need coffee.

I walk into Ponderosa's on a mission—first, to acquire caffeine, second, to secure Ginny and Brad's allegiance in the fight against Kings.

There are a few people in line ahead of me, and I listen to their conversation rather than stay alone with my thoughts for a single second.

"It was good," one of the women is saying to the other. "Like, really good."

"Like there's gonna be a fourth date good?" her companion asks her.

"Like one hundred percent makes up for the next twelve dumb

things he says good," the first woman says in a tone that makes the other one giggle.

I tune out as quickly as I tuned in. Other people have sex. That's fine. My desires are leaves on a stream.

But it turns out meditation and nonattachment are much easier in your bedroom than out in the world. In practice, it seems I'm still more likely to drown in my river than to let my thoughts float gracefully across it.

This woman is having sex with a man who says dumb things. She seems happy. Her skin is glowing, she's smiling and planning future meetings without getting in her head. More than that, she's here with her best friend talking about it normally. Giggling. Standing close. Not kissing her and having to awkwardly apologize later or hyperfixating on dreams and fantasies that won't leave her alone.

I wonder what I did to cast myself out of this wonderland. The one where you just do what works and don't overthink it.

The women make their orders and move off to the side. I do my best to prod the leaves of my musings along as I approach Ginny behind the counter.

"Hey, Cash," she says. "What can I get you?"

"Hey, Ginny," I say. "I'd love a large black coffee and to see if you and Brad are up for a little small business subterfuge."

"Black coffee coming up," she says, punching in my order. "And I'm officially intrigued. Is this about Kings?"

"It is," I say, a little quieter even though no one is listening to me. "They're planning to pitch their franchise and the big old parking lot that comes with it at the city council meeting in three weeks. Inez and I have plans to renovate Joyce's, make it competitive so the money guys back out. But we need a little help."

As a high school kid pours my coffee, I lay out the plan for the fundraising festival to Ginny, who is ecstatic.

"We're in," she says, the minute I'm done. "I can put together a raffle prize basket, and Ponderosa's can serve coffee at the event too, all profits go to Joyce's renovation. I'm so glad you guys are fighting back."

By the time I'm back out on the sidewalk with my coffee, I think turning people against Chase and Kings is a much more effective strategy than meditation. If I can just have a conversation like this with a Ridley Falls business owner every four minutes I should be good to go.

On the way back to open the bar, I think of the to-do list and am genuinely thrilled that we're nowhere near done. Maybe by the time the to-do list is accomplished I'll have made more headway with my meditation.

Back at Joyce's, I arrive just as Stitch-n-Bitch is getting set up. Brook hands me a warm blueberry muffin on my way in.

"Love what you guys are doing," she says with a megawatt smile. "Down with the man, right?"

Thinking specifically of Chase, I return the smile. "Absolutely."

"My wife, Willa, and I would love to help any way we can. Happy to set up a little pastry table, or maybe offer some kid-friendly activities for parents who need a break? We'll be wrangling our little one anyway, so the more the merrier."

The little map of the event I've been constructing in my head sprouts a little kids' activity table like a mushroom after rain. "That would be incredible," I say. "As an event organizer *and* the parent of a rambunctious six-year-old."

Brook laughs. "Zephyr is almost five, good to know we have another year before the rambunctiousness slows down."

"And counting," I say with a weary chuckle. "But I wouldn't trade it for anything."

"Me, either," Brook says with an equally weary nod. "Gotta keep Ridley Falls in good shape for them, don't we?"

"We do," I say, liking Brook more with every interaction. "I'll give you a call about the kids' area, let me know if there's anything you need. And if you want to do pastries maybe you could coordinate with Ginny at Ponderosa's? They'll have a coffee setup, seems like a perfect match."

Brook gives me an earnest little salute. "Can't wait for the event," she says, then turns back to her truly catastrophic-looking knitting project, which Mrs. Blair is patiently helping her untangle.

Inez is behind the bar when I make my way back. "That looked like it was going well," she says with a hopeful expression. "Brook and Willa?"

"Pastries for the Ponderosa's table *and* a kids' play area," I confirm.

"You know what this means, right?" Inez says with a significant look. "Willa Cross is Sammy Espinoza's best friend. If they're in . . ."

"I'm trying not to think about it," I say, shaking my head. "It's intimidating enough calling her up and asking for signed bands that cost thousands of dollars to book, to come play for free at some little townie party."

"Excuse me," Inez replies, puffing up indignantly. "This isn't some *little townie party*, okay? This is the first annual Joyce's Jubilee."

We've been brainstorming names for days and nothing has quite stuck, but the second the words are out of her mouth I know there's nothing else this thing could be called. It's perfect.

"You're a genius," I tell her, then I try it out myself just for fun. "*First annual Joyce's Jubilee.*"

Her answering smile is a little shy. "We don't have to use the 'first annual' part, I just couldn't stop thinking that if we pull this off, it would be a great way to keep the town involved, to show our gratitude for their help year after year. We could raise money to help other businesses, or good causes . . . anything we want."

There are at least fifteen people in here, including Inez's grandmother, but in this moment it's the greenhouse all over again. It's the climactic moment of all my dreams. The part where I'm so filled with this surge of emotion that I don't care that I'm straight, or that she's my best friend and it could ruin everything. I want to kiss her anyway.

Desires are thoughts and thoughts are temporary, I tell myself. *Observe them and let them pass on the stream of your consciousness.*

"No, I'm all in," I manage, a beat too late, willing myself not to blush. "Today an upgraded kitchen, tomorrow world hunger."

She claps her hands in excitement, not seeming to notice my struggle. "Okay good, because I already have Mars working on a logo and I was afraid you'd say I got ahead of myself and—"

I interrupt her by stepping forward to hug her. This does not help the leaves in my stream drift away any faster, but I'm doing it before I can stop to worry about that. "You're amazing," I say, smelling chamomile and roses. "I couldn't do any of this without you."

When I step away, her face is a little pink. "It's important to me," she says, holding my gaze. "Joyce's, Ridley Falls, you. I wouldn't let you do it alone."

Just then, Granny O'Connor calls out for a towel, having spilled a mimosa on her quilt square. Inez takes it to her and the moment passes, the leaves making their way down the stream. But I have a feeling there are more where those came from, and I still have no idea what it means.

It's easy to blame my subconscious when this stuff happens in my dreams, but now that it's bleeding into my everyday life I don't know what to think.

"Earth to Cash?" Inez says, bemused. She's standing across the bar from me and I have a feeling this isn't the first time she's said my name.

"Sorry," I say, shaking my head like there's water and not errant fantasies stuck in my ears. "I didn't sleep much last night."

"I just asked if you think we should strike while the iron is hot," she says. "Make an appointment with Sammy and ask her about the event."

It's not a bad idea at all. I was hoping to have all the rest of the business owners confirmed before we approached her, but there's no doubt we've made a lot of progress. And if we can show up to Badger's business owners' night with Sammy and Max and all their star power on our side? It's hard to imagine anyone would bet against us . . .

The Verdad Records offices are right downtown, in a space that used to be a Christian bookstore. The front is gorgeous, with tons of plants in the window and the logo frosted into the glass, but they also don't look like they think they're better than the rest of the neighborhood. They fit here, elevating the area instead of outshining it.

I step inside to a homey-looking waiting room—cozy gray furniture with throw pillows that look like woven tapestries. Rugs. A counter that I recognize as an antique bar top.

It feels like the living room of the coolest person you know, and instead of being intimidated I notice some of this morning's confidence returning.

"You must be Cash," says the girl behind the counter. "Sammy's expecting you."

She gets up to escort me down the hallway. There's a gorgeous studio just across from an office with her nameplate on it, and even after wheeling out little speakers and a karaoke mic for the past few years I can appreciate that this equipment is incredible. Top of the line.

The receptionist taps twice on Sammy's dark wood door and leaves me to wait. Only a second or two later, she calls, "Come in!" and I step through it into her private office.

This room looks a lot like the lobby, making me think she decorated the whole thing herself instead of hiring some corporate interior designer.

The difference is, the wall behind her desk is covered with photos in different-sized frames. I recognize Max in several of them, vacations and date nights and a large one from their wedding at the falls.

In a few of the others I see Brook from Stitch-n-Bitch with an adorable woman that must be her wife, Willa.

By far the most represented human is a little kid with bright blonde hair, who grows across the wall from a squishy little infant to a toddler to a kid in overalls and pigtails nearing kindergarten age.

Sammy herself sits behind her desk in a big, cozy-looking chair with an afghan over the back. She smiles as I take in the photos.

"Cute kid," I remark.

"My godchild," she acknowledges with a smile. "If these two are half as great as Zephyr I've got a smooth ride ahead." She gestures down to her massive belly, smiling fondly.

I think privately that based on the half-wild joy in Zephyr's face in every photo, Brook and Willa might have longer than a year to wait for peace and quiet.

"Twins, huh?" I ask Sammy.

"That's the diagnosis," she says with a wry smile. "It was a shock, but now I can't imagine it any differently."

I nod, thinking of Parker. How quickly my world—so not set up in any way for a child—expanded to fit her. To become entirely about her.

"Everything's a shock, I think," I find myself saying. "But then they're so perfect you wonder how you ever could have wanted anything else."

"How old is yours?" Sammy asks, gesturing to a seat across from her, which I take.

"Parker," I say. "She's six. A ball of chaos and sass and I wouldn't have it any other way."

"Well, I hope I'll get to meet her one day."

"If she has her way she'll be recording here by her tenth birthday," I say, smiling.

"So," Sammy says, leaning across the desk. "You're here about the Joyce's fundraiser."

I nod. "We've got some great support from quite a few local business owners already, and my"—I panic slightly as I attempt to mention Inez. My friend? My partner? The only adult person I always like?—"business partner, Inez, has an amazing space on the outskirts of town where we can host. It'll be booths, games, a karaoke contest, and if this meeting goes as well as I hope it will, a Verdad Records headliner."

She smiles as I wrap up my pitch—which I practiced in the Jeep on the way over here. "It sounds amazing," she says. But she doesn't immediately agree to help.

"If there are any questions I can answer for you I'd be more than happy to," I say, trying not to panic.

"No questions," she says. "But I do have some advice for you if you don't mind."

"Of course not," I say quickly.

"This is an amazing plan," she says. "And I think it's so cool you're fighting back. I love this town, and I want the same things you want. But I would do your best to get the town's community pillars on board as quickly as you can."

"What do you think I'm doing here?" I ask with a small smirk.

She nods with a smile of her own. "I'm something of a special case. People still see me as an outsider, you know."

"A beloved one," I argue.

"Thank you," she says. "But I heard through the grapevine that this is going to come down to a city council decision about a parking lot, and I'm afraid I won't be much help with that."

"I'm hoping to talk to Robin at Badger's on Sunday," I offer, feeling slightly intimidated now. "And my business partner got Roark from Roark's Hardware, that was a big score."

"Wow, Roark is so crusty," Sammy says. "Your business partner must be incredibly charming."

"She's the most charming person I've ever met," I say without hesitation, and then I feel incredibly silly.

"But I'm not just talking about businesses. I'm talking about Judge Patterson, and the city council members, and the mayor. People with power and influence to help get this Kings parking lot thrown out."

If I felt silly for complimenting Inez too enthusiastically, I feel absurd now. Of course we should have been targeting people besides business owners. We've been thinking way too small.

"The reason I say this," Sammy goes on, "is because there's a little weasel in a suit going around town making quite a case for Kings. He was in here this morning promising me that the franchise will make money for the town. That if business owners don't take advantage of the tourism now by getting some reputable businesses in here they'll lose all the progress they've made."

My blood starts to pound in my ears. I wish I were anywhere else so I could scream, or punch something. Fucking Chase. Of course he wasn't just going to disappear.

"I'm guessing by the impressive shade of purple you just turned that you know this weasel?"

"I do," I manage. "And I wish I could say I'm surprised."

"I lived in Seattle for a long time as a music writer," Sammy says, with the air of a cool big sister being utterly frank. "I know Kings. They have great marketing but they're not a good business. I don't want them in town any more than you do. But again, I'm coming from a place of privilege. Most of the other businesses here need this to stop turnover, and bleeding during the slow seasons. He's making a compelling argument."

"He's an ass," I mutter before I can stop myself.

"That's the impression I got, too," Sammy says, and I picture Chase schmoozing Max Ryan at karaoke night. The little lemmings with their bucket of Coors Light inviting him.

But Max had sided with us.

"So . . . can I ask what you told him?"

"He offered to book Verdad bands as openers for the first year of operations," she says. "And to book my headliners in their Seattle locations. I told him I love this town too much to make a deal that could ruin it, but like I said, I'm fortunate enough to have financial security that doesn't come from tourism in Ridley Falls. And I'm positive I'm not the only person he's approaching with this pitch."

"I can't offer anything like that," I tell her frankly. "I can't promise to fix all the problems businesses here have. But I do know that letting big corporate chains come in and run us out of town won't stop here if we let it happen. They're so greedy there'll be a Starbucks across the street from Ponderosa's if they think they can make a profit here. A Cheesecake Factory where Badger's used to be."

The moment I'm finished, I'm prepared to apologize for the rant. I'm here to ask about a band, not vent all my frustrations about gentrification on this poor, busy pregnant woman. But when I lock eyes with Sammy she's smiling.

"*That*," she says. "That's what you say to anyone who needs convincing."

15

ON THE WAY home, I take out my phone to text Inez to meet me at my house after her shift. But before I can hit send, I realize that might not be the smartest decision. Feeling like I've lost something precious, I put it away. I'll tell her in the morning. Maybe if I don't see her tonight I'll actually get some decent sleep for once.

But before that, I get to tell Parker about the party.

"Oh-em-gee," she says when I've finished explaining the plan. "I thought I was in trouble for lying and now we get to actually have the party? Am I dreaming?"

I laugh. "You weren't in trouble," I tell her. "It's normal to want to make people happy by telling them what they want to hear. But you've learned your lesson, and Auntie Inez and I think the party will be a great way to get people to help us with some things we need to do for Joyce's."

It seems obvious we'll have to repeat this part of the conversation, because it's clear she hasn't heard anything I've said since "party." "Will there be donkeys?" she asks.

"Yes," I say. "It's at the farm, so the donkeys will be present."

"And a stage?" Parker asks.

"Yes."

"Ice cream?" she asks, ticking off on her fingers as I answer.

"Unconfirmed, but I'm sure we can figure something out."

"There *has* to be ice cream," she says.

"I know there will be pastries," I offer.

Parker looks mollified by this, at least momentarily. "How many friends can I invite?"

"As many as you want," I answer, thinking that Parker's class-mates will bring their parents and their parents might make dona-tions. "But remember, it's not *your* party, it's a party for Joyce's, so let's practice telling the whole truth when you invite people, okay?"

She nods impatiently. "How many of my friends can go in the VIP section?" she asks.

My head is officially spinning. Even George and Linda didn't ask this many questions. "How do you know what a VIP section is?" I ask a little wearily.

"Madison," Parker says nonchalantly, as if Madison weren't persona non grata just a few days ago.

"Since when are you and Madison so chummy?"

"Well," Parker says, carefully avoiding her green beans in favor of potatoes. "She said she liked my moxie, so even though I defied her I could still come to her party. But now I'm having an even better one." Her smile turns a little maniacal before she catches my eye. "*Joyce's* is having an even better one," she amends quickly.

"Good," I tell her. "Now you just need to remember that at school tomorrow, okay?"

Parker taps her temple. "It's all up here," she says. "Now, will there be a bounce house, yes or no?"

* * *

I finally get her to bed around eight. I know I should be brain-storming ways to get the Ridley Falls pillars on board, but it feels weird to plan for something Inez doesn't even know about yet.

At nine, I go upstairs with no small amount of trepidation. I can't remember the last time I went to bed when the clock was showing a single digit, but there's no doubt I could use the sleep after last night's meditation podcast binge.

I turn off the lights and unlock my phone to try a bedtime guided meditation, which I'm hoping will lead me to a dreamless sleep. Once the soothing voice is playing beside me, I close my eyes, thinking of leaves on streams, and donkeys, and bounce houses, and anything at all except my best friend doing things best friends shouldn't do . . .

At eleven-thirty, my phone rings, startling me out of my suc-cessfully dreamless sleep. My heart is hammering hard; who would be calling me this late? Is one of the vendors pulling out? Did Chase do something to ruin all our plans? Is Joyce's on fire?

I grope for my phone in the dark, flipping it over to see Inez's photo lighting up the screen. Still groggy, my mind reaches for reasons she might be calling—she's usually a text-first kind of girl. I'm doing my best to let the fantasy my mind conjures float away on the stream. Inez, up late, thinking about me . . .

"Hello?" I answer, trying not to sound too husky or expectant.

At the sound of her voice on the other end of the line, the leaves in my stream depart at top speed. She's panicked, clearly crying.

"Cash?" she says. "It's Granny. She fell on the steps of her cot-tage and we're waiting for the ambulance. She has to go to the hospital."

The sleep-grogginess is gone. As soon as the words register I'm out of bed. "What can I do?" I pull my jeans on over the boxer shorts I sleep in. "Anything, seriously."

"There's nothing really, god, I'm sorry, I shouldn't have called. The ambulance is coming and I'll ride with her there. It's just . . . no one else is home. Jaz is at drag night and Mars is working and Gladys is on another date and I . . ."

"Should I come there or the hospital?" I interrupt. "You shouldn't be alone."

"Hospital," Inez says, like a sigh of relief. "Thank you, Cash, I'm so sorry I know Parker's probably asleep and I have no right to ask I just really need you right now."

"Hey," I say. "You deserve support. You don't have to apologize for asking for it."

She lets out another shaky breath. "Okay," she says. "Thank you. I'll see you there, the ambulance is pulling up."

"Hang in there," I say. "I'll see you soon."

Even though it's late, Juliana's mom says she's awake watching TV and sends her over to sit with Parker. I make up the bottom bunk as silently as I can, give her an extra twenty up front, and I'm on the road in fifteen minutes.

The Ridley Falls Hospital is a dingy little place, but I've been here a few times and I know there are some genuinely good doctors here. I look for Inez's Bug in the lot before I remember that, of course, she came in the ambulance.

She's there in the waiting room when I walk in, tear-streaked face, the outfit she was wearing at work today rumpled. Blood on the shoulder of her cardigan.

Seeing me, she staggers across the floor, collapsing into my arms. I catch her, hugging her tightly, rubbing her back like I do Parker's when she's shaking and sobbing after scraping a knee.

"It's going to be okay," I say. "Granny O'Connor is the toughest person I've ever met in my life. She's going to be just fine."

Inez pulls away then, wiping her eyes. I shove down the urge to take her in my arms again, telling myself it's concern. Instead, I sit with her in the cold bucket seats beside the window.

"What are they saying?" I ask.

"Nothing yet." Inez sniffles. "I don't know what made me go down there to check on her, but I was feeling weird about the empty house and just *off* in general. There's a little set of steps up into the cottage and she'd slipped walking up them after watering her garden out front."

"Was she conscious?"

Inez nods. "Bossing around the paramedics, totally lucid. But her arm was bleeding and I think her wrist might be broken." She breaks down again and I put my arm around her, trying not to enjoy the way she snuggles into my side.

"Juliana is sleeping in Parker's room so I'm good to stay as long as you need," I say. "This place is depressing enough, I don't want you to be alone."

"I feel awful," Inez says. "You barely sleep as it is."

There are a lot of things I could say to this. Things about why I haven't been sleeping, and the barrier between my waking and dreaming lives that seems to be more permeable by the day, but it's not about me tonight. "I want to be here for you," I say instead, taking her hand and squeezing it.

"Okay," Inez says, with a soft smile that makes it all worth it.

We sit in silence for a while. I take her phone when she tries to WebMD and do my best to keep her mind off things.

After what feels like forever, a doctor comes out and Inez jumps to her feet, leaving my arm cold where she was leaning on it.

"You're the granddaughter?" he asks brusquely.

"Yes," Inez says. "But I mean, she raised me, she's practically my mom and there's no other family who will show up so . . ."

The doctor, who I already don't like much, holds up a hand to stop her. "Her wrist is broken," he says. "And she's lucky that's all it is. She needs a ramp at the very least, but at her age . . ."

"I know," Inez says tearfully. "I'll do it right away."

"I think it's time to consider assisted living," the doctor says, ignoring her promise. "And the sooner the better. Bones don't heal the same at her age, and it could easily have been a hip. We'd be in a much worse situation then."

Inez's jaw tightens, her face going pale. "I understand," she says. "Can we see her?"

"She's sleeping now," he says. "She's sedated, so she'll probably be out all night. We're going to keep her a few days. Her blood pressure's low and she was a little disoriented. Probably nothing to worry about but she's safer under observation. I suggest you go home and get some sleep, come back in the morning when she's awake."

He walks off in that same brisk manner before Inez can ask any follow-up questions. She drifts back to our little bucket seat island looking utterly lost.

"This is all my fault," Inez whispers, collapsing into the seat next to mine again. "She just seems so competent. But I know she's getting older. I should have gotten her a ramp. I should have known she was ready for assisted living."

"We only know what we know," I tell her, in as soothing a voice as I can manage. "You couldn't have known she'd fall. And it's not like Granny is in the habit of letting other people make decisions for her."

"I didn't know she wouldn't fall," Inez says miserably. "She's almost ninety years old. I should have insisted she stay in the big house. I should have . . ."

I put my hand on her shoulder bracingly. "You heard him," I say when she trails off. "We got lucky. It wasn't her hip, or her head. Now there's time to figure the rest out."

Inez nods. I settle back in my chair, assuming she'll want to stay until morning, but she surprises me by putting a hand on my arm.

"Do you mind if we go back to your place?" she asks, eyes liquid, hair falling across her face. "The doctor's right, I need to sleep if I'm going to be here for her tomorrow, but I can't be at the farm by myself."

"Of course." I put my hand on top of her hand. I tell myself these are friendship sparks that I feel in my palm, traveling all the way across my skin.

"Thank you, Cash," she says, and I feel her gratitude like a kindling fire. Warmth coming off her in waves.

My friend Inez is sad, and I want to take care of her, I observe. And then I take her home.

Part of me thinks Inez will conk out immediately on the couch downstairs, but once she's dressed in her standard Joyce's shirt and a pair of my sweatpants she curls up in the corner of the couch with a mug of tea and starts talking.

"There was this time right after my parents kicked me out," she says, eyes fixed on some indeterminable point. "I had expected to feel so good after coming out, but I was low. I'd known my parents' rejection was coming, but there was this small part of me that hoped I'd have that heartwarming coming out story. The one where your strict Irish Catholic parents surprise you by putting a Pride sticker on the car . . ."

I just listen, sensing this is less about conversing and more about purging.

"So anyway, it hadn't been very long. They'd called Granny to tell her she was forbidden to give me any money, or to offer me a place to stay. That if I wanted to choose a life outside God's light I would have to make my own way."

"Telling Granny O'Connor what to do," I say. "They must have been braver than I am."

She laughs a little tearfully, then continues. "So I'd been moping around for days, feeling awful for dividing the family. She and my parents had had an all-out screaming fight, sworn never to speak to each other again. Anyway, Granny goes out for a few hours and comes back with an internet printout and a bag of clothes from the thrift store. She drags me out into the living room and tells me it's time to decide which kind of lesbian I'm going to be."

Inez is giggling now, and it's so hilarious and absurd that I can't help but join in.

"She'd gone to the public library, and printed out this horribly outdated list of like, lesbian *types*, probably with the assistance of some scandalized old help desk volunteer. And there's like, butch, femme, sporty, goth, and she literally has an outfit for each type in the bag."

We're both laughing so hard now that she can barely finish the story. About how she tried on every single outfit, and Granny rated them out of ten, and it was the first time Inez had smiled since her parents rejected her.

In the midst of all the laughter, I imagine it. A scared, teenaged Inez determined to be herself even if it meant losing everything. I think of myself, with my ridiculous hair Elmer's glued into spikes, telling my own parents I'd never be back.

It's stupid, but I wish we had known each other then. That we'd been able to count on each other like we do now.

"What are you thinking?" she asks when I've been quiet a long time.

"It's stupid," I say, but she waits anyway.

"I was thinking about when I left home," I say when I realize I'm not gonna get out of it. "How it would have been nice if we'd known each other then."

Inez smiles. It's my favorite smile of hers. Kind of tender. "I would have had such a crush on you," she says, that sparkle in her eyes.

Snorting with laughter, I shake my head, trying to ignore the words and the place where they settle. "You would not have. I was a very try-hard suburban punk. There was lime-green Kool-Aid hair dye involved. Literally everything I wore had studs."

I'm giving her an out, but instead of taking it she shifts closer to me on the couch. "It wouldn't have mattered," she says. "Studs or no studs, I would have been twitterpated."

We're very close to each other now—almost as close as in the greenhouse. I know how easy it would be to cross the distance; I've already done it once. But even if it was remotely appropriate, I don't want her to think today's support is contingent on something as fleeting as attraction. Another leaf floats away on the stream.

"You should get some sleep," I say gently. I lean forward and kiss her lightly on the forehead. "I can take you back to the hospital as early as you want."

"Okay," she whispers. She doesn't move back. I have to be the one to stand up. To walk away from her even though it feels like something inside me is stretching to its breaking point as I do.

Back in my room, I can feel something unraveling at my core. Some idea of who I am that I've always believed to be true, now unmoored on the tide of feelings I can't bring myself to ignore anymore.

I take out my phone. *Can you be straight but be attracted to one woman*, I type, feeling utterly absurd.

The first headline appears like a lifeline: HELP! I'M A STRAIGHT WOMAN BUT I'M ATTRACTED TO ANOTHER WOMAN!

Okay, I think, clicking on it, my phone illuminating the pitch-darkness of my room. At least I'm not the only one who's had this problem.

The article is extremely comprehensive. It asks a lot of questions to contextualize your experience of attraction, which feels grounding to me as I begin to answer them in my mind. Surely by the end of this I will realize everything is normal, and nothing is changing, and this is just a strange blip in my life that I'll someday look back at and laugh.

Have you felt this way before? That one's easy. Definitely not. Part of what's so destabilizing about this is that I have nothing to compare it to.

Next, *Do you still find men attractive?* This one is a little tougher. I'm forced to admit it's been a long time since I felt genuine attraction for a man. Especially when I consider the failure to launch with Chase in his car, and the image of Inez that interrupted it . . .

I decide to put a pin in that one. Come back to it later. I'm sure it's an anomaly. The rest of my answers will make this seem silly and inconsequential.

Is this attraction emotional or physical? There's a case to be made that it's mostly emotional, I argue. I mean sure, there are the dreams, and the fantasies, and the kiss, but couldn't those all be considered reactions to emotions? Maybe?

I put a pin in this one, too. Two anomalies. Not a big deal.

When I get to the next question, I decide the quiz is rigged. There's no way this was meant for women like me, who are really just dealing with a wildly out of character series of intrusive thoughts. I'm sure plenty of straight people would answer like this, too.

I toss my phone across the bed, like physical distance from the quiz will help me untangle the ever-worsening knot snaring itself in my chest.

But I forget to lock it, so the question glares accusingly at me anyway:

Can you imagine having sex with her? The description is burned into my brain, damning, demanding I consider things on a deeper level than I've let myself so far. This quiz was supposed to let me off the hook, but I can't help feeling like it made things more confusing than ever.

Finding a woman attractive doesn't necessarily mean you're queer. There are all kinds of attraction. If you find yourself drawn to a woman but the idea of having sex with her still doesn't feel right compared to imagining sex with men, you're probably just reacting to some super-charged charisma.

There's no doubt Inez has supercharged charisma, but there's also no denying I *have* imagined having sex with her. Almost endlessly for over a week now. Imagining that went from my subconscious to my inconvenient conscious.

So what does that mean for me?

16

THURSDAY NIGHT KARAOKE passes in a blur. I can't shake the feeling I had answering those questions last night. The feeling that something big is about to happen and I'm not remotely ready for it.

Chase doesn't show his face at Joyce's, which is for the best, but Sammy and Max aren't there either. Inez, using her connections with Cindy at City Hall, does get a number of city council members to come. I move them shamelessly to the top of the list and smile widely through their heartily lackluster performances.

Anything for Joyce's.

The mayor doesn't show, but no one really expected her to. In the end, I tell Inez to take the night off, feeling horribly guilty for doing so. She's happy to spend the night at the hospital reading *Us Weekly* to Granny, but to be honest my motives weren't entirely altruistic.

My entire life is changing. Whether or not we save Joyce's, things are going to be different in this bar. Ridley Falls isn't the sleepy, small town it once was. The presence of the label and the new tourists are changing that, too. Parker is getting older, she's a whole new kid every day.

Isn't that enough transformation for one era? Whenever I'm

around Inez lately, I feel like I'm under a very bright spotlight, exposing things I don't even know about myself. Things I'm not sure I want to know.

I know avoiding her forever isn't an option, but for right now it doesn't feel bad to take the night off of endlessly introspecting.

But near the end of the night, I get a text from her anyway. My stomach erupts in butterflies, which I try ruthlessly to tamp down before I read it. Luckily, the text itself does the trick:

Just saw Sasha at Safeway when I was shopping for Granny.
She says Robin is supporting Kings. What do we do??

My formerly butterfly-filled stomach now feels like it's full of lead. Robin is supporting Kings. Which means Kendra, editor of the *Gazette*, will most likely follow suit. Badger's is the biggest local business we have, and the newspaper is exactly how we get through to the community pillars. Is it possible we really lost them both before we even got a chance to speak to them?

I manage to get through the rest of karaoke night. Lots of people come up to me, mentioning their excitement for the party, their delight that we're attempting to take down Kings. I'm so grateful—for that and the tip jar that's overflowing tonight— but it's like Sammy said, without the support of the community pillars, Kings just has the stronger message.

And worse, I find I can't even blame Robin. Stability for small businesses at the mercy of the tourist season roller coaster? A chance to bring in the kind of concerts and events that will attract young people to Ridley Falls? A connection with Seattle that will make us a true tourism destination? If I wasn't managing the direct competition, could I really say I wouldn't be tempted?

That night, after I check on Parker and Juliana—fast asleep in the bunk beds—I sit up for a long time. I wonder if this was all selfish of me. The hope that I could turn Joyce's into a place I love at the same time as I helped the town that's come to feel like home.

Is a new-and-improved Joyce's really what's best for the town? I have to wonder. Or is it just what's best for me? Maybe the future really is in big businesses like Kings that will draw outsiders to a town we can't keep afloat ourselves. No matter how much we might want to.

The only upside to this melancholy self-reflection, I think as I drift off to sleep, is that I haven't thought about that stupid article at all.

I get through Friday and Saturday on the wings of Parker's enthusiasm alone. It's shaping up to be a truly awesome event, and I start to believe that even if we can't get Kings thrown out, we might be able to raise the money to compete with them.

At the very least, we'll have a hell of a farewell party.

Also, I feel terrible admitting it, but a few Inez-free days have done wonders for the state of my tangled insides. She texts occasionally, but less now that Granny is back home and mobile again. Presumably because she's following her around like the guardian of an extremely bossy toddler.

Without the constant pressure to examine my reactions to her and the feelings they kick up, I'm feeling more normal than I have in weeks.

Or at least, that's what I tell myself. On Sunday morning, as I'm setting up the bar, the door flies open and there she is in all her red-tank-top, hoop-earrings, checkered-Vans glory and it all comes crashing back.

God, she's beautiful, I think, helpless without the chance to steel myself against her arrival. It feels like a punch to the stomach, but at the last second the punch turns to champagne and bubbles pleasantly through your blood.

"Surprise!" she calls, holding what appears to be a bottle of champagne and a box of donuts. "Did you miss me?"

I splutter, mostly. "How's Granny?" I finally manage, but I can see the answer on her beaming face as she sets down her bounty on the bar top.

"So much better," she says, her excitement contagious. "She's off her painkillers and on Tylenol now, and get this—she's *thrilled* about the idea of assisted living. She says she'll be ruling the roost by week three."

"I'm sure she's not wrong," I say. I want to walk around the bar and hug her, but even the sight of her is sensorily overwhelming. Best to take it in little steps, I tell myself.

"It is," she says. "And I think I have enough in savings to get her over to Meadow Lake at the beginning of the month, so until then we'll just have to take extra good care of her."

"I'm so glad," I say, feeling slightly tongue-tied. Like after not seeing her for a few days I've lost my tolerance and her presence is making me woozy.

"Brought an apology for leaving you high and dry all weekend," she says, sliding the champagne bottle toward me and opening the donut box.

I take a donut as she pops the top of the bottle, missing my mouth twice before banning myself from looking at her. "Okay, so. We gotta talk about Robin," I say, hoping that grounding ourselves in strategy will be enough to dispel the bubbles.

"We do," Inez replies, taking a sip right out of the bottle and passing it to me. "I haven't seen anything in the *Gazette*, and Granny gets it every morning, so that tells me there might still be time to get to her tonight."

"So we're still on?" I ask, taking a polite swig of the champagne even though I don't need any help in the surreal and loopy department. "For tonight, I mean? I wasn't sure with Granny."

"You're not getting out of it," she says, pointing her half-eaten donut at me. "Gladys is going to hang with Granny, and Mars and Jaz are coming with us. We're gonna be the hottest thing that's ever rolled into business owners' night and that's a promise."

"Good." I try not to picture what she'll be wearing. How she could possibly look hotter than she does right now. "What's the plan?" I ask, finishing a glazed donut and taking another one, realizing I fed Parker breakfast but forgot to feed myself. "It better be good, because we have less than two weeks until the party and there's no way we can get the mayor without the *Gazette*."

Inez leans across the counter, fringe falling into her eyes. There's a tiny bit of chocolate frosting clinging to the corner of her lip and before I can point it out she licks it off. Slowly.

It's like the intro to one of my dreams. I pinch myself surreptitiously just to make sure. It hurts. I feel like one of those horrible cartoon animals with the bobbing Adam's apple.

"We get there, we show Robin how integral Joyce's is to the community, we show we're not intimidated in the slightest, and then at an opportune moment of your choosing you corner her and give her that speech."

"That speech?" I ask, slightly bemused by her confidence.

"You know, the speech," she says. "The one that knocked Sammy Espinoza off her feet."

"Oh," I say, missing my mouth with my donut again. "That speech."

Sundays are always dead, so I close Joyce's at four and head home to dismiss Juliana. Inez and I spend the rest of the afternoon going over the to-do list, which is looking pretty great actually.

We're entering the final stages of what we can accomplish ahead of time. Chairs are rented, speakers are handled thanks to Mars and their friend, and Gladys and her new *friend* (a carpenter from the next town over named Betty) are hard at work on a little expansion for the stage using donated materials from Roark's. Ponderosa's, Sassy's, Mystical Moments, and Burro's Burritos are all planning to set up at the festival. Sammy is looking for the perfect band to headline.

I'm looking forward to telling Parker all systems are go before she leaves for tonight's sleepover, but I find her looking uncharacteristically somber as Juliana heads home with barely more than a grunt.

"What's up, pal?" I ask, taking a seat across from her at the table as she finishes her apple slices.

"Mama," she says. "I need to negotiate with you."

It's all I can do to stifle my laughter. "Okay, shoot."

"You want this party to involve the *whole* town, right?" she asks.

"Of course," I say. "It's a celebration of the community. Everyone should be represented."

"Good," Parker says, and to my immense surprise, she hands me what appears to be a first-grade version of a business proposal.

It's made from multicolored construction paper, three-hole-punched and tied together with red yarn. The first page, in clumsy block letters, says:

WHY OUR CLASS SHOULD BE ALLOWED TO PERFORM AT THE PARTY

I do my best to flip through with a serious expression. The following pages highlight, in full illustrated glory, the talents of the various first-graders of Ridley Falls Elementary. The pictures mostly show them singing, dancing, hula hooping, building with Legos, and, of course, at the very end, jumping rope.

"Kids are part of the community," Parker says as I finish reading. "And if you let us perform it'll help build our con . . . confidence. Plus we'll do a really good job."

What's truly hilarious about Parker's proposal is that it's a fantastic idea. If we get the kids involved, their parents will be duty bound to come watch. Plus it solidifies Joyce's as a place that supports our whole community and not just the drinking crowd.

Setting the proposal back on the table, I stick out my hand for Parker to shake. "You know what, Parker? You've got yourself a deal."

In lieu of shaking my hand, she launches herself into my arms, squealing and giggling.

"Mom, you are the best. The very best. The extreme best. Do you even know how much everyone is going to love me for this?"

"Beautiful and beloved," I say, kissing her on the nose. "Madison better watch her back."

A little while later, Isabella R.'s mom arrives to pick up Parker. I'm braced for an ordeal. This is her first sleepover outside our house, I expect a little drama. Some nervousness, a little clinging.

I haven't ruled out the possibility that I'll have to cancel the whole thing.

Instead, she gives me a high five and hops into Mrs. R.'s minivan like we're college roommates. Doesn't even look back.

All in all, I think I'm more nervous about tonight than she is.

Back inside, I have two hours before I'm supposed to meet Inez, Mars, and Jaz downtown. I already have my outfit picked out— I took Mars's advice and ordered a few shirts from Wildfang— so I don't have to worry about melting down over wardrobe this time.

I am nervous, but as I get dressed, I realize it's not because of the stakes. Robin and Kendra. Kings and Joyce's and city council. It's because of Inez.

Another thing about being a single mom is that you're almost never alone. Even in the shower you're usually answering shouted questions through the door for half of it. But faced with more than an hour of quiet, I think maybe it's time to be honest with myself.

Clearly, there's something going on here. Google hasn't been able to answer it to my satisfaction, but that doesn't mean I can just dismiss it. Whatever it means about my long-held notions regarding my sexuality, I have developed some kind of feelings about my best friend.

I think of my high school self for the second time this week. Elmer's glue hair spikes and punk patches on every inch of my clothing, giant boots that clomped in my parents' suburban hallways. That kid was so desperate to break out of every box that might confine her. So why am I so desperate to stay in mine?

What if I really am attracted to Inez? I ask myself, forcing myself not to shy away. What if, instead of being totally straight, I'm just 99.9 percent straight. Would that really be so bad? I'm still an adult with agency. I don't have to act on it. But maybe the process of trying to repress the feelings is what's making them so powerful.

I can hardly be the first person who's indulged in impure thoughts about a platonic friend. What if I just . . . let myself have them? Stop worrying so much?

Tonight is the perfect time to practice, I tell myself. I have other feelings I don't act on all the time. The creepy guy who works the counter at the Chevron gas station often makes me want to punch him in the face. I don't force myself to repress that thought, but I also don't punch him. This will be just like that.

Feeling confident about my new plan, I finish getting ready and leave for Badger's right on time. Tonight is going to be a victory. I will successfully not punish myself for thinking about Inez *or* act on any of those thoughts. And I will manage to win over Robin Knight to the Joyce's cause.

Piece of cake.

I check my reflection in the Jeep's rearview mirror before heading inside. My button-down shirt is navy blue with bright red lipstick marks all over it, and I like the way it fits. I also snagged some hair goop that looked relatively similar in texture to the stuff Inez loaned me on the night of my disaster date. I'm still not sure it does anything, but it smells like sandalwood, which is nice.

For a minute, looking myself over, I feel like a totally different person. Someone who is capable of accomplishing all the tasks I've set for myself tonight and then some. It's a nice feeling. Maybe I should get out more often.

This self-appreciation fest ends abruptly when Jaz raps on my window—resplendent in sequins with a long blonde wig I've never seen her in before—and it's time to put all this hypothetical confidence into practice.

"Stop preening and get out here!" she calls, and I do, locking the Jeep behind me.

"Yes, because I'm sure your look requires no preening whatsoever," I say with a smirk.

She drops her jaw in mock horror. "*My* look is worth the time," she says, fluffing her hair as if to prove it.

"Don't be a jerk, Jaz, Cash looks damn good!" Mars is climbing out of the backseat, and I laugh when I realize we're dressed almost identically. They're wearing the shark shirt this time, but it's still close enough.

"Sorry, I totally bit your style," I say.

"Imitation is the sincerest form of flattery," they reply, brushing off their shoulders.

I'm just thinking that it feels nice to be standing in a group of people I don't work with when Inez gets out of the Bug driver's seat and all thoughts leave my head entirely.

When they recover enough to be vaguely word-shaped, I think I might be in over my head with this *let the thoughts happen* plan. She looks amazing. Short black dress that flares out above her knees. Embroidered bomber jacket. Hair in two braids, bright white sneakers. Her legs are long and tanned, as is the shoulder that peeks out of the jacket where it's sliding off just a little.

Her lips are shiny. I wonder what the shiny stuff tastes like, and as per the plan I don't wonder what it means that I'm wondering or try to stop myself from doing it.

The unforeseen problem with this plan is that the thoughts get out of hand quickly. I swallow hard, then glance around to see if anyone notices. Jaz is tapping away on her phone and Mars is looking over her shoulder, so I'm safe for now.

"Hey," I say to Inez, as casually as possible.

"Hi."

I'm sure there's something else I'm supposed to be saying, and even if not I'm sure I'm staring. Is it my imagination or is she blushing a little in the evening light?

"So, are we gonna do this or are you two just gonna make moony eyes at each other all night."

"Oh god, stop," Inez says, swatting at Jaz. "You know it's not like that."

The casual way she brushes this comment off helps me get ahold of myself. *She doesn't think of me that way,* I tell myself sternly. Which is absolutely for the best.

Badger's is packed. I've never been here for one of these before, but it's clear they're a town favorite. I see Ginny and Brad near the window, Amy from the grilled cheese place, even Larry Cross is holding a beer by the firepit.

No sign of Robin yet, but that's okay. We have all night.

"Okay, remember," Inez says, her face close to mine. "We're not intimidated. We're confident. We're gorgeous. We're just having a great time, and then?"

"Boom," I say, mimicking an explosion with my hands. "Speech."

"Exactly," Inez says with a smile that makes my knees a little wobbly.

"I put stuff in my hair," I blurt. "It's new. Maybe it's too much."

Her answering smile is so warm, so affectionate that I feel it in my chest. "No," she says. "The hair stuff is great. You look amazing. And you're going to kill it tonight, and Parker is going to be fine at her sleepover, and you have nothing to worry about. Let's have some fun, okay?"

"Okay."

She removes her hand from my shoulder and turns to Mars and Jaz. I shake my head a little to dislodge the thought of other kinds of fun we could be having. There's a no repression policy tonight, but I do still have to function.

Badger's goes all out for business owners' appreciation night. They do it the last Sunday of every month, and I've never been. For one, I'm not a business owner—though it's not like George and Linda are going to show up to attend on behalf of Joyce's. And for another I usually spend Sunday nights at home with Parker.

There are at least thirty people in here. No one is seated, they're all just milling around with drinks in the low light, spilling out onto the patio, chatting in small groups. It's pretty tame, given it's barely eight, but if I know this group it'll loosen up after an hour and a couple of drinks.

Sasha is holding court at the bar as usual, and with a stab of rage I notice Chase leaning over the counter chatting with her. Even though I expected it, it feels entirely presumptuous for him to show up here. At least I *run* a local business—all he does is attempt to destroy them.

I'm about to do a lap and look for Robin, but my phone buzzes with a text from Isabella R.'s mom, Sarah. It's a picture of the girls eating pizza at their well-appointed dining table. Parker is smiling with all her teeth (and lack thereof).

"Ready?" Inez asks, looping her arm through mine. "I think I saw Robin on the patio."

I'm not sure if the sudden nerves are about the close contact or the fact that I may soon be delivering a speech that my entire livelihood hinges on. Maybe both. "Let's get a drink first," I say, stowing my phone. "Then we'll divide and conquer."

"You read my mind," Inez replies with a wicked smile.

Chase has abandoned the bar by the time we reach it, and Sasha gives me the discount on my sweet potato fries even though I'm not technically a business owner. "We all know you run that place," she says with a wink.

For a brief moment, I'm transported back to the article. *Do you find other women attractive?* I've never thought about it before, but now I find myself looking at Sasha. The tight-fitting, high-waisted pinup pants, the red lipstick. I stop short of answering the fantasies question, but there's no doubt there's something here.

I shove that thought aside for later obsession. I'm not here to solve the question of my misbehaving straightness tonight.

"Thanks," I say, "I'm not sure how much longer it'll need someone to run it, though."

I'm trying to prompt her into giving me the dirt about Robin's support of Kings, and I see a wince of pity cross her face. "I'm really sorry about all this," she says, and it seems like she means it. Inez, in possession of her glass of rosé, moves over to chat with Barry from the donut shop.

I lean across the bar to speak more quietly to Sasha. "Give it to me straight, yeah? Is Robin really buying into the whole Kings thing?"

Sasha glances furtively around, only answering when she clocks her boss moving out onto the patio. "It's pretty compelling, you have to admit," she says finally, like she's confessing to a crime.

"I get it," I say. "I don't think they'll live up to the stuff they're promising everyone, but I get why it's hard to turn down. It's just . . . if Robin and Kendra are on board, we don't have a chance of getting their city council pitch thrown out."

Sasha nods. "I know she feels shitty about hanging you guys out to dry," she says, even quieter now. "And don't tell her I told you this, but she said something today that made me think it's not a done deal. You should talk to her. She's good people."

"Thanks, Sasha," I say. "You're good people, too."

"By the way, love the look," she says as I turn to walk away. It's nothing compared to how I feel when Inez smiles at me, but I can't deny it does something . . .

I make my way around the room a few times, letting Robin see how many friends I have here before approaching her outside by the firepit.

Inez, seeing me heading out, gives me a double thumbs-up that I return subtly.

Robin is a tall, broad-shouldered woman with a severely short haircut and a perpetual sunburn on her nose and the back of her neck. She wears work pants and a Badger's button-down. She speaks in a loud, booming voice.

I hang around, making casual small talk with Larry and a couple of people I don't know at the opposite firepit until Robin's conversation concludes, then I make my way over.

"Robin?" I say as I approach. "Cash Delgado, Joyce's."

"Cash," Robin says, reaching out her own beer to clink with mine. "Of course. How are George and Linda?"

"Good," I say. "On a cruise up in Alaska with their son. If we could all be so lucky."

She laughs at that, and I know I could ask how things at Badger's are, make some small talk, but you don't work as a career bartender without learning to read people's cues, and I sense Robin is a woman who doesn't appreciate idle chitchat.

"Well, Robin, I came over here to ask you a question, so I guess I'll just ask it instead of wasting your time. Are you and Kendra thinking of supporting the Kings franchise?"

I know immediately that I gambled right. Robin nods in appreciation. "Look, I can't deny the suits did their homework. I know it's a raw deal for you guys, but it does feel like a good move for Badger's. Kings isn't our competition, so the crowd they draw for big shows can only benefit us. I've got a kid in college, my wife needs surgery on a slipped disc. This tourism roller coaster doesn't do us many favors, and it's hard to pass up the opportunity to solidify things around here."

"I really hear you," I say.

I take a deep breath, drawing on the confidence I felt in Sammy Espinoza's office. On that face Parker makes when she thinks I can solve any problem, no matter how complex.

"But if you have a minute, I'm going to tell you why I think supporting a corporate franchise is bad for Badger's *and* Ridley Falls." I don't bother waiting for her to respond. I just go. "If Kings comes in, if the chains start to see they can succeed here, they're not going to stop at putting Joyce's out of business. There'll be a Starbucks on the corner next, competing with Ponderosa's. Then a Cheesecake Factory on that corner competing with you."

I can tell I have Robin's attention with *Cheesecake Factory*. When I pause for breath she doesn't cut in. She waits for me to continue.

"You know what these corporate guys are like," I tell her. Just her and me, a few casual small-town folks. Us against them. "They don't care about small-town economies or businesses. They care about making a buck. And if that buck comes at the expense of this town's culture and community, they're fine with that. And if, in a few years, the tourism slows down and they're not making a profit? They'll cut their losses and get out of here. On to the next place with promise. Only by then, it'll be too late for most of us to rebuild our businesses. And what happens to Ridley Falls then?"

Robin nods thoughtfully, takes a long drink of her beer. I know it's time to go in for the kill, so I do.

"Small towns like this one don't thrive because we court big businesses," I tell her. "We thrive when we have each other's backs. When we help each other through the tough times. When we act like communities. We have some heat right now because of the record label and the tourism, let's use that to support each other, to build some reserves. Because once we start down this road, we can't turn around. I can't promise you supporting Joyce's will make things stable or easy forever, but I can promise you this: When those Cheesecake Factory corporate monkeys come sniffing around here, they won't be drinking at my bar."

At this, Robin laughs. A deep, loud bark of a laugh. "Kid, I gotta tell you, that was a hell of a speech. Whatever George and Linda are paying you, it's not enough."

I laugh, too, glad to shake off the tension. To know I did my best, for better or worse. "I love that place," I tell her. "And this town. I've lived in big cities before, but this one is home. I don't want to lose it."

Robin nods, then claps a hand on my shoulder. "Let me think about it, okay? You've got spunk, and you're making some good points. I'll call you."

"Thanks, Robin," I say sincerely, reaching out to shake her hand.

"You got it. I hope you get your own place someday, Cash. You've got the heart for it."

I walk away feeling lighter than I have in weeks. I can't be sure, but I think I just knocked it out of the park with Robin. I have the same feeling I did in the greenhouse, back when we came up with the idea for the party in the first place. Like I'm floating just a little above the ground.

There's only one person I want to tell, and she's coming toward me across the bar.

"I got Barry!" she says as she reaches me. "There was a fair bit of intimidation involved, but he's bringing donuts to the festival *and* donating a basket for the silent auction."

"You're incredible," I tell her.

"Okay, enough of that," she says, waving a hand, her cheeks bright pink from the heat in the room and the wine. She leans in very close to ask: "How'd it go with Robin? Chase was glaring daggers at you two."

"It went well," I manage, dazed again. "She said she likes my spunk and I've given her a lot to think about. She's gonna call me."

"Oh my god, Cash, that's incredible!" She launches herself into my arms. She smells so good. Her skin and hair are so soft I'm almost lost in the sensory experience of her and this time I don't try to pull myself out.

I tighten my arms around her just a little. I feel loopy from the beer and the victory with Robin. My body barely feels like my own, like someone else is at the controls and they don't care what the consequences are.

My phone buzzes in my pocket, startling Inez who's still pressed against me. She disentangles herself, leaving space for me to pull it out.

"Sorry," I say, nerves jangling. "It's Isabella's mom."

"Go, go," Inez says, and I make my way outside, the anxiety of what could have gone wrong mixing with the intoxication of the moment until I feel muddled and dizzy and strange.

"Hello?" I say when I'm out front, away from the noise.

"Hi Cash, it's Sarah."

"Hey, is Parker okay?" I ask, heart hammering.

"Oh, yeah, she's great," Sarah says. "She just wanted to say goodnight if you have a minute."

Relief floods through me. That Parker is okay, and also that she still needs to say goodnight to me.

"Mom?"

"Hey, pal," I say, smiling, the cool night air doing wonders for my mixed-up emotions.

"Is it a little kid thing to have to call your mom at night?"

I laugh, wishing suddenly, fiercely, that we were just at home together. Eating frozen mozzarella sticks and watching *Moana* again.

"Not at all," I say. "It's a very big kid thing to even be at a sleepover. Calling your mom is a thing you can do anytime. Even when you're eighty."

That gets a giggle from her. "Okay. I'm having a lot of fun."

"Good! I'll be there to pick you up after school tomorrow and you can tell me all about it. Sound good?"

"Yeah!" Parker says, sounding much brighter now. "I gotta go; we're gonna tell scary stories. Can we say goodnight?"

"Of course," I say. "Silly voices or normal?"

"Silly, of course!"

We say goodnight in our chicken voices. Mine is loud. Several people from the patio look over. But I'd do anything for Parker.

"Love you, pal," I tell her.

"Love you more."

"That's impossible."

And then she's gone. I stand outside for a few more minutes, almost wishing I still smoked cigarettes just to have a reason to stand out front for a little longer.

"Hey," comes a voice out of the shadows as Mars approaches around the building. "Just didn't want to startle you."

"Oh, no worries, just saying goodnight to my kid."

"Cute." Mars apparently doesn't share my qualms about smoking and life expectancy, because they light one and lean against the wall. I'm actually thankful for this, standing with someone who's smoking gives you the same amount of legitimacy as doing it yourself.

"Having fun?" I ask.

Mars yawns. "I was hoping to see some new blood in there but it's just the same old crowd. Dating in this town is miserable."

"Tell me about it." I lean against the wall beside them.

"So, Inez says you're straight," they say, taking a drag.

"Yeah," I answer automatically, but my mind pushes back, a little rebellious. *Are you sure?*

"Are you sure?" Mars asks, echoing my thoughts. They raise an eyebrow, and it suddenly occurs to me that they might be flirting with me.

In the spirit of the evening, I let myself think about it. Mars and me, kissing against this wall right now. The thought doesn't remotely repulse me, but my first thought is that I couldn't, because Mars is one of Inez's best friends.

"Actually," I say, realizing I haven't said this out loud to anyone yet. "Lately I think I might . . . I don't know. I might be less sure than I used to be."

Mars's mischievous smile deepens. "Yeah, I have that effect on women," they say. Flirting, no doubt about it.

"How did you know?" I ask. "Is it even possible, at my age?"

Mars laughs. "Oh, you're having, like, a moment," they say. "My bad, let me take off my flirting hat and put on my counseling hat."

I laugh. "I'm so sorry," I say. "You don't have to answer. I'm fine. I'm just . . ."

"Fantasizing, googling shit, feeling like a mess?" they ask, in a significantly less sultry tone.

"Yes," I say. "All of that."

"Yeah, girl," Mars says. "I mean, you are whoever you want to be. But there are some signs that are pretty universal. And with the wild way this society forces everyone into their little cishet boxes, there's no shame in figuring yourself out at any age, so don't let that trip you up. It's better to live any of your life authentically than none of it."

These words connect somewhere deep. I nod, but then it starts to become overwhelming again. The idea of changing what I fundamentally know about myself. The potential consequences for me, for Parker. "I mean, I'm not even sure it's anything," I say. "I'm going through a lot right now, I might just be freaking out over nothing."

Mars holds up their hands. "You take your time. But just know you have some friends who have been through it. You don't have to do it alone. *If* you're doing anything," they finish with a smirk. "Which you're *totally probably* not."

"Thank you," I say. "It means a lot, even if . . ." I trail off.

"Even if," Mars says. "And you know, to put my flirting hat back on for a second, if you think you might be queer . . . the easiest way to find out is just to experiment."

I laugh. "I'll keep that in mind," I say.

"Do that," Mars replies, winking. When they head back inside, I follow them, feeling both better and more confused than ever.

17

THE MOMENT I get back inside, my head entirely full of what feels like uncooperative mush, I'm confronted with Chase making his way to the door.

"Cash," he says, pausing as Mars disappears into the crowd. "I'm surprised to see you here. I didn't know they let *employees* in on business owners' night."

"Chase," I say in my most withering tone. "I didn't know they let gentrifiers in either. It's a banner night for both of us. I suggest we enjoy it."

He rolls his eyes. "It really didn't have to be like this, you know? We could have worked together. And now I'm going to make absolutely sure that Kings sucks the life out of that little backwoods karaoke hovel."

I laugh out loud. "Good luck," I say. "You're going to need it."

Without waiting for his response, I push past him, but he reaches out and grabs my arm. "Yeah, hurry back to that little girlfriend of yours. You know, I've been curious, when you're fucking . . . which one of you pretends to have a dick?"

The only thought in my head as I pull my arm away and whirl

around to face him is that I want to hit whatever part of him I can reach. But before I get a chance, a booming voice fills the entryway.

"Son, my *wife* and I don't tolerate language like that in our establishment." Robin steps between us then, nearly as tall as Chase and about ten times as intimidating. There's not a hint of laughter in her eyes now. "In fact, we've got a zero tolerance policy for bigotry of that kind and any other. I'll thank you to get the hell out of my bar and not come back."

"Robin," Chase says, turning on his schmoozing voice. "I think there's been a misunderstanding."

"There must have been," she agrees. "Or you wouldn't still be standing here."

There's nothing for him to do then but to walk out the door, muttering under his breath all the way.

I turn to Robin once he's gone, not at all sure what to say. I'm not sure whether to feel grateful for the fact that she defended me, or like an impostor because I probably didn't deserve it.

"Don't worry about assholes like him," she says, before I can work it out. "Industry's full of them. I've never let them bother me."

"Thank you," I say, and suddenly that feels like enough.

"Don't mention it. Grab a beer on the house, huh? I'll be in touch." And she makes her way out into the night.

I'm barely inside ten seconds before Inez, Mars, and Jaz are all over me. "What the hell happened?" Inez asks. "Someone said you and Chase got in a fight in the entryway and Robin punched him?"

It can't have been more than thirty seconds. The Ridley Falls gossip engine is clearly running efficiently tonight.

"He made some shitty comment," I say. "Robin threw him out. It was no big deal."

"What comment?" Inez asks, but I don't want to get into it. Not here.

"Honestly, I'd love to get the fuck out of here," I say. "You guys with me?"

"Going home at ten is a tragedy," Jaz groans. "But there's nowhere else to go, so call me Juliet." She mock swoons, and Mars steps forward to catch her.

"Let's not go home," I say, struck with sudden inspiration. The last thing I need to do is go home and worry about everything that's happened tonight in my dark, quiet house. "Come on, don't you remember what we used to do to before we were old enough to go to bars?"

"Sell fake IDs out of my locker?" Jaz asks.

"Get my slightly predatory twenty-eight-year-old boyfriend to buy us liquor?" Mars offers.

"Shoplift?" Inez guesses.

"Wow, you were a bunch of degenerates," I say, even though this is a real pot-calling-the-kettle-black moment. "I just meant drinking in the baseball dugouts."

Everyone is enthusiastically on board. We all pile into the Jeep, stopping by Safeway where we obtain beer and wine coolers (by legal methods, we are adults and pillars of the community now after all) and then head for the Little League dugouts across town.

The place is deserted. Mars carries the beer and Jaz, who's been sober for years, volunteers to drive us home. Even with all the precautions, I nurse my first beer as we settle in on the benches. There's too much going on in my mind right now not to have my wits about me.

It's an absolutely gorgeous night. Almost summer, when the nights are warm enough to be out but there's still a little bite in the air that makes you want to huddle up next to someone. Or, at least, it seems to make Inez want to do that, because she presses the length of her left arm into my right.

I don't acknowledge it except to drink slightly clumsily with my left hand.

Within minutes, a tipsy Mars is talking with Jaz about their gender-awakening stories, and I'm grateful that the pressure of Badger's is off. That it's okay for me to just listen. To enjoy the feeling of Inez's warm body pressed against mine. To be in this liminal space that feels separate from my real life and all its consequences.

"I was five," Jaz is saying, plucking Mars's cigarette from their fingers and taking a long drag. "I was at soccer practice, absolutely hating every second of it—those ugly cleats and polyester uniforms, the screaming little heathens everywhere. Someone's mom came to pick them up with a big sister in tow. She was probably eight, coming from ballet class. She was wearing a tutu and tights and a tiara and something just clicked. I could *see* myself in that outfit. But more than that I could see myself as *her*. As *a* her. Even then I remember it making perfect sense."

"It took me so much longer," Mars says, a little maudlin, snagging the cigarette back. "I mean, in some ways I always knew, but I just didn't let myself acknowledge it. Couldn't own it. I thought I was a lesbian, but even that never really felt right. I liked guys, but it didn't feel the same way it felt when my cis female friends talked about it."

They take a long swig from their beer, staring out into the field. Inez is turned toward Mars, listening, giving me the chance to look down at her without being noticed. My whole body feels oriented to hers, like she's exerting some gravitational pull over me.

My friend Inez is warm and soft and curvy and beautiful, I think, but it's far from a detached observation floating away on the stream of my consciousness. I can feel every word beating along with my pulse.

"I was in college, twenty-one I think, when some frat threw a gender-bender party. Everyone I knew was borrowing clothes from boys they liked. I'll never forget it. I wore gray wool slacks and a button-down black shirt. Red suspenders. My friend wrapped my chest with an ACE bandage because there was no one to tell us that's wildly dangerous. I remember feeling so confident. So *present* in my body. I stalked my friend's Facebook just to stare at the pictures for weeks afterward."

They put out the cigarette in their empty beer bottle and reach for another.

"It still took me five more years to come out as nonbinary," they say with a chuckle. "Probably three years before I could even think the word to myself."

This last sentence snags like a sweater on a nail. *Before I could even think the word to myself.* I want to ask if it felt like a wave rearing up inside them. Too big. Too much. If they shoved it down again and again. How they knew it was the right time.

Jaz makes a sympathetic sound, petting Mars's head. Inez stirs beside me.

"I had my first girl crush when I was ten," she says with a nostalgic smile. "Keira Phillips. Fourth-grade queen bee. I worshipped her in secret until seventh grade, never said a word, and then cried when I saw her kissing Blake Daniels after our first boy/girl dance."

"Devastating!" Jaz exclaims.

No one looks at me during all this. Inez's token straight friend would never be expected to tell a queer awakening story. But I find I wish I had one. Something in my history I could point to and say here. Here's where the story starts to make sense.

Half an hour later Mars falls asleep, and Jaz says we should call it a night. I'm panicking, thinking of my real life as a box I don't want to fold myself back into. Not yet. Inez must be feeling the same because she turns to me. "Stay a little longer?" she asks. "We can call Larry or walk?"

I don't even hesitate, just toss Jaz the keys to the Jeep and ask her to leave it outside Badger's when she gets the Bug. In minutes, Inez and I are alone, and when she looks at me with a mischievous sparkle in her eye, I know I'm about to say yes to whatever she proposes. And maybe even the thing after that.

"Up for a light misdemeanor?" she asks, bumping my shoulder with hers.

"With you?" I say. "Anytime."

It takes us twenty minutes to walk to the Palm Motel. Along the way, Inez disappears into the bushes behind someone's large back-yard and emerges with four eggs.

"Do I want to know?" I ask mildly as she rejoins me on the street.

"Probably not."

We continue down the road, not speaking again until the Palm is in view. It's the only motel in town—tourists who aren't staying at Max Ryan's swanky recording retreat out of town are stuck here or at Mrs. Blair's B&B, which smells like cats, I'm told.

"What are we doing here?" I ask Inez as she prowls through the parking lot, clearly looking for something.

"I know it's here somewhere," she says. "He wouldn't stay

with mommy and daddy. Aha!" We round the corner and her plan becomes clear. Chase's overly shiny rental car—the one I'm disgusted to admit I let him kiss me in just two weeks ago—is outside room five. It's empty.

Do you still find men attractive? The internet listicle asks in the back of my mind.

There are lights on in Chase's room, the sounds of laughter. The TV? I wonder. I can't imagine he found someone to accompany him in his exile from Badger's.

"Oh my god, he left the windows down!" Inez whispers as we approach the car. She pulls the eggs out of her tote bag purse and hands me two of them. They still feel warm.

"You can't be serious," I say.

She holds them threateningly at the open window. Her expression says she'll do it. "Tell me what he said or I'm egging it," she threatens.

"What?"

"Chase said something that made Robin kick him out of the bar," she says, enunciating clearly despite the whispering. "What was it?"

I can feel my face going hot. There's a reason I didn't tell her in the first place. There are a hundred reasons.

"Okay," she says, a response to my silence. "Here goes." She pulls back the arm holding the first egg. I have a vision of Chase coming outside, calling the cops, the mayor hearing we were arrested for vandalism and rejecting our plea to have the Kings parking lot denied on sight.

"He called you my girlfriend," I blurt out. "Asked which one of us pretended to have a dick when we fuck. Robin overheard. She threw him out. That's the whole thing."

Inez's eyes go wide. She lowers the egg. "Wow," she says. "Are you okay?"

I think about it, instead of just saying yes by default. I think back to the first time Chase insinuated that there was something going on between Inez and me. The way I bolted. How ashamed I felt. Then I think about tonight, the anger, the feeling of solidarity when Robin stuck up for me.

"Not really," I admit.

Solemnly, eyes reflecting the lit windows of Chase's motel room, Inez gestures down at the eggs.

I feel electric as I crack the first one against the edge of the window, letting the yolk run down into the passenger seat. I laugh without thinking about it, and Inez shushes me, giggling, too.

Together, we fill the driver's and passengers' seats with raw egg goo, tossing the shells onto the floor mats before bending over in near-silent hysterics.

"I have egg all over my hands," Inez says, gasping with repressed laughter. She turns to hold them up, walking toward me like a zombie. I stumble back, laughing quietly, and my foot catches on something.

Inez lunges to catch my outstretched hand but it's too late, my back thuds into the car and immediately the sound of an alarm fills the air.

"Oh shit!" I say, scrambling to my feet. "Oh shit!!"

Inez is laughing, grabbing my hand despite the egg. We run as the door to room five opens. There's no time to look back but we can clearly hear Chase shout, "What the fuck?" as we scramble around the corner.

The Palm campus takes up a whole block, and Chase—clearly planning on needing his privacy this week—took a room on the far side. Inez and I, carless and scrambling, stick to the shadows until we make it around back of the office.

Before us, glowing in the pre-midnight darkness, is a pool surrounded by a low fence. Potted palms stand in every corner, as tall as we are.

I'm amazed by the agility with which Inez hops the fence. I clear it, too, bringing back memories of the hopped trains and raided house parties of my youth.

Still giggling, Inez takes my hand again, pulling me behind one of the palms, crouching down.

It's a tiny space. We can't make any noise. Our bodies are pressed together and she looks at me sideways. Mischievous. Crackling with that energy that's always drawn me to her.

If I don't kiss her now I'll die, I observe, trying to keep my mental tone as even as my meditation recording.

She licks her lips. The entire surface of my skin feels charged, like static. If she touches me anywhere, I'll disintegrate.

"Cash," she whispers, and the sound of my name in her voice is a bolt of electricity straight between my legs.

I'm about to say her name. To close the incredibly minimal distance between us and damn the consequences, when a flashlight beam crosses the pool area and two voices ring out across the water.

". . . the hell are you doing for security around here, do you even know how expensive that car is? I don't have time to get it detailed before I drive back to Seattle tomorrow. Am I supposed to sit in *egg* the whole way back?"

I can practically see the unattractive shade of bright red Chase must be turning in his anger. It's all I can do not to giggle.

Inez reaches forward as if she can read my thoughts, covering my mouth with her hand, locking her eyes on mine as mirth dances through her expression.

"Sir, we don't have security. Guests are responsible for their own belongings. It's in your agreement."

"Well, where the hell are the people who did this then? Do you have cameras? Anything?"

The long-suffering voice of the old woman who runs the motel desk is a few minutes in coming.

"I assume your egg vandals are either high school students who ran home to their parents because they have class in the morning, or you have some very immature enemies who had the good sense to drive off in a car of their own."

Chase actually growls in frustration. "What do you suggest I do then?" he asks in his icy corporate manager voice.

"I suggest you get a bottle of cleaner and a towel or you're not getting your rental deposit back. Now, if you don't mind, I'm going back to bed."

The shuffle of house slippers on asphalt. Chase, storming off to the other side of the motel property. Within minutes, Inez and I are alone again.

I'm almost sorry when she takes her hand off my mouth.

"You know what I really want to do right now?" she asks in a low, sultry voice that makes me forget my own name.

"What?" I manage, my whisper fracturing halfway through the word, forcing me to clear my throat.

She sparkles at me for a long moment before she says: "Go swimming."

Without waiting for a response, she's up, whipping her dress over her head and diving soundlessly into the dark water.

I've never been jealous of chlorinated liquid before, but as I imagine it wrapping around every inch of her newly bare skin I realize there really is a first time for everything.

"You coming?" she says, and I'm up before I can even interrogate it. It's automatic. A reflex. An instinct.

My trousers and button-down shirt are in a pile beside Inez's dress. I watch the rest as if from above: I'm approaching the water. I know I should test the temperature first. That it's stupid to just leap without knowing what's below.

Instead, I jump into the deep end feet first. I never learned how to dive so I just keep myself as straight as possible to avoid a splash that might attract the manager.

The water is perfect. There was nothing to fear. Just a little warmer than the air. I stay under for a long time, opening my eyes to see Inez's body, mermaidlike as it comes toward me.

By the time I surface she's already there. So close. Water clings to her lashes, her lips, the tip of her nose.

"Hi," I say softly.

"Hi."

There's a long silence while I adjust to the closeness. The barely there clothing separating our bodies. The waves of want sweeping through my body.

"Can I ask you something?" Inez says.

"Sure."

"Why did you really kiss me in the greenhouse that day?"

"Because I wanted to," I say, hoping she'll leave it at that.

"I wanted you to, too."

Another wave. Gravity, pulling me closer to her as we tread water, facing each other.

"Can I ask *you* something?" I counter.

She nods.

"Have you ever been with a straight girl before?"

Her expression turns thoughtful, like when Mars switched from their flirting hat to their counseling hat. I wonder if this is something all queer people can do. If it's something I'll be able to do, one day, if I discover I am.

I can almost hear Mars's voice before Inez formulates her response. *The easiest way to figure out if you're queer is to experiment.*

"Yes," she says finally. "I've been with straight girls before."

"So it happens," I say, more to myself than to her.

"People are curious by nature," Inez says. "Women are beautiful. It's more common than you think."

She drifts over to the side of the pool. I follow closely to the place where our feet are on solid ground again.

"Why do you ask?" she challenges. We're close still, despite the location change. Any shift of movement and we'd be touching beneath the water's surface.

"I can't stop thinking about you." It's such a relief to say it that I feel dizzy. I let my gaze rake across her body without justifying or minimizing it. The ripple that passes through me leaves me dry-mouthed and breathless.

"Thinking about me what?" Inez asks, eyes all wide and innocent. She bites her lip.

"In lingerie," I confess, my voice rough and low. "In a bathing suit. Between my legs on the bar. Sliding into my bed in the middle of the night."

Her unflappable cool breaks then. She takes a shaky little breath. "Cash," she says. A whisper I can feel across every inch of my skin. "What are you saying? If I needed you to spell it out . . ."

I'm so turned on I seem to have lost the ability to be embarrassed. "I'm saying I want you so badly I can barely be normal anymore. I'm saying curiosity doesn't begin to cover it. I'm saying I've listened to twenty-nine hours of guided meditation to try to stop wondering what it would be like to touch you, and it hasn't done a fucking thing."

Blush spreads across her cheeks. "I've thought about it," she admits quietly. "You and me. I've thought about it on your couch, knowing you're asleep upstairs. I've thought about it in the bar. In the passenger seat of the Jeep. I've thought about making you come for me in ways a man never could."

"Fuck," I whisper. "Fuck, Inez. Don't say it unless you mean it, because I can't take it anymore. I feel like I could lose it right now just from the way you're looking at me."

A wicked smile spreads across her face. The way my body feels right now makes me wonder if this is the first time I've ever properly been aware of it. Every cell is demanding, needy, pulsing and throbbing and pounding.

"One time," she says. "Just to get it out of our systems. That's all it can be, okay? We're best friends. We work together. We do it once so we can stop thinking about it, and that's it."

"Yes," I say in a rush. "Just once. We release the pressure and get back to normal. Nothing changes."

"Nothing changes," she echoes, moving an inch closer. Her hand grazes my hip beneath the water. "Promise me nothing changes."

"Nothing changes," I say, and I can see it reflected in her eyes. That hunger that's been eating me alive for every second since that first dream. I take her face in my hands and kiss her the way I've wanted to for hours. For days. Weeks. Longer. Forever.

This isn't the sweet, exploratory kiss from the greenhouse. This thing has heat. Its own agenda. It snakes inside me to all the places I've been trying so hard to repress and seizes control.

With the low gravity of the pool I lift her, pressing her against the wall, feeling her smooth legs wrap around my back. I can't help it, I grind my hips into hers, desperate for friction.

Her mouth drops open and I take full advantage, our tongues tangling. Her hands reach up and grip my hair in the back, tugging gently, making me moan into her mouth.

My hands run up and down her back, memorizing the feel of her body. A landscape that I've admired so many times it's become more familiar to me than any other. Shoulders, spine, hips. Inez responds eagerly, arching into every place I'm touching her as her mouth continues to probe mine relentlessly.

When I reach the soft swell of her ass I pause, pulling away from the kiss to whisper "Is this okay?" in her ear, surprised (though I probably shouldn't be) by the harsh and ragged quality of my voice.

"How about this," she murmurs into mine. "Unless I say stop, you can do whatever you want to me."

I laugh, my voice still low and rough in her ear. "For that, we'll probably need a change of venue."

"Well," Inez purrs, walking her fingers up my neck. "We *are* at a motel."

"Good reminder," I say. "I kind of forgot we were even on earth."

With permission obtained, I let myself cup the glorious expanse of her ass, squeezing, pulling her into me as she giggles and kisses my neck.

"If you don't stop that the change of venue part is going to become much more difficult to manage," she says.

Only the promise of more, elsewhere, can convince me to untangle our limbs. To climb out of the water and struggle back into my clothes. I don't bother to button my shirt, just leave it open over my sports bra as she turns to face me, her dress clinging to her wet skin.

I step forward helplessly, letting my hands roam her body as I kiss her again, not able to stay away even for the time it would take to get to the front desk, into a room . . .

Seemingly on the same page, Inez backs me into a lounge chair near the edge of the pool. I sit down roughly and she climbs into my lap, straddling me, her perfect breasts pressing against my chest as she grinds against me.

My whole body feels like a raw nerve. Anywhere she touches me has a direct line to the electric current of desire running through me.

She slides her palms into my open shirt, tracing my chest, my stomach, my shoulders and collarbones as I lie helplessly beneath her, pinned and rapturous.

I don't know how long we map each other's damp skin before the sound of a throat clearing shocks us back into our separate bodies.

Scrambling to right myself, imagining Chase or the police or one of Parker's teachers or worse, I'm almost relieved to come face-to-face with the elderly proprietor of the Palm in her dressing gown and slippers.

"I think the phrase the kids use is *get a room*," she says dryly. "And wouldn't you know it, you're about thirty feet from the right place."

18

IT TAKES A few minutes to get checked in. I use my credit card, and the old witch of the Palm—who Inez calls Barb as if they're old friends—hands us two room keys and a stack of towels with, you guessed it, palm trees on them.

"Check out is at eleven," she says. "And keep the noise down. In case you didn't know it's after midnight."

We make our way through the winding stairs and sidewalks until we reach room fourteen. I let us in with my key, holding the door for Inez who flips on the lights to reveal a room with little more than a bed and an ancient TV.

The air-conditioning is on full blast and I turn it off, adjusting to the change in atmosphere.

"Do you mind if I take a shower?" Inez asks, rubbing her arms, which I can see from here are covered in goosebumps.

"Of course not," I say. "I'll just wait here. I bet *Jeopardy!*'s on."

"Or . . . you could join me?" She asks this a little shyly, despite the very public antics we were just getting up to in the pool and surrounding area.

I understand the shift. Out there in the dark everything felt reckless and rebellious. Like a fast-moving train we had to hop on before it sped away. In here, with the lights on and the bed beckoning, it feels more like a choice than a happening.

"I would love to," I say, stepping out of my trousers for the second time.

She steps forward and removes my shirt herself before pulling off her dress again. We're down to our underwear, hers a set of royal blue that makes her skin glow. Mine the traditional boxer briefs and sports bra I wear every day.

I think almost deliriously back to choosing them, with absolutely no idea how this night would end.

I step forward, closing the distance again, reaching behind her to undo the clasp on her bra. Pausing to give her time to say stop if this is moving too fast.

She doesn't. Her breasts spill out and I have to swallow, hard. The perfect teardrop shape of them. The smoothness of her skin. The round, dark nipples. I caress them, feeling like I'm trespassing on holy ground.

Inez moans when my thumbs brush her nipples. A small, whispery thing that sounds involuntary and sends a shiver of pleasure through me.

I take off my sports bra next while she steps out of her thong. Once my briefs are gone we're fully naked, taking each other in.

"Goddamn," she says with a smirk.

I do my best to find a witty retort, but mostly I just gape like a fish.

She laughs. Bells chiming through the room. "I'll take that as a compliment."

Out of sheer habit, my mind tells me not to stare as she moves around the room, turning on the shower, putting the towels on the rack within reach. It takes me a few minutes to remember that I'm allowed to look at her this way. Allowed to want her so much it feels like a new heartbeat under my skin.

Just for tonight, I remind myself. *Nothing changes.*

Once the shower is steaming, she slides the glass door aside and lets me watch as she climbs in. Beneath the hot water we warm up in more ways than one. Her skin feels different in hot water than in cool. I kiss down her neck, across her chest, finally taking her nipple into my mouth and grazing it just a little with my teeth.

"Stop," she says, hand tightening in my hair. "No teeth, please."

"Noted," I say, kissing it softly as if I can erase the hurt. Moving on to the next one, learning the rhythm of her breath when she's enjoying herself, the little gasp that means I'm doing something she likes.

I let her lead, stepping out when she turns off the water. Following her to the bed.

There's no awkwardness now, no shifting and no pause even as the scenery changes. We're in this new world we've created together and she doesn't seem any more eager to leave it than I am.

I meant to tell her I've never done this before, but of course, she knows. And anyway all I can manage is "Tell me what you want," as I move breathlessly across her skin. "I want to make you feel good."

She guides, instead of telling. Her hand on mine, moving it across her skin. Showing me where to apply pressure, where to circle, where to pull back. I listen with my whole body. I might not have much experience, but I've always been a quick study. Soon enough she's lost in the sensations, releasing my hand, trusting me to remember the rhythm.

"Oh my god," she says, breathing the words in, barely a whisper. "That's good, that's so good . . ."

A wave of pleasure like nothing I've ever known pulses through me at the thought that I'm causing this. That I'm making her feel this way. This level of arousal is so intense it goes beyond urgency. I understand, for the first time, why people brag about fucking all night.

She kisses me deeply, fisting her hands in my short curls, pulling me closer as I trace every curve, dip, and swell. Once, she reaches lower, but I shake my head. "Not yet," I tell her, and her head falls back in relief, surrendering to the sensations.

When I'm confident in my understanding of the routes, I begin to kiss down her body, stopping at her nipples again, feeling the impossibly soft skin of her breasts against my face. But this time I don't stop there.

Inez is panting before I even reach the apex of her thighs. "Please," she whimpers. "Oh, god, please."

Another wave courses through me. I have to focus not to unravel just from her encouragement. No touching required. I take a deep breath to steady myself, and then I'm lost. My tongue remembers the path my fingers took, and it's a miracle because everything about this is distracting. Overwhelming in the best possible way.

I think, almost deliriously as I taste her, that I've never been this close to another person. That this is the most intimate thing a person can do. That it never felt this way going down on a guy. This feeling is beyond arousal, beyond pleasure. It feels more like reverence than anything.

There's no wishing it was over already, no counting down. I don't know if it's been a minute or an hour when her breathing speeds up, when her hands scramble frantically for purchase in my hair. She pushes me closer to her center, begging me without words to go deeper, faster.

I forget the map. The routes. I'm operating on instinct alone. I feel her thighs clenching, the map changing as she swells and peaks and finally contracts, tight as a bowstring as I ride the waves of her climax with her. Every one of my nerve endings is on fire at the knowledge that she's unraveling beneath me. Around me. *Because* of me.

When she's still I kiss back up her body, living for the long, shaky exhales.

"Pretty good for your first time," she pants, smiling in disbelief.

I want to be with her in this liquid moment, but I feel like I've been dropped back into linear time now that she's sated, and all the urgency that felt unimportant in the beginning hits me like a train.

I've been literally dreaming of this moment for weeks, getting close and being denied. I've become fairly accomplished at repressing these urges, but right now that's impossible. I feel primal. Creaturely, as I grind myself against her thigh, kissing her again, harder this time, begging without words.

Inez understands the assignment. The languorous post-orgasm smile focuses into something with a glint of steel as she realizes the power she holds over me right now.

"Fuck," I grunt without giving myself permission. "Fuck, I need . . . please . . ."

She doesn't need me to finish that unintelligible sentence. She also doesn't require a road map. Her fingers find the place where I'm swollen and slick from months of frustration and wanting. From weeks of almost and false promises of release. I grind into her, straddling her thigh, my mouth hungry on hers as the friction of her fingers and the rhythm of my thrusting hips begin to build to a peak so high I'm afraid to look over the edge.

"It's okay," she whispers roughly in my ear, as if my thoughts are painted across my naked body. "You can let go."

I know it's only been minutes. Maybe less. I'm almost embarrassed to be losing it so soon, but there's no doubt that I am. Every sensation in my body is focused on the place where her fingers are rubbing against me, and when I finally let myself surrender it's almost too intense, at first. Not fireworks but genuine explosions, boring through stone toward my molten center.

This doesn't just feel like my first time getting off in a few months. Or my first time with a partner in a year. It feels like the *first* time, and when the intensity subsides, I know I'm not the same. Of course I'm not. How could I be?

I wake more than once in the night, like my mind needs to confirm she's really here. That this really happened. Every time she's next to me. Once, she has an arm thrown over my belly. Once, a leg wedged between mine. I know tomorrow will be hell, but I can't help but watch her, charmed at how messily she sleeps.

As I drift off for the last time before morning, I have the vague worry that this isn't how people having a one-night stand with their best friend feel in the middle of the night . . .

When I wake up in earnest, I'm alone in the bed. We never even made it under the palm tree duvet. Once I stand up, it will be as if we were never here at all.

For a second, I panic. Did Inez already leave? Given how we set this up, would it be weird if she had? Or would it be weirder that I'm panicking about it?

My questions are answered, and my anxiety momentarily quelled, by the sound of the shower. I'm a little embarrassed by the relief I experience, but it's enough to get me out of bed, still naked, and halfway across the room to the bathroom door.

That's where I stop. Remembering last night. The guidelines we set up to preserve our friendship through this night of potentially ill-advised experimentation.

This was a one-time thing, I tell myself sternly. Nothing changes. We promised each other that.

Instead of following Inez into the shower, I get dressed. Check my phone for messages about Parker. There's a photo from a few minutes ago, the girls eating pancakes in their pajamas. I send a heart emoji, but I feel like I'm half dreaming. Like I belong underwater and I'm surprised to find myself on dry land.

Grasping for something in the pro column, I can confirm that the low-level (okay, sometimes high-level) horniness that has been buzzing relentlessly through me for the past few weeks has been satisfied. I feel clearheaded for the first time since I woke up gasping from a dream of Inez and my whole world turned upside down.

But Mars's words are there again. The ones that made me take this leap in the first place. *The best way to find out you're queer is to experiment.* I never let myself wonder what would happen if I liked it. If I felt transformed by it. If the whole world looked different in the morning.

Just then, Inez steps out of the shower already dressed. "Morning!" she says cheerfully, like she just walked into the bar and not the motel room where we brought each other to dramatic climax just a few hours ago.

"Hey," I say, trying to match her tone. "Sleep okay?"

"Hell yeah," she says, flashing a smile. "How about you—are you okay?"

I feel so cared for by the question, and still I have no idea how to answer it. Is it my best friend Inez asking? The person I tell everything to? Or is it the girl I spent the night with last night who's making me rethink everything I thought I knew about my sexuality?

I'm too aware of the promise we made each other. Just once and nothing changes. But is telling her I'm unraveling a little a change? Or is acting normal a change?

"Yeah," I say finally. "I'm good. A little tired, but good."

"Okay," she says. There's an unfathomable look on her face as she seems to wait for me to say something. I feel like I used to in school when the teacher called on me and I didn't know the answer. Is there some protocol I'm missing?

But before I can ask, the expression is gone.

"Okay!" she says again, brightly. Maybe too brightly. "Well, I should go. I'm sure you want some time to yourself before we're back at the bar all day."

"Sure," I say, feeling lost, like I'm scrambling for purchase as the ground crumbles away beneath my feet. "And um, about last night . . ."

She looks at me with an eyebrow raised. The unfathomable look is back, just for a second. Only I don't know what to say.

"Did you . . . are you . . . ?" I don't complete the sentence because I can't. I don't even know what comes next. Some intangible feeling I can't put into words. Do you feel the same as you did yesterday? Are you fundamentally changed?

"Oh," Inez says, smirking. "Are you asking if I *enjoyed* myself?"

I can tell she means physically, but to correct her would mean to articulate my own feelings, so I just nod a little helplessly.

The smirk widens. "It's so like you to want a progress report," she teases. "Let's just say I never would have known it was your first time."

It's nice to hear, even if it doesn't get close to the core of what my stuttering question was trying to ask. "Oh, well, good," I say. "And you were . . . I mean that was . . . Wow."

She laughs. It's a laugh I've heard nearly every day for years, but it sounds different today. "Please, I feel like I barely even got to show off, you're easy to please."

I stall momentarily at this, wondering how I could possibly explain that the reason there was so little to do with her hands was because of everything she did with her presence. Her moans and pleas. Her mouth falling open in pleasure. Her eyes rolling back in her head . . .

Instead, I clear my throat. These aren't the kinds of things friends who did it once to get it out of their systems say to each other. Inez is putting her earrings in, fluffing her hair, picking up her purse.

I'm still so lost in the memories of last night, of her, that I can't even contemplate an after. But it seems like I don't have a choice. I've never done this kind of get-it-out-of-your-system thing before, but I assume this part—the part where it feels like the whole thing is tattooed on some secret piece of your soul—will fade after a few hours. And maybe some coffee.

"You heading out?" I ask, trying to sound extremely casual.

"Yeah, I called Larry," she said. "Unless you don't want me to . . . ?" Inez looks at me quizzically. Waiting again as I try to sift through the rubble in my head and heart.

What can I possibly say? That I feel like sleeping with her knocked something loose in me and I'm about to totally fall apart? That I want her to stay in this room with me while I try to put it all back together? That I'm afraid if she leaves now it'll be like this never happened?

Those aren't the kinds of things someone says when they did something once and nothing is going to change.

"No, it's totally fine," I say, waving her off. "You go. I'm gonna shower and maybe nap before work."

"Okay," she says. "You sure?"

"Totally sure."

"Well, don't forget to eat something and let me know if you need anything, yeah?"

I nod. "Yeah, of course I will."

Her phone buzzes. She looks down. "He's outside," she says, but she doesn't walk to the door. I know I could still stop her if I said something. The window is open for a few more seconds.

"I'll see you at the bar," I say.

Inez gives me one more long look. "See you at the bar," she replies, and then she's gone, and the door is closing behind her, and absurdly, for the first time in a year, I start to cry.

19

IT TAKES ME at least twenty minutes to stop crying, and another ten to figure out why it's happening. I don't feel sad, I just feel . . . full. Overflowing. Overwhelmed in the most extreme sense of the word.

I feel like I've been climbing up the wall of my house every day and shimmying in through a barely big enough hole in the roof and I just realized this morning there's been a door the whole time.

I'm sitting on the floor with my back against the bed. I can't look at the bed itself. I don't even consider leaving, because in this anonymous motel room I feel like I might have a chance to figure things out. But back in my house, or the bar, or any of the places I normally go I know there'll be excuses to hide behind.

I know, because I've been doing it for weeks. For years, maybe. For my entire life.

Last night, I had sex with a woman, I think. But it's not enough, so I say it out loud: "Last night, I had sex with a woman." I was mostly sober, I think, and in full possession of my faculties. I made the decision to do it, but more than that, it felt as natural as breathing. Much more natural than the weeks I've spent thinking about it and not doing it. Or the years before that when I didn't even know it was something I could want.

I've spent so long trying to convince myself I was still straight because I didn't want anything to change, but all that did was delay the inevitable. So I finally take out my phone, and I type the most important words of my life so far into the search engine that's seen more than its fair share of justifications this month.

Is it possible to discover you're gay later in life?

I sit on the floor for an hour reading every post in order. Articles about compulsory heterosexuality, which Inez told me about. How it can trick people into conforming to a hetero norm so thoroughly that they hide their sexuality even from themselves. Threads on reddit with desperate, married thirtysomethings asking if it's possible they've been wrong about themselves their whole lives.

There are advice pieces about coming out in your late twenties and thirties. Feel-good human interest pieces about people who thought there was something wrong with them until they realized they'd just been queer the whole time.

In the second hour I realize I'm crying again. Silent tears streaming down my face as I read a long article in *The Guardian* titled: "Why it's never too late to be a lesbian."

The article is about a woman who was married to a man for nearly thirty years. Two kids. Picket fence. And one day at forty-four she woke up and realized she'd been hiding from herself her whole life.

She put up flyers, asking other lesbians who'd been married to men to contact her. She got enough replies to fill a book, which I can't bring myself to order yet, called *Married Women Who Love Women*. There were so many responses that the author says she never could have spoken to them all.

Checkout time approaches. I call down to the front desk and ask for an extra hour, which the old woman grants. I text Inez and tell her I overslept, that I'm running late. I abandon the Google search and start really thinking about my life. How easy it was to meet men in a society geared toward hetero relationships. How I never really bothered to ask myself what I wanted, just followed the script in front of me. How I could never relate to the intense emotional pain of other people's breakups. How every relationship I've ever been in started with some man initiating and me just going along because it was easy. Because it was expected. Because it was supposed to make me happy.

As I force myself to get up, collect my things, and leave the motel room where my life changed forever, I wonder how something like this is even possible. How I could have been holding one end of a thread that could unravel my entire sense of myself all this time . . .

With one minute remaining before checkout, I step out into the harsh light of late morning. I don't close the door behind me until the last possible second, because once I do it will be over. The one night we agreed on. Portal closed, normal life resumed.

Except my life will never be normal again. Because I'm not even remotely the person I thought I was.

"I'm a lesbian," I say in the softest voice I can imagine, sending the words into the room and closing the door to lock them inside.

I intended to call Larry or grab a bus, but I find myself walking back into town, so lost in my own thoughts that I don't even bother. Mostly I wonder how I could have lived my whole life without knowing such a core part of myself. I mourn all the years I could have spent happy. I know that part will likely go on a long time.

But once I've wrung my brain out like a sponge, once I've gotten as close to acceptance as a person can possibly hope to get in one morning, I hit what feels like an insurmountable obstacle: How can I ever tell Inez? I promised her nothing would change. *Surprise, having sex with you made me gay* is kind of the epitome of change.

And even if she doesn't mind, what does it mean for us? Did sleeping with her bring about this monumental change because of who she is? Or because she happened to be the first woman I ever felt safe enough to try it with? Is there a difference? And if so, how can you tell?

Finally, after telling your best friend you realized you were a lesbian after having sex with her, which one is worse: Saying you have feelings for her? Or saying you don't?

And does any of that matter if I can't untangle it all myself?

I'm downtown by the time I reach the end of this seemingly endless question list, passing Mystical Moments, just across from Ponderosa's.

Coffee, I think. Coffee won't fix this, but it'll help. It'll sort itself out, I tell myself as I push through the door. It has to. I promised Inez nothing would change between us.

"Hey, Cash!" says Ginny, genuinely beaming to see me. "So great seeing you out last night. We're getting so excited for the party."

In the shadow of everything that came after, I'm almost surprised to remember that we were so successful at the night's original intent. Robin is considering. Chase made an ass of himself in front of her. There's no way to explain this, however, so I smile widely back, feeling like a rusted old machine part clunking reluctantly into gear.

"We're glad, too," I say as sincerely as I can. "And no matter how many people get on board, we'll always remember you and Brad were some of the first to support us."

Good, I tell myself. Normal-sounding. Nice work.

"We're honored," she says. "What can I get you? It's on the house."

Another ten minutes later I'm vaguely alarmed to find myself at my Jeep, which is parked outside of Badger's. I remember checking my reflection in the mirror, Jaz teasing me through the window. It feels like a scene from another life.

My twilight zone moment is interrupted by another arrival to the walk of shame street-parking club. Sasha, wearing the same outfit she was last night, makes her way to her little Datsun pickup looking decidedly worse for wear.

I'm about to wave in solidarity, but then I see the car on the corner, just pulling away from having dropped her off. It's shiny and gray, and I choke back a giggle when I imagine its front seats full of eggs last night . . .

Sasha and Chase, I think, watching her hop into her truck and drive away.

Why not, I guess?

My phone is in my hand before I can think twice, my brain already drafting a text to Inez. But I stop before I can even type the first word. Can I casually gossip with someone I just hooked up with? Can I tell Inez Sasha slept with Chase without telling her I think I'm a lesbian and it might be because of her but I'm too mixed up to tell?

This spiral goes on for several minutes before I remember. She was the one who made me promise. One night and nothing changes. This is just me sticking to the rules.

You won't believe who that was in Chase's room last night, I type before I can second-guess it again.

She replies immediately: Who???

We spend a few minutes going back and forth about Sasha. Inez feels sorry for her, saying no one that cute should be doomed to like mediocre men. I pause to experience another sigh of relief/panic attack about possibly never having to date another man again before replying with something casual that indicates nothing about any of that.

By the time the conversation is over, I feel better. Or at least, I feel like it's possible for us to be normal with each other. For me to be normal with her. It's almost nice to recall that Inez didn't want anything more. That no matter what my absolutely snarled subconscious reveals about my feelings (or lack thereof) for her, it won't matter, because I made a promise to her.

We're best friends, I tell myself as I drive to Joyce's. *Everything else might be a mess, but that part will never change.*

Turns out things are much more of a mess in person.

After stopping at home to shower and change, I'm feeling more like myself than ever. I walk into Joyce's with all the unearned confidence of someone who's had several cups of coffee and thinks they can compartmentalize a life-changing, earth-shattering realization in one morning.

"Honey, I'm home," I call out. Our standard greeting, except I cringe the moment the words are out of my mouth. After last night? What a nightmare.

But Inez only smiles. "Glad you made it in one piece." She's changed into ripped jeans and an emerald-green T-shirt. Her hair is in a messy topknot. Her sunglasses are heart-shaped.

My heart stalls like a faulty engine at the sight of her. I've been so busy processing the ramifications of last night that I almost forgot about the details. But the details rush back unhelpfully now, mocking me by displaying just how weak my barriers were.

I can feel her skin under my hands. Hear her whispered pleas in my ear. Taste her—

"Love the glasses," I say, glancing up from my list with what I hope is a normal amount of enthusiasm.

"Thanks," she says, reaching up to touch them where they're perched on her head. "Uh, what's on the agenda this morning? Or are we taking a day off?"

"No rest for the resistance," I say, getting out the to-do list I'm planning to armor myself in today. "We have to get a final budget for supplies, confirm with the sound guy, check on the permits—"

"—Please," Inez says, holding up a hand. "Three things at a time."

"Budget," I say as she comes around the bar to peer at my list. "Sound. Permits."

She's next to me by the time I finish. I fight the urge to shove the list back into my bag, as if it says the words I MIGHT BE A LESBIAN on it in bright red ink. Her arm presses against mine. She smells different, like motel shampoo instead of her normal chamomile and roses. Proof that it wasn't a dream, like all the other times.

Would I pull away normally? I wonder as she grabs a pen and checks off the things she's already done. Even after years of friendship I can hardly remember what things were like before I realized I wanted to kiss her.

Does that mean I always did?

"Heard from Robin yet?" Inez asks, putting the pen down and standing up, stretching her arms over her head.

"Huh?"

"Robin," Inez says, lowering her arms. "Has she called?"

"Not yet," I say with some effort. "I don't want to call her and look eager so I guess we have to wait."

She smirks at me. "I don't think looking too eager is something you struggle with."

My brain is immediately whirring at full capacity, trying to decode what she means by this. But friend-Cash wouldn't ask, so I just chuckle. "Well, you know what they say, keep them wanting more."

This time it's her turn to not respond. It's almost satisfying, in an odd way, this evidence that I might not be the only one feeling a little wrong-footed. Of course I feel immediately guilty for thinking that. I'm the one who promised nothing would change.

Still, the rest of the day feels endless. Every interaction that was once easy now feels like a minefield. I've never done this much overthinking in my life. With men it was always whatever. They wanted it more than I did. When they weren't in front of me I wasn't thinking about them.

I feel ridiculous for this several times over the course of the afternoon. Should it have been a sign? Isn't feeling indifferent about men one of the things at the top of the list?

Even though it feels like tapping out, I ask Inez if she minds me being on call for the evening instead of coming back after Parker pickup.

"It's been awhile since I didn't see her for a whole day," I explain. "But I can totally come back if you need me."

She's already shaking her head. "No, of course you should hang with Parker. I think I can handle Mo and Charlie until ten."

"You wish, sweetheart!" Charlie calls from the dartboard.

"Thanks," I say, though in the grand tradition of today the opposite of bad is still somehow bad. What did I want? For her to be sad? For her to break the agreement we had and make everything weird like I seem so determined to?

"Anything for you." She blows me a kiss as I gather up my stuff.

Tomorrow will be easier, I tell myself. Like a mantra.

20

NONE OF THE following tomorrows are any easier. In fact, they seem to be getting harder.

Even the dreams have deserted me, and I find I miss them. That I wish I could have her back even if I know it won't last beyond waking.

It's a strange dichotomy, because everything else is coming together. Folks drop by the bar all week to deliver prizes for the raffle and the silent auction, the phone rings all day with people who have heard by word of mouth and want to help.

The only person we haven't heard from by the end of the week is Robin, which gives me some pause. After my speech and Chase's total meltdown on Sunday, I assumed we'd be a shoo-in, but Kings is a big company. Someone as smart as Robin might not throw in the towel because they hired one problematic lackey.

Even without her, though, the permits are approved. Chairs rented. Speakers tested. Best of all, Parker's class has been diligently rehearsing their performances, and I've gotten several calls from parents thanking me for including the kids.

Everything outside is great.

Except inside is a big mess.

I somehow manage to make it through the week, despite getting no relief from the ache that sprung into being the moment Inez left the Palm Motel. In fact, the ache only grows deeper and more complex with every shift I spend with Inez. Everything I do that reminds me of us, together. Of her. Of how I feel.

This week is enough to prove me entirely wrong about my feelings fading with time. I try to tell myself I just need more of it, but every day brings deeper conviction that I've been living without a key piece of myself. I filter every experience, past and present, through this new lens, feeling like someone's flipped the lights on in a dark room.

I'm a lesbian, I think to myself in wonder at least ten times a day. The fear begins to recede, leaving relief in its wake. Leaving something suspiciously like joy. That is, unless I'm in the same room as Inez, and then the joy becomes torture.

It's starting to become clear to me that sleeping with Inez was not, in fact, just a vehicle for my sexual awakening. That whether they're real or just a product of the tender new part of me, unarmored to her charms, I have unruly, uncontrollable feelings about doing it again. And again. And again.

But it doesn't matter, because those feelings are not reciprocated. I replay what she said to me in the pool again and again. *One time . . . that's all it can be.* And I agreed. Which means I have no right to change the rules now that I got what I wanted.

Inez is my best friend. She's the piece that makes my life work. At home with Parker, at Joyce's with all the upheaval and change. If I can't break the promise that nothing changes between us, I'll just have to try to act like I did before until it feels natural again.

So I hear myself saying the things I would normally say. Acting like it's all the same. Putting on the best show of my life. Telling myself that someday it won't be a constant effort not to touch any-place her skin is exposed. Not to kiss her impulsively when she slides past me behind the bar. Not to tell her she's the sexiest person I've ever seen.

And somehow, though it's the most difficult thing I've ever done, keeping my cool around her isn't even the hardest part of all this.

The hardest part is the fact that I'm shifting tectonically in a way that makes me feel so proud and so brave and so *myself* and I can't tell her. Because how could I tell her I'm a lesbian without telling her how I feel about her?

It would be impossible. And I can't tell anyone else, either. The only people who would understand are so intertwined in the far-reaching web that is our friendship that it would get back to her, and finding out from someone else would be worse than hearing it from me.

So after thirty years of being in the closet, even to myself, I can't walk out into the sunshine. It's all my own fault, of course. Ensnared in my own web. But it feels more constricting every day.

By the time our last pre-festival karaoke night rolls around, I'm a zombie again. It should be common territory by now, but I'm tired in a way that makes me miss the less complicated tiredness of a few weeks ago. The kind that can be easily solved by a nap or a giant mug of coffee.

As good as I usually am at hiding any complex adult inner workings from Parker, even she's not immune to the sight of me after another sleepless night.

"Mama, no offense, but are you okay? You look like *death-warmedover.*"

She says this last part like it's one long, jumbled word.

I raise an eyebrow at her as she eats her oatmeal. "Where on earth did you learn that expression?"

"Granny O'Connor," Parker relays promptly. "She volunteered for story time. I heard her say it to Miss Fitz and asked her what it means."

Wearily, I sit down across from her. "Okay, what does it mean?"

"It's like when someone looks really tired or like they need to make different life choices." She slurps another big spoonful, kicking her legs under the table.

I laugh. "Well, it's not a modern expression, but it's probably not inaccurate."

"So," Parker prompts when she's swallowed her bite safely. "Why are you warmed over?"

It takes me a solid twenty seconds to come up with something that's both not a lie and not completely inappropriate developmentally. "Nothing you need to worry about," I settle on. "It's just a lot of work planning the party."

Parker nods sagely. "Yeah, I've been feeling pretty warmed over myself lately."

"Why's that?" I ask, as seriously as I can manage.

"Madison's got us all working hard on the jump rope thing and I'm not sure my legs can hag it."

Does she mean hack it? I think, not sure I'm up for another round of where-did-you-learn-that-expression. Luckily, there's a more pressing issue.

"I thought everyone was doing their own stuff," I remark. "Isn't Madison the only one jumping rope?"

"Ohhh yeah," Parker says with a slightly guilty expression. "About that . . ."

"What did Madison do now?"

"Well, she said not to tell you so it would be a surprise. But she thought it would be more . . . co-cheese-ive? If we all did the same thing. Like a real performance. So we're doing that now."

I look at the clock on the microwave, debating whether I have time to dig into all the reasons manipulators like Madison need strong boundaries and friends who tell them no sometimes because *clearly* their parents aren't doing enough of it.

We have to leave in four minutes to have a prayer of being on time for drop-off, so I do the condensed version:

"I'm all for whatever feels fun to you, okay? And if you want to step outside your comfort zone and improve your jump-roping skills I think that's awesome. I just want to make sure you think about what *you* want to do, and not just what Madison wants to do. Got it?"

Parker chews thoughtfully for a minute, like she's really taking this in. "I guess I kinda forgot about that part."

"It happens," I say, ruffling her hair. "Just remember you can't get what you want from people unless you tell them what you want."

"Roger," says Parker, inexplicably saluting me and hopping off of her chair.

As I follow her to the Jeep, I think about my own advice, wishing it could still be as simple for me as it is for her.

By the time I need to set up for karaoke I feel like it's been three days since I woke up this morning.

Maybe this is a new strategy, I think as I step out the door. Exhaust myself to the point where I'm too tired to think about Inez.

She's getting out of the Bug as I approach the back door with the keys. The new strategy immediately proves as useless as all the ones that came before it. The low-level static that's just her name on repeat in the back of my mind increases in volume, tunes itself so the specifics of my thoughts are impossible to miss.

"Hey!" she calls, locking the door. She's wearing jeans with holes in the knees again. A cropped T-shirt with a band name I don't recognize. Hair in two braids I just want to grab and tug until her face is nose-to-nose with mine.

"Hey. Ready for karaoke tonight?"

"Totally," Inez replies. "If the response we've been getting this week is any indicator it's gonna be a huge night for the bar."

"That's great," I say, falling into step beside her. Trying not to look. Failing. Trying again. "It's the last karaoke night before the festival. If we're not going to get Robin and her newspaper editor wife on board we should probably start advertising somehow. Maybe flyers or a website or something?"

"Yeah, about that," she says, rummaging through her bag as we get inside. She pulls out a copy of this week's *Ridley Falls Gazette,* hot off the presses.

Bewildered, I reach out a hand to take it from her. Our fingers brush, and I can barely hide the fact that my whole arm erupts in goosebumps.

For a blessed moment, though, thoughts of my impulses are pushed to the side. Because there, on the front page, is a headline that makes the days I've waited to hear from Robin feel totally worth it.

FRANCHISING IN RIDLEY FALLS? THE COMMUNITY SAYS NO.

Underneath it is a photo of me at the karaoke mic, smiling.

"Does this say what it looks like it's gonna say?" I ask Inez, not trusting myself to fully comprehend it with her standing so close.

She's grinning from ear to ear, dimples popping out on her cheeks, her eyes all crinkled up in a way that makes my stomach swoop. "Yep," she says. "Complete with a quote from the mayor about the importance of maintaining Ridley Falls' close-knit community. I guess all those calls we made to their office paid off. And look—"

Inez reaches out and unfolds the paper in my hands without taking it from me, which requires more physical contact than I feel equipped to handle. But it's weirder to back away, it reveals too much, so I just stand there perfectly still.

"Right there." She jabs a finger at the bottom of the page where a big ad displays the date, time, and location of the festival this weekend.

"Joyce's Jubilee," I read out loud. "Who made this? When—"

She's grinning again. The mischievous one with an edge that makes me shiver. "You had a ton on your plate and I wanted to surprise you. We had the name already, so I told Mars to hit the gas with the design, but if you hate it we can totally change it before—"

I interrupt her with a hug that crushes the paper between us. Today's feelings-suppression strategy was built around minimal contact, but right now I don't care. "It's perfect," I say. *You're perfect.* "Thank you."

Her arms reach up to encircle me immediately. I tell myself I'll let go when she does.

But she doesn't.

We stand there with our arms around each other and I swear I can feel her pulse. My whole body is aware that there's no distance between us anymore. I could kiss her. God, I want to kiss her. But before I can obey the impulse hammering through my veins it comes back in full force, like she's saying it right now in my ear.

One time. That's all it can be, okay?

Reluctantly, I disentangle myself. She lets go when the pressure lessens and steps back. I think her face looks flushed but I don't trust myself to examine her too closely—my willpower is hanging on by a thread as it is.

Inez clears her throat. "Well, I'm glad you're happy," she says. "You deserve it."

"Yeah." My voice is too low. Too rough. I clear my throat, too. "I think it's gonna be good. The event. Seems like we really pulled it off."

"I should probably get inside," she says, exactly as I'm saying, "I think I'll call Robin."

We laugh. Then we both step in the same direction as we're trying to pass each other. Then we switch directions and do it again.

By the time she's safely out of my eyeline I'm so flustered I have to take three deep breaths before I do anything. I know I'm in no fit state to talk to Robin just yet, so I pull up Sammy Espinoza's contact instead.

Did you see the Gazette this morning? I type, unable to stop myself from grinning. Hope you've got a hell of a headliner.

Despite how busy she must be, the little dots that mean she's typing appear right away.

Never been so glad to have to pull off a miracle last minute, she says with a winking emoji. And then, a few seconds later: Do you trust me?

Implicitly, I reply.

Then just tell me when and where, and prepare to be amazed.

I text her the details for the festival—the address, where to park any large vehicles, the performance time, and happily leave the rest in her capable hands.

After that, sufficiently calmed down from my encounter with Inez, I dial Robin's number. The paper shakes a little in my hand.

"Cash," Robin answers, no nonsense. "I thought I might be hearing from you today."

I tear my focus from where Inez has just disappeared through the bar's back entrance, forcing myself into the moment.

"I don't even know what to say," I manage, chuckling in disbelief. "Thank you. Truly, thank you so much."

"You really got me out of my rut the other day, kid," Robin replies with a chuckle. "I wanted to show you I appreciate you not letting me get complacent about our community."

I'm about to thank her again, but apparently she's not done.

"Listen, I also have a check for five thousand here that I want to donate to the reno costs, and I've already sent Sasha over with some gift certificates for the raffle."

My head is spinning. I've barely heard anything since *five thousand*. That gets us to half of our budget minus the cost of the festival. It's enough to build the new stage on its own.

"*And* I called up the Kings corporate offices to give them a piece of my mind. Told 'em there'd be lots more unpleasantness where yours came from if they don't back off on this Ridley Falls idea."

"Robin," I croak. "I don't even know what to say."

She laughs. "Kid, you've got what it takes. I can tell. So just promise that when you've got your own place and you're one of the old folks like me, you'll remember how you feel right now. It's easy to lose your fervor for community justice when your bones ache and your kid's in college and your wife needs back surgery—but it's not any less important now than it was when I had the energy for it."

"I'll remember," I promise her, but I can still hear her saying *your wife,* and I'm thinking of Inez, and the hole is back in my chest like it never left.

"Good. Now, this article went up online last night and you've already got a ton of support. People are coming from three counties to this party of yours, and I'm planning on staying up past eight, so you better make it a good one, you hear me?"

"I hear you," I say, not even daring to believe this is real.

She hangs up without a goodbye, and I stand there for a long moment, fizzing like a shaken-up soda can. This is exactly what we wanted. Exactly what we've worked for. But there's part of me that feels like something's still missing . . .

The internet says time heals all wounds, but the internet has never met Inez.

21

I'VE NEVER SEEN so many people packed inside Joyce's as there are when I turn on the karaoke machine that night. I'm intentionally not counting heads because I'm afraid we're past capacity.

People started showing up at four—a good two and a half hours before the usual busy time. More than one of them had a copy of the article. Mrs. Blair from Stitch-n-Bitch asked me to sign hers, right under my picture.

Inez has the donation jar out on the bar top and I can see from here that it's already almost full. Half of me feels entirely giddy. Accomplished. Genuinely happy for the first time in longer than I can remember.

The other half is just a blast crater where Inez's and my one-night stand took place.

It's an interesting emotional cocktail to mix, to say the least.

I shrug on my leather jacket. Close my eyes for a second, trying to let go of Cash Delgado, sappy lesbian bartender with too many feelings. Tonight, I need to be Cash Delgado, community organizer. A person with a plan and their picture in the paper.

Just as it did when I was a teenaged punk about to go onstage and scream, it works. Everything melts away—though I know it'll be waiting for me the moment I step back into my real life. For the time being, this momentary break from the reality of my impossible feelings is overpowering.

"Wow," I say when the microphone is on. "Y'all, I don't even know what to say."

Cheers greet this. Loud ones. Every face in the room turns to look at me.

"A few weeks ago, I got up here and asked you for help. I didn't know what would happen. To be honest, I rarely ask for help. I never really learned how." I chuckle self-deprecatingly. "But the people in this room—this *community* that I'm so proud to be a part of—stepped up in ways I can't even imagine."

More cheers. This time I don't stop them. They're cheering for one another. For all of us. And they deserve it.

"I know this is just a little dive bar along the highway, but it means more than that to me. To my daughter. To my friends, and to all of you. I wanted to save this place, yes, but I also wanted to show corporate dicks like Kings that Ridley Falls isn't for sale."

Knowing it's a gamble, I glance at the bar. At Inez, who has a line of at least eight people and a frantic-looking Eduardo behind her. But she's looking right at me. Looking at me with an expression that says I'm the best thing she's ever seen. As a friend, of course.

"I'm so excited to hear some karaoke tonight, but I'm even more excited to see all of you this weekend at the farm for what I very much hope will be the *first annual* Joyce's Jubilee."

Folks have been signing up all this time. The list is already a page and a half long. As they cheer one more time, as Inez turns back to the soda hose, I glance down at it and call the first name.

After years of running karaoke in a tiny bar in a one-horse

town, it's rare I see anyone I don't know approaching the little cardboard stage. That's when it becomes fully real to me, when the name I read is a total stranger's, and the person who takes the mic is someone I've never seen before.

This is Robin's doing, of course, but it's also mine, and I stand back with pride for the length of one song—trying to focus on that feeling, and not the hollow one that comes from trying not to see if Inez is looking at me.

The first disastrous thing doesn't happen until almost ten. We're on page two of the karaoke sheet when I see it, my heart dropping. "Next," I say in what I hope is a normal tone. "We have Chase. Come on up, Chase."

I'm hoping beyond hope that it's a different Chase. A Chase who lives two counties over and loves online newspaper articles written by middle-aged lesbians.

Inez's eyes snap to me when she hears it, and I feel our hearts are beating in sync as we watch the crowd parting from the back corner of the bar behind the pool table.

It's clear he's been drinking. A lot. He must have snuck in sometime after I came onstage, when it was too crowded for me to notice. I remember the last time I saw him, berating the owner of the Palm Motel about the eggs we smashed in his rental car.

He was supposed to be leaving the next morning. The morning I was waking up across the parking lot with my life suddenly strange and unmanageable. So what is he doing here?

"Would you look at that," I say sarcastically into the mic as he approaches. "Not just any Chase, but Chase Stanton—our former manager."

The applause is tepid at best, and I can tell it's only coming from out-of-towners. Ridley Falls is a polite town, but they're here because they've chosen our side. Joyce's side, against the evil Kings empire. They're not any happier to see him than I am.

"Looks like you didn't put down a song," I say when he reaches me. "Can I suggest 'Loser'?" Chase sneers. His eyes look out of focus, his mouth twisted in a petulant pout that says making amends isn't his purpose tonight.

"I'm not here to sing."

He grabs the mic out of my hand. Like, actually grabs it as a toddler might grab another toddler's toy. I'm so surprised I just let go.

"I just want you to know," Chase slurs into the mic, "what total backwoods, ignorant *hicks* you all are. I mean, you could have had a real place! A place with real drinks! And food! And, like, music that doesn't sound like a cat *dying*."

"Okay, Chase, that's enough." I step up and reach for the mic, but he spins out of range, wrapping the cord loosely around his ankles.

"Cash, everybody, Ridley Falls' second-favorite dyke. Your first-favorite is that bitch at Badger's who called my boss and got me *fired* this week."

The room is totally silent as Chase looks over his shoulder at me with crossed eyes.

"We used to fuck, you know, me and her. When I worked here. Is that what turned you queer? Couldn't have me, so no man would do?"

I don't even think about it. I punch him. My hand hurts like I broke a knuckle. It's been a long time since my last bar brawl. He's drunk and not expecting it, so he goes down immediately, tangling himself in the cables.

Eduardo and Inez make their way to the front. Chase scrambles to his feet and tries to dodge them but he trips over the mic cable, unplugging it from the karaoke machine. Eduardo heaves him up and Inez sees them to the front door, tapping Larry Cross on the way, who will drive him back to the Palm in his car.

He disappears through the doors. I know I need to plug the mic back in. Get the crowd back on board. This week is too high-stakes to let this stupid performance of Chase's derail it. But half of them are already looking at me. Whispering. About what Chase said, no doubt. About me being a lesbian.

Ridley Falls is generally friendly toward all stripes, but it is rural, and I can tell there are a few people here who aren't pleased. Suddenly my heart is beating too fast. I feel like my persona was torn away when Chase hit the ground. Before, I could have brushed it off, but being called out publicly as something I haven't even told the world I am yet feels destabilizing in the worst way.

When this night began, I was so high on the feeling of community. On this little town I made a home of. But right now, with a third of its inhabitants staring at me like I'm a two-headed calf in a field, it feels too small.

Inez is back, beside me before I can let on that I'm panicking. She's plugging in the mic and saying something that doesn't quite penetrate. Everyone's laughing—and not in a point-and-laugh kind of way, but in a let's-collectively-move-on-from-this way that relaxes me just a little.

"What do you say, Cash?" Inez asks, bringing the room back into focus.

She's looking at me, eyes wide and heavily lashed. She's smiling a little. I don't know what she said but everyone's watching—and it probably wouldn't matter if they weren't.

"Yes," I say, grinning at her. And then the music starts to play.

It's her favorite song, so it makes sense that she picked it, but right now I'm so bowled over by the irony that I almost miss my cue. That acoustic intro I've heard in her car a thousand times.

I drop my voice into that low, scratchy Tracy Chapman register and start to sing.

"You got a fast car, I want a ticket to anywhere."

For the next four minutes, I forget the crowd. It's just Inez and me, a single mic, and one of the most iconic lesbian love songs of all time.

When we're done I can't look away from her. The outro plays. And then the whole bar bursts into the loudest applause I've ever heard within these walls.

Inez recovers first. She blows me a cheeky kiss and tosses the mic, turning around to saunter back to the bar where there's an absolute pileup. I don't stutter too much as I return to the list. The night is salvaged, but at what cost? I feel like my heart has just been through a meat grinder. I make it through the rest of the night on autopilot, devoutly thankful that I've done it so many times it barely requires consciousness.

As I'm calling names and cracking jokes, inside I'm entirely focused on suppressing the way I felt being close to her. Singing with her.

And I had a feeling that I belonged . . .

It's almost two before the place clears out. Definitely a record in Joyce's history. I try to keep busy until the last second, hoping Inez will get tired of waiting for me. Of course, I'm not that lucky. When I come back from counting every remaining Tater Tot in the walk-in she's at the bar alone, sorting change from the beer pitcher that tonight's crowd absolutely filled with cash tips.

I want so badly to say something normal. Something to defuse the tension that's been building in me for days—that caught fire tonight during that duet. But I can't think of a single word.

I'm just considering booking it for the back door. Pretending I didn't see her. But she spots me, and she calls out.

"Hey," she says. "Are you okay? I wanted to check in so many times after Chase, but the crowd was so massive I never caught a break."

"I'm fine," I hear myself say. *Just act normal.*

"He's disgusting," she says, voice heavy with disdain. "Lying about you, dragging your personal history through the mud in front of all those people. I wanted to strangle him."

I nod, but all I can think is that he didn't lie. He was cruel, but he didn't lie. I am a lesbian. And now it's all hitting me. Everyone in town knows. Parker's teachers and the parents at her school. I'll have to tell her before someone else does. The days I've spent unpacking this on my own terms are officially over, which means I have to tell Inez, too.

And all of this is colliding horribly with the effect of her body on me. Her closeness. Her eyes, liquid with concern, trained on mine. I can't even breathe. But I have to. Before it's too late.

"Inez," I say in a tone much lower and huskier than I mean to. I swallow hard. "I have to tell you something."

"Anything," she says, her eyes wide. Her lashes impossibly long. She abandoned her flannel shirt at some point, and the way she's leaning across the bar in her tank top is doing dizzyingly wonderful things to her breasts—exactly like my first dream. The one where she wore a red negligee right on this very bar. "But can I say something first?"

I nod, eager to put my thing off as long as possible. That is, until she moves closer. I can feel her breath on my cheek. See my knuckles as I grip the bar, white from the effort of not reaching for her. I know that if either of us moves a fraction of an inch all bets and confessions will be off.

"It's just . . . I know what we said," she begins. "One time only."

"Nothing changes," I confirm.

"But I've been thinking," she continues, a little smirk now playing at the corner of her lips. "You didn't even get the proper straight-girl-experimenting experience. Last time? That barely counted. You were so gone you lasted all of three seconds, and I don't feel I was given a chance to properly represent my community."

As I process what she's suggesting, I lose all necessary blood flow to my brain. I can feel my pulse everywhere.

"I'd argue that you represented your community so well that it *resulted* in me lasting three seconds," I manage. "But I'm obviously not the experienced one here, so I'll defer to your judgment."

"Well then, I judge that you're in need of a continuation," she says. The smirk is no longer just a hint. She knows she has me. And she does. She probably always has. "It doesn't have to be a big deal. Not even a second time. Just an . . . epilogue. Then back to business as usual."

I know logically that this is a terrible idea. That doing it again will only make it harder to compartmentalize everything. To separate who I'm becoming with how I feel about her. But I feel like a teenager again, all logic going out the window. It doesn't matter that it's a terrible idea.

We're kissing before I can figure out who started it, and I know

I'm not the only desperate one this time. Inez stands up, reaches for me across the bar, cups my face in her hands as her lips slide against mine, tongues and teeth tangling like we really are teenagers in the backseat of someone's car.

It's not long before the bar between us is too much space. I swing myself on top of it and she pulls me toward her, settling between my legs, kissing me like her life depends on it.

My hands slide into her hair, tugging at the base of her neck, making her moan into my mouth. Her fingers are digging into my thighs through my jeans, close, but not close enough to the place I need them.

I almost can't believe how good it feels to give in. To let myself touch her. The feelings flooding through me are so much more than desire, they're a culmination of everything I've thought about her these past few days.

Her fingers inch closer to the place I'm throbbing for her. She tilts her head to look up at me, wordlessly asking permission to take it further. But suddenly all the pent-up emotion is welling in me, and my throat is full of words that I absolutely can't allow to leave my lips even though I know in this moment that they're absolutely true.

I love you.

I love her.

And with those words, the teenage haze lifts, and reality comes crashing back in. I love Inez. I'm in love with her. I'll never be satisfied with one more time, no matter how many of them there are.

I pull away abruptly, overwhelmed by the force of feelings that I can't explain to her. If I tell her I love her there are only two options. One, that she doesn't feel the same way and our friendship is ruined. Or two, that she *does* feel the same way and she wants to be with me as much as I'm realizing I want to be with her.

But I'm not ready for that. I know I'm not. I've only known who I am for a few days. I haven't even told anyone. I can't give her what she deserves in a partner, and if I try I'll probably only ruin it. Destroy our friendship, Joyce's, and probably break Parker's heart by ruining things with the one adult she could ever rely on besides me.

Before I know it I'm sliding back across the bar, away from Inez, whose gaze has gone from liquid to confused. Hurt.

"Did I . . . ?" she begins as I climb down the other side.

"No," I say, shaking my head. "It's not you. It's just . . . I'm sorry, I can't do this, Inez. I just can't."

And before she can respond, or do anything but stand where I left her and gape, I scramble to the back door and let myself out without looking back.

22

I DON'T SLEEP all night. In fact, I don't even try to go to bed. I just sit on my couch as the night deepens and finally the sky begins to lighten again.

No one has ever been stupider or more wrong than I am in this moment, I tell myself again and again. I love Inez. How long have I loved her? It would be easier to say it started in the greenhouse, but I think it started way before then.

I think back to the first dream I had about her, but I'm sure that wasn't the beginning. Just the moment it finally broke through. Does it go all the way back to the first day I met her? And what does it mean if it does?

There's an almost desperate longing in me to return to the way I felt a few days ago. When I knew that I just had to starve the crush, ride out the detox. That things could just go back to normal if I tied myself up in knots and waited.

But if I've always loved her, *will* I always love her? Either way, it seems clear that the do-nothing option isn't an option anymore. As long as we're in the same place I will want her. And that leaves me in the same catch-22 as tonight. If she doesn't want me the way I want her, it's ruined. And if she does and I'm not ready, it's ruined.

I can't bank on happily ever after. Not with how rare it is. Not with everything I have at stake.

So that leaves me entirely out of options, then.

Can't tell her how I feel. Can't keep lying about it. Can't keep sleeping with her. Can't date her. Apparently can't even be *around* her without ending up with my tongue in her mouth.

But where does that leave me? And Parker? Where does it leave Joyce's and our plans for a hundred more Jubilees?

I don't have a single answer. Only a million questions that desperately need them.

Joyce's Jubilee is tomorrow, I tell myself a few minutes before Parker needs to get up for school. No matter how battered my heart is or how jumbled my thoughts, I absolutely cannot avoid going in today. I'll just have to do my best.

But when I walk in, braced for the worst, Inez isn't there. She doesn't show up all day. She doesn't even call to say she won't be here. And I hate myself just a little for being relieved.

It's easy to get caught up in plans for tomorrow. Most of the folks who will have booths at the festival or baskets in the raffle trickle in throughout the day to drop things off or check in. Some of them stay for a drink. Almost all of them congratulate me on the article.

Over the course of the day, I start to realize I'm breathing easier than I have in a long time. And that makes me think.

Yes, the situation is incredibly sad. I've done the one thing I promised myself I wouldn't do and irrevocably altered my relationship with my best friend. This past week, I've been trying to ignore that fact. To convince myself that the molecular rearrangement that happened could somehow be centralized only to my identity. That I could be a lesbian and *not* in love with Inez and we could go back to the way things were.

But by the end of my shift, my thirty-sixth hour without sleep, I realize something that's sad and freeing all at once. There is no *the way things were* to go back to. I think I've loved Inez in some form or another since the moment I met her, I was just too stubborn to admit it to myself because she didn't fit the script I'd been given about what love looks like. And if us being together isn't a possibility for me, maybe it's time to let that go. To let *her* go.

The idea is a knife in my chest, but knives can do more than wound. They can also cut through the ties that bind you.

Later that night, I'm at home going over my list for the three-thousandth time when the phone rings. I jump, picturing Inez, calling from outside ready to unravel my willpower for the second time since last night.

But curiously, the name on the screen isn't Inez's. It's Robin's.

A new panic enters the chat. What if Robin is calling to withdraw her support? Her donation? What if, at the eleventh hour, it all falls apart despite all our hard work?

"Hello?" I ask, trying to keep my voice from betraying my spiraling thoughts, or the many, many hours I've been running on coffee and willpower alone.

"Hey, kid, sorry to call so late."

"No problem, is everything okay?" I can't stand not knowing for one more second.

"Oh yeah, we're all set for tomorrow, no worries there."

The relief is a dunk tank, and I'm briefly submerged. I break the surface just in time to hear her continue.

"Listen, I'm calling about something else. There's a bar owner over in Chinook River. Gator's, do you know the place?"

"Can't say I do . . ."

"Well, it's owned by another couple of queers, and you know we keep up with each other. The thing is they're thinking of getting out of the game. Getting on with that retirement they keep promising each other. And until they saw the article we ran on you they were considering cashing out to some big franchise that's been buzzing around."

My head is still swimming from insomnia and heartbreak, and the added complication of how much I like it that she considers me one of her people. One of the queers that keeps up with each other. "Interesting," I manage.

"It is, but only because your article shook them up a bit, just like your speech at Badger's did me. Chinook River's a little bigger than Ridley Falls, but they've got a nice little community over there. They said they hadn't thought of how franchising the place would affect the rest of the business owners, and now they're thinking of going in another direction.

This time, I just wait for her to continue. Apparently Robin, when you're on her good side, can be very chatty. My to-do list swims in my peripheral vision, reminding me I'll be up another five hours even if everything goes perfectly right.

"Anyway, I'll cut to the chase here," she says, mercifully. "After reading the article they called and asked about you. They say they want to pass the place on to someone who can fight for it. Be an asset to the town instead of showing up to change it. And, of course, keep it safe for folks like us. When I heard that, I told them I think it's high time *you* had a place of your own."

Before she says this last bit, I'll confess I'm only paying about

40 percent attention, my mind following other simultaneous threads about paper cups and the raffle table and Parker's class performance. When she says *a place of your own,* though, the thread tangles in a hopeless knot as I return almost painfully to the present.

"M-my own bar?" I splutter.

"Your own bar," she agrees.

I'd be lying if I said I hadn't thought about it. I mean, I've been running Joyce's. But it's different when the bills come in your name. Different when it's all yours.

"I know Chinook River's fifty miles from here, but I didn't think you had any family in the area tying you down. And look, if I'm way off base here let me know. I just know it's gotta be tough, with your instincts, to have George and Linda to answer to."

"No," I hear myself saying, as if it's someone else answering her. "You're not off base. I don't have family here. The only thing is . . . I don't think I can afford it. A down payment and all that. There's no way I'd qualify."

"I thought you might say that," Robin agrees, sounding totally unfazed. "But they said if they found the right person they'd be willing to work something out. Listen, don't answer now, just think on it and give them a call when the fundraiser's behind you."

"Okay," I say, still feeling like I'm looking down on myself from up high. "Wow. Yeah. I will. Thanks, Robin."

"We gotta have each other's backs," she says, and then she hangs up.

As soon as the line goes silent, I slump back on the couch, feeling entirely saturated. No more room for thoughts. But these thoughts won't wait. They come up like mushrooms, thick and fast and everywhere.

Before this week, I never would have considered leaving Ridley Falls. It's my home. The home I made for Parker and for me. But now, with this new opportunity floating tantalizingly in front of me, I know I need to look at the situation dispassionately. I have no family here. I love Joyce's, but it's not mine, and when George and Linda are ready to officially retire it'll probably go to one of their many adult children, not to me.

Parker isn't old enough to have made lifelong social connections yet. In a lot of ways it's the perfect time to start over for her.

And me? A week ago I would have said I had a lot, even besides Inez. A community. The farm. Mars and Jaz and Gladys. Sasha. Robin and Kendra. Even Granny O'Connor.

But it all looks so much more nebulous in the aftermath of the lightning bolt that recently cleaved my heart, and my life, in two. The truth is it all comes back to Inez. She took my hand when we met and pulled me into a world I'd never have found on my own. Without it, without her, maybe Ridley Falls isn't a place I can imagine myself in anymore.

My email pings about an hour after Robin and I hang up. It's the contact info for Trixie and Lex Sullivan, owners of Gator's in Chinook River.

Would it really be so bad? I ask myself. To start over somewhere new? Somewhere I can just be Cash the lesbian and no one will know that I once hooked up with my apparently homophobic sellout of a co-worker or fell in love with my best friend on a dare.

My own bar. The support of queer folks who want to help someone succeed. And fifty miles of distance from the thing ripping my heart into pieces.

I tell myself I'll call, once the Jubilee is done. Just to see. But even that feels like an awful betrayal.

23

SATURDAY DAWNS CLOUDLESS and warm, with just a little hint of a chill on the breeze. The perfect kind of day for an outdoor party. The hardest kind of day to say goodbye.

Parker is up with the sun, and my completely wacked internal clock has me feeling very close to human after four hours of sleep. I'll take it, even though I know it's not sustainable.

Maybe in Chinook River I'll sleep better, I think as I cut a banana into bite-sized chunks for cereal. I keep trying it out, waiting for the moment when it doesn't feel like something's being physically torn from me when I think of leaving.

"Are you excited for the party, Mama?" Parker asks when I set her cereal in front of her, settling across the table with my own bowl and what can only be described as a bucket of coffee.

"Very. How about you?"

Her grin widens in a mischievous way that terrifies me. "I have a surprise."

There is no parent of a six-year-old in history who has felt positively about these words. Especially when combined with that facial expression. "What's the surprise?" I ask, trying not to appear too wary.

"If I told you it wouldn't be a surprise," Parker says in a sing-song voice. "But trust me, you're gonna *love* it."

"Okay." I try to balance my desire to know everything immediately with my desire to foster her burgeoning independence. "Is it a performance-related surprise or another kind?"

"Performance," Parker says decisively. "And you're not gettin' any more clues out of me." She pantomimes zipping her lips, but it's all right. I'm mostly satisfied that it will be harmless. After all, the teacher will be supervising and the stage isn't very tall . . .

"I'm looking forward to it," I say as diplomatically as possible.

"Now, let's talk about *you*," Parker insists, leaning across the table with her chin resting on her little chubby fist. This is a common tactic when she's afraid she might be told no or get in trouble for something. "What's on your mind?"

I laugh, but actually, now doesn't seem like the worst time to tell her what's on my mind.

"Well," I say. "Let me answer your question with a question. How do you feel about living in Ridley Falls?"

"Let me answer *your* question with a question," she replies. "I like it a lot."

Stifling another laugh, I press on: "Well, how would you feel about maybe trying living somewhere else? You know, taking our show on the road. Trying a new town."

I expect thoughtfulness, or a silly answer. Basically Parker's two speeds. What I don't expect is the adult-level expression of pity she levels at me as I finish this question.

"Ah," she says in a tone of deep knowing. "Did you and Auntie Inez break up?"

"*What?*" I ask, doing a terrible job of disguising whatever the hell emotion is now making my face go slightly numb.

"Did you and Auntie Inez break up?" Parker asks again, patiently, as if I haven't heard her. "Ruthie at school—she's new— she says she moved here because her mom and dad broke up and her mom didn't want to see the ghost of their love around every corner."

Privately, I think this is a lot of information for Ruthie's mother to share with a first-grader, but the current conversation requires too much focus and careful stepping to worry too much about that right now.

"Okay, sure," I concede. "But what gave you the impression that Auntie Inez and I were the kind of together where we could break up?"

"Oh!" Parker says, slurping her sugary cereal milk. "Lizzie at school says that when you're in love it's like best friends but extra. Like you're best friends, but you have sleepovers a lot, and you make each other laugh *a lot* and you're, like, even better best friends than the best best friends."

Draining the last of my coffee in one gulp, I'm forced to accept that this is a more succinct definition of what being in love with your best friend is like than any of the ones I found on the internet.

"Anyways when she told me that I was like, oh *duh*, my mom is *so* in love with my Auntie Inez! They're *the* best friends and they laugh and they have sleepovers. Also I love her and she loves me and you said you'd never fall in love with someone who doesn't love me."

She seems so utterly certain about this that her logic starts to make sense to me against my will. I don't know whether to tell Parker that Inez and I were never anything more than friends, which sort of feels like a lie, or to follow her lead here.

Because in a way, she's right. This doesn't feel like a friendship that took a weird turn. It *does* feel like a breakup. I sigh. "It's all a little complicated, pal," I tell her. "I wish I could do a better job of explaining it, but the truth is I don't even have it all figured out myself."

The pity in Parker's tiny, cherubic face only deepens. "Sometimes you're supposed to have something for a little time, and sometimes a long time, and sometimes forever," she says sagely. "Remember when I left Princess Twilight Sparkle out in the sun and she melted?"

"I do," I reply, not sure whether to laugh or cry. It had been pretty horrifying, the little lopsided pony with its face half-puddle on the driveway.

"You told me that just because she was gone didn't mean I wouldn't have all the good memories we made together. And those were precious. And remember we drew pictures of the memories and put them on the fridge."

"I remember," I say, and I'm definitely trying not to cry now.

"Do you want to draw a picture of Auntie Inez and put it on the fridge?" Parker asks, her head cocked to the side out of curiosity. "Or should we just move away for now?"

"Let me answer your question with a question," I reply. "How would *you* feel if Auntie Inez and I were together romantically and we were breaking up? I know you love her. Wouldn't that make you a little sad?"

I wait with bated breath for the answer to this question, which suddenly has more significance than a six-year-old should be able to control.

Parker waves a hand nonchalantly. "I mean, no offense, Mom,

but Auntie Inez isn't breaking up with me. Only four more years until I get a phone and then we can text. Or we can have sleepovers when you're busy meeting a rebound guy like Ruthie's mom. Or a rebound girl," she adds diplomatically. "Or even a them."

I make a mental note to limit Parker's exposure to Ruthie and her oversharing mom, but after that I feel something give way in my mind. Something I've been holding tightly to for a very, very long time. Parker is okay, I realize. She's a well-adjusted, under-standing, wise-beyond-her-years little person, and she's right.

In my two doomed options catastrophizing, I forgot to account for something important. That even if I do ruin a relationship, now or in the future, Parker will be okay because she'll have me to guide her through it. Even if it hurts her, I can't protect her from the harsh realities of love and loss forever. Ruthie's mom seems determined to make sure of that.

I did an okay job navigating her through the melting of Princess Twilight Sparkle, didn't I? Who's to say I couldn't do the same with a real breakup? What if I'm a good enough parent to keep her safe without giving up my chance at being happy, too?

As Parker hops down from the table and goes upstairs to try on her costume again, I sit boneless at my kitchen table as my care-fully constructed objections wobble like a Jenga tower that's had a central block removed.

If I don't have Parker to worry about, and I've already proven to myself that there would be life beyond Joyce's by considering this Chinook River situation, then the only people left in this decision-making process are Inez and me. What if she understands that I'm new at this? And a bit of a mess? What if she's willing to take a chance on us anyway?

Suddenly, the door leading to Chinook River closes tightly in my mind's eye, and another, infinitely more terrifying one opens beside it.

Because if this revelation can be trusted, if I don't have Parker or my little heteronormative box to hide behind, there's only one real obstacle in the way of Inez and me. If I want to get past it, I'm finally going to have to be honest with her. About everything.

Before I can overthink it, I take out my phone and text her with my heart in my throat.

Heading your way soon. Can we steal a couple minutes? I really need to talk to you.

Upstairs, Parker sings *Moana* songs off-key, and I think that if the surprise she's planning for the performance is anything like the one she just detonated at our kitchen table, Joyce's Jubilee is going to be one memorable event.

By the time Parker and I get to the farm, Inez still hasn't texted me back. I tell myself she's probably just busy with the setup. I'm sure people started showing up at the crack of dawn even though we told them noon was plenty early enough.

The place looks incredible. I can't even believe the difference. A massive Joyce's Jubilee banner hangs over the driveway. Flowers are blooming all along the field they've designated for parking. Tables and easy-ups and tents have sprouted like mushrooms on the massive lawn, and as I hop out of the Jeep to unbuckle Parker I just catch a glimpse of the stage down the hill.

"Gladys!" Parker shrieks before I even see another soul. The second her feet touch the ground she's running, all sequins and sparkles and tutu lace and, of course, her dinosaur rain boots.

When I turn, Gladys is, indeed, making her way down the

porch steps from the house. She accepts Parker's chaotic gremlin embrace with what appears to be genuine enthusiasm.

"Morning!" I call with a chuckle. "I think she might be happy to see you."

"The feeling is mutual," Gladys says, booping Parker on the nose and making her giggle. "I can take this little one down to see the stage if you like? None of the other kids are here yet but I've volunteered to help with the performance, so I can get her where she needs to be."

I'm about to ask Parker if this is okay with her, but the way she's velcroed herself to Gladys's side and is already talking a mile a minute about her costume, and her boots, and her big surprise answers that question well enough.

"Doesn't seem like she'd have it any other way," I say, and Gladys winks at me.

"She's a special one," Gladys whispers over Parker's head. "You're doing a great job."

I nod my thanks, thinking that before this morning I might not have believed her. But today I do. And I have to, if I'm going to keep believing in what I've decided to do next.

To that end, I call Gladys back before Parker can pull her into the mayhem. "Oh, Gladys, you haven't seen Inez anywhere, have you?" I remind myself this is a totally reasonable question, as we are putting on this event together. That there's no way Gladys can tell the last time Inez and I saw each other was under less than professional circumstances.

"Oh, she's around here somewhere," she says, vaguely waving the hand that isn't attached to Parker's. "Been running around like a chicken with her head cut off all morning."

"Thanks!" I say, as if this answer is totally satisfactory. As if every second I don't get to say the words burning in my chest isn't literal agony. "I'm sure I'll run into her."

I have a to-do list as long as my arm. I need to text Sammy a picture of the stage, and measure the area behind it to make sure a van can fit back there. It's killing me not to know what she's planning, but I know whatever it is will be better than anything I could have come up with on my own, so I have to let it go.

The raffle prizes that were dropped off at Joyce's yesterday are all in the back of the Jeep and need to be arranged attractively somewhere. I have a roll of tickets bigger than my head and a can for cash with a little Parker-handmade sign on it that says FIVE DOLLARS, but I can't for the life of me remember who's supposed to be selling them.

Above and below and around everything, though, is a sense of urgency, pounding in my chest like a drum. I have to find Inez. I have to tell her how I feel. I have to find out, once and for all, if this is something real.

Unfortunately, I don't encounter her once as I take pictures of the stage or measure the area behind it. I catch a brief glimpse of her through a window on my way back up to the house, but by the time I get there there's no sign of her.

Jaz approaches as I'm doing my level best to arrange the raffle prizes on a folding table near the entrance to the booths, coming up from behind with a sigh.

"Honey, you might have learned how to dress a *little* better, but you need to leave things like this to a professional if you want anyone to buy one of these things."

I turn to face her, shoulders slumped in defeat. I had a vision for how I wanted it to look, but so far it has fallen woefully short.

"This is not my area of expertise," I say with a self-deprecating chuckle.

"That's obvious," she agrees with a pitying look—but there's a smirk hidden in there somewhere. I take it as a good sign. "Hand it over."

I do, and gladly. There's only an hour left before the kids and the rest of the setup crew arrive, and only three hours until we're open to the public. I have to find Inez if I want to have any chance to talk to her before the chaos makes it impossible.

"Jaz?" I ask before she loses herself in the artistry of arranging raffle prizes. "You haven't seen Inez anywhere, have you?"

She gives me a long look up and down before she answers. This time, there's no hidden smirk. "That girl is one of the best, biggest-hearted people I've ever met," she says instead of answering. "You better know what you're doing before you go looking for her."

There was a time—basically until this morning, really—when I would have pretended not to know what she was talking about. Or would have worried endlessly about whether she was right. But I know what I want for the first time in what seems like my whole life.

I smile, and she must see something in my expression because she relents. Smiles back. "I do," I say. "This time I really do, I promise."

"Last time I saw her she was checking on Granny," Jaz says, and it feels like permission. "Good luck."

"Thank you," I say, and I turn and actually *run* into the house.

24

I REALIZE WHEN I get inside that Inez has actually given up her own room to Granny O'Connor. The door is still painted emerald green. I did it for her just a few weeks after we met—I remember she asked if I was *as handy as I looked*.

Knowing what I know now, I wonder if she was flirting with me. How long did it take me to tell her I was straight? How many other potential moments have I missed over the years we've known each other? And would it have even mattered before I was willing to accept who I am?

I tap gently on the door. My heart is beating way too fast. I feel like a teenager knocking on her door for our first date, nervous to mess it up in front of her parents.

"Come in, come in," Granny grumbles from the other side of the door. I wait for Inez's giggle. Something to signify that she's here. But there's nothing else.

When I open the door my heart sinks. She's not here. It's starting to feel intentional.

"Hey, Mrs. O'Connor," I say with my best attempt at a smile. "I was just . . . coming to see how you are since the fall."

The old woman is sitting at Inez's old-fashioned vanity, putting on lipstick with a surprisingly steady hand. The other one is still in a cast. I can see bruising peeking out through the hole and I feel a pang of affection for her. Soon she'll be ruling assisted living, but it's a big change for someone who's been in this house her whole life.

"Coming to check on me, a likely story," she says when she's puckered her lips in the mirror. "Looking for my granddaughter's more like it. And after you turned her down flat."

I'm so thrown off by this that I'm literally speechless. Did Inez come home from karaoke night and tell her grandmother what a jerk I was? Did she think I'd turned her down because I wasn't interested?

Also, does the fact that she was upset enough to tell her grandma point to deeper feelings than a one-and-a-half-night stand would indicate? I feel like a jerk for wondering this. If I really hurt her I should feel terrible, not hopeful . . .

"It was more complicated than that," I manage at last. Granny's shrewd stare is offering me no easy outs.

"That's what people always say when they break your heart."

"I'm sure you don't know much about that," I say wryly. "Somehow you strike me as the breaker not the breakee."

"Shows what you know," she says, spinning around in Inez's chair to examine me even more closely. "I've had my heart shattered more times than I can count. It's all part of being alive."

I think about this for a long minute. The truth is, I don't think I've ever really had my heart broken. "I didn't really learn how to risk mine right until recently," I say, not sure if I meant to say it out loud or not.

"Inez is worth it, you know," her grandmother says. "She deserves someone who's sure about her. Who accepts and loves themselves enough to love her right. If you're not that person you need to leave her be."

"You sound like Jaz," I say with a self-deprecating chuckle.

"Who do you think taught her?" Granny replies, affronted. "After that last awful boyfriend of hers we went through four boxes of tissues and eight pints of rocky road."

I laugh, picturing the two of them. Tough Jaz, heartbroken. Granny O'Connor dabbing at her false eyelashes. "You know, I've always been pretty terrified of you," I say conversationally. "I always got the impression you didn't approve of me."

"Pah." She waves a hand as if I've missed the point entirely. "Everyone's afraid of me until they're ready to hear the truth."

"Well, I'm ready now." I don't know if I even want to hear it, but I feel like this trial might be part of it. The road I have to walk to be worthy of Inez. And I want that more than almost anything in the world right now, so I wait for my judgment to be handed down.

Granny O'Connor takes a deep breath. Her shrewd eyes bore, if possible, even deeper into mine. I get the uncomfortable sense that she's excavating something even I haven't had a chance to fully examine yet.

"You're a good mother," she says at last. Decisively, like she's rendered a final verdict. "But you've been hiding behind that little girl of yours. Behind wanting to give her a 'normal' life. Only she doesn't want normal. She wants you. It's important to put them first, but she's looking to you to do more than tell her how to live. She needs you to show her."

I think of Parker at the table this morning. How deeply *okay* she was with everything I'd tried so hard to protect her from. "That's true," I say quietly.

"If you live a life of repression and self-sacrifice, all you're going to show her is that she should do the same. I know that's not what you want for her."

"It isn't," I say automatically. I've never thought about it quite this way before, but I know she's right. That whatever reasons I had for believing in my heterosexuality were compounded by my desire not to make things complicated for her.

"Every good parent wants to save their children from the things that hurt them," Granny goes on. "But our children aren't us. They need different things than we did. I can see that you really needed parents who would put you first. That you needed more proof that they loved you, more investment in your happiness."

Unbidden, my eyes are misty. I don't think about my parents much after fifteen years away from them, but Granny O'Connor is absolutely right. They knew what they wanted for me, but they never bothered to know me. Never wanted to invest in my happiness. Were never curious about my dreams. It was always the two of them, an immovable force shoving me toward something I never wanted.

"But your little girl is so free to be herself. She speaks her mind. She knows she's loved, and that the people around her are interested in what makes her special. Using her as an excuse to close yourself off from the world is selfish, Cassandra, and you're better than that."

This seems to be the concluding piece. I feel a bit like a carpet that's been beaten clean over a porch railing. A little battered, but better for it.

"She's avoiding me, isn't she?" I ask, not quite meeting the old woman's eyes.

"Of course she is," Granny replies. "Wouldn't you be avoiding you?"

"I guess so."

"If you want to find her, you will. But you have to be brave."

"I will," I say, smiling at her. "Thank you, Mrs. O'Connor."

She smiles that freshly lipsticked smile at me, and for a moment I can see what she must have looked like when she was much younger. Inez resembles her. I never noticed that before.

"You can call me Granny," she decrees. "Now, get going before you mess it up for good."

I don't need to be told twice.

I find her in the greenhouse. Because of course I do.

Between her determination to avoid me and the fact that I get stopped every ten feet to grab a table end, or taste a pastry, or find tape for a sign, we only have a few minutes left before the Jubilee opens to the public.

It'll have to be enough.

The door opens soundlessly. Someone fixed the knob after I was here last and I feel a pang that it wasn't me. I want to fix everything for her.

Inez is facing away from me, standing right where she was when I kissed her for the first time. She doesn't turn toward me. Her arms are crossed tightly, her head bowed.

"Hey," I say softly. I was worried I wouldn't know what to say when I found her, but it turns out the opposite is true. I have too much to say, and only a few minutes to do it in.

"You tracked me down," she says joylessly. Her nose is stuffed—has she been crying?

"I've been looking for you for hours," I say, halting before I reach her. If she's this upset I don't know how close I have the right to be.

"Well, I wasn't going to make it easy for you."

"You never do," I agree, hoping to inject a little humor. "But I really need to talk to you."

This, finally, gets her to turn. Her eyes are red and puffy, her normally rosy cheeks pale, like she didn't sleep last night. "I know you do," she says. "And I kind of can't believe you chose today of all days to do this, but clearly I can't stop you, so just go ahead and say it."

She sounds angry. Whatever I expected, it wasn't this. The two possible futures I saw were enthusiastic agreement (ideal) or pitying kindness (disastrous). But anger?

"I know we said nothing would change," I begin. The only thing I can imagine is that she's upset that I'm going back on the deal we made at the Palm Motel's pool. My promise. "But . . . things did change. It was stupid and naïve of me to pretend they wouldn't, so first I should say I'm sorry for that."

Inez's red eyes are still narrowed in my direction. She's so beautiful, even puffy and furious. I don't want to talk anymore. I just want to take her in my arms. Kiss her until she forgets there's anything to be angry about.

"And you couldn't talk to me about it?" she asks. "You had to make some huge, life-changing decision without even asking how I feel? That's pretty selfish, Cash. This affects me too, you know."

It's a fair criticism, even though I wasn't expecting it. It would have been better to work all this out together. "I'm sorry," I say, meaning it. "I just really needed to figure out how I felt first. It wouldn't have been fair to you otherwise."

When I saw her standing in here, I'll admit my hope was bigger than my fear. But now, listening to her anger, seeing how closed off she is with her arms folded across her chest, I'm forced to confront the idea that this might be too little, too late. Or that she never felt that way about me at all, and she's furious at me for ruining our friendship over it.

The thought sinks like a lead balloon in my stomach.

"And this seems more fair to you?" she asks, sinking it even further. "Springing it on me today? Right when things were about to get better?"

"I know the timing sucks," I say, struggling to get to the point. My hope might be dwindling, but the urgency is there. As strong as ever. This truth is like a toxin I have to expel from my body. Even if it doesn't go the way I want it to, I have to tell her. I've come this far. "But once I was finally sure, I had to find you. To tell you . . ."

"Well, let me save you the awkward confession," she says, and the last of my hopeful balloon shreds are incinerated by the look on her face. The cruelty of these words. "You're leaving for Chinook River. I'm staying in Ridley Falls. Everything we've been building together all these years is over. Did I miss anything?"

It takes a few seconds for the confusion to lift, and then I start laughing. I can't help it. "Who told you that?"

Inez's mood is not improved by my laughter. "Well, I couldn't nurse my rejection wounds at the only bar in town last night, so I went to Badger's with Mars to have a glass of wine and mope. You'll imagine how thrilled I was to find Robin positively bubbly about you *buying* some dive in Chinook River. Finally cutting off the deadweight of Joyce's. Getting a *fresh start*."

"She picked a great time to become the town gossip," I say.

"This isn't *funny*," Inez says. She actually stomps her foot. It's so adorable I nearly split open at the seams. "It's tragic. After how long I waited for you to finally open up, after—"

"Inez," I interrupt. "I'm not going."

She stops in her tracks. Her eyes—narrowed from the moment I walked in—open wide at last. "Excuse me?"

"I'm not going to Chinook River." I take a step forward. "Robin told me about the offer, and I'm not going to lie to you, I was considering it. But I decided this morning that I can't leave Ridley Falls."

Inez takes a step toward me, too, almost as if she's sleepwalking. "Why not?" she breathes.

I take a deep breath. Steel myself. I had a whole speech planned—about realizing I'm a lesbian, and how long I've probably wanted her, and about Parker, and everything— but really what it boils down to is very simple.

"Because I love you."

Her eyes widen farther. I can see her breath catch. "What did you just say?" she asks, and I can't tell one way or another how this is going. I don't know if she's about to kiss me, or slap me, or walk away from me forever.

"I said I love you," I repeat, reaching out for her. To take her hand. To touch her anywhere just to prove that she's real. That she's really here. That I really said it at last.

But before I can reach her, before she can react at all, the door opens behind us and a frantic Mars sticks their head in. "There you both are!" they say in a much higher-pitched voice than normal. "People are starting to line up outside, and Jaz doesn't know how to run debit cards for raffle tickets, and we're gonna need overflow parking, and Cash you need to sound check for the karaoke contest, and everyone's kind of losing it out here."

I devoutly hope that Mars will withdraw for a moment after this proclamation. Give us thirty seconds to wrap this up for now at the very least. But they don't. They just stand there with their big, round panic eyes until we have no choice but to exit the greenhouse.

To split up as Inez heads for the raffle table and I head for the stage. The event won't be over until the last band finishes playing, and that could be midnight for all I know.

Until it's over, I realize with a horrible, sinking feeling, I'll have no idea where we stand.

25

EVERY MOMENT OF the Joyce's Jubilee is absolutely perfect, and I can't wait for it to be over.

There's a line of cars all the way down the road by the time we start letting people in. Everyone who signed up to provide food, drinks, or coffee runs out of supplies in the first hour, and Mars (as the only person smart enough to keep their car from getting blocked in) spends half the party just running back and forth into town for more.

Claudette sets up her grill for burgers an hour in and serves 150 of them before two.

Gladys joins Willa and Brook in the kids' zone, where they do sack races and bubble-blowing contests and storytelling with the kids, assisted by Parker's teacher and a few of the other parents who jump in when it's clear every child in town is here.

Jaz comes up with a brilliant plan for a poster of how much money we need to raise to fully renovate Joyce's, and she colors in the bar every hour to show the progress we're making. I can't make myself look very often, but I know the green has eaten up a lot of the white by the time I need to start our karaoke sing-off.

The place I want to look more than anything is, torturously, just out of view. Inez is manning the raffle table and there's a tree right between us. Not that there's much I'd be able to tell from this distance, anyway.

I take the stage to tumultuous applause from the gathered crowd. There are so many people I feel overwhelmed, grateful to nearly the point of tears. But I manage to keep it together as I click the microphone on.

"Hello, Ridley Falls," I say. I'm not wearing my leather jacket today. It's just me, and it feels right. "I don't know how to thank you all for coming out. It's incredible to see all your faces. To know you care about Joyce's enough to be here with us today."

Plenty of people cheer. Anyone who's not already gathered at the stage looks up, starts drifting in our direction. The sun is blazing, it's a warm day for springtime in Washington. And there, for just a brief second at the coffee stand, I see Inez's white shirt. My stomach does a backflip.

"Anyway, you're not here to listen to me get sappy," I say, chuckling, wondering if Inez can hear me. I have a wild urge to ask her to join me on the stage. To say I love her again in front of everyone, through our borrowed stacks of speakers. To get my answer once and for all in dramatic fashion.

But I can't, and I know it. Making it public diminishes her choice. She knows where I am. She knows what I said. All I can do is wait for her to say how she feels.

"Who wants to sing some karaoke?" I ask, and the crowd—as they say—goes wild. I give them the logistics—sign-up sheet at the edge of the stage, five dollars a song to support Joyce's. Everyone will be organized into heats. The winner gets the raffle prize of their choosing *and* number one spot on the list at Joyce's karaoke for a month.

I think it'll be a relief to hand the microphone over for the first heat, but as soon as everyone's eyes are off me my thoughts return to Inez. To the greenhouse. To the totally less than ideal conditions of me at last admitting I love her.

From this angle, I can almost see her at the table. Just a peek of her white eyelet shirt from time to time behind the massive trunk of the alder tree. I know Jaz is there. I've seen Granny O'Connor puttering around. Has Inez told them about what I said? Are they all laughing at me? Or trying to talk her out of it?

And what am I going to do if she turns me down after all this? Is leaving town still an option? Could I keep working with her every day knowing she didn't feel the same way?

The first heat is over, and I announce the winner before setting up the second. This day is going to be endless.

During karaoke intermission, Parker's class is set to perform. I'm so nervous for her that I almost forget to be nervous for myself for a few minutes. I stand on the side of the stage watching as their teacher gets them all in formation, each wearing a complementary costume and holding a jump rope.

I can tell which one is Madison immediately. She tosses her hair in a way that tells me exactly what kind of person she's gonna grow up to be. Parker, as always, is one of the shortest, but her boots stand out.

Her eyes scan the crowd for me, and light up when she finally finds me on the side of the stage. That toothless smile breaks my heart. I want this to go well for her so bad.

She gives me the thumbs-up. I return it. And then the performance begins.

At first I think everything's going to go better than anticipated.

The teacher gives me the signal to start their song—that same one Parker was singing in the car the other morning. "If You Said Yes" by The Walking Wild. I have to admit it's pretty good.

They're all jumping rope, mostly on time, too. Of course Madison is the standout. She's front and center doing some pretty fancy footwork.

That's when it happens. Parker misses a step. Her rain boots are too clunky for jumping and her legs are a lot shorter than the other kids'. I'm ready to run out and rescue her, but she's on her feet in no time, and she's smiling.

I think she'll get back to the routine, but instead she walks to the front of the stage. The other kids keep jumping. I lower the volume of the music instinctively, wondering if this is her big surprise.

She's right at the front. The crowd is watching, giggling, and then Parker yells, "Hey, what do you call a fly without wings?"

One of the other parents yells, "What?" and I swear I could kiss her.

"A walk!" Parker answers, giggling at her own joke.

There are some laughs from the crowd. It's chaos now, as some of the kids are realizing Parker's no longer jumping. They're splitting off to do their own things, too.

"What do you call a fairy that doesn't like to take a shower?" Parker shouts to the audience.

This time, multiple people call back in answer.

"A STINKERBELL!" Parker says, and this time the other kids are laughing, too. One of them is pretending to be a frog, hopping around the stage on all fours. One of them is doing cartwheels. Two of them are holding hands and spinning in circles. One girl near the back has started to sing, very shyly.

It's the most hilarious, terrible, perfect performance I've ever seen. Halfway through I'm crying and laughing at the same time. Madison is clearly furious, if the speed of her jump rope smacking the stage is any indication.

But at the end, the other kids all dogpile Parker with hugs and gratitude and congratulations. I'm clapping so hard my hands sting, and I wonder how I ever could have worried that she wouldn't be okay. She's so perfectly, beautifully herself. And if Granny O'Connor can be believed, no small part of that is because of me.

As if to put the perfect cherry on the ice cream sundae of this moment, I catch Inez's face in the crowd, and she's looking at me, and she's smiling.

I'm not off duty until I announce the winner of the karaoke contest, which ends up being Mo with a surprisingly emotional rendition of Johnny Cash's "I Walk the Line."

I'm sure Charlie will never let him hear the end of it, but he looks happy up there as he accepts his raffle prize—a guided fishing trip in the bay—and I'm happy for him.

At this point, a black van pulls down the driveway heading for the stage, and soon it'll be time to find out who Sammy's mystery headliner is at last . . .

The sun is setting. It's been an absolutely beautiful day. And to top it all, when I hop down off the stage, Inez is running toward me.

It's all I can do not to run, too. To meet her in the middle of the field. To get my hopes up for the kind of cinematic *I love you too* movie moment I couldn't have even dreamed of a few days ago. I tell myself to be patient, to let her say what she needs to say, but I can't deny the hope is there—ready to be dashed.

Maybe this is what love is, I think as she gets closer. Giving someone this power. Hoping they don't use it to destroy you. I wouldn't know. I didn't even know how to fall in love right until a month ago when I first dreamed of my best friend.

Inez skids to a stop in front of me, out of breath, her expression unreadable.

"Hi," I say.

"Hey."

There's a pause, and I can't tell if it's awkward or full of possibility. Either way I can't take it for long. "Look," I begin, running a hand through my hair. "I'm sorry if I put you on the spot earlier. You don't have to say—"

"George and Linda are here," she interrupts me.

"Oh," I reply, struggling to switch gears. "They didn't tell me they were coming."

"Well, they're over by the raffle table and they want to talk to you."

She starts walking, and I can't do anything but follow. I'm torn between anxiety about what George and Linda cut their vacation short for and the agony that is still not knowing where I stand with Inez.

The ball is in her court, I remind myself. *Don't be pushy.*

"Did they say what they wanted?" I ask, trying to be normal, jogging up to walk at her side. The crowd is still lively, all the booths packed. People are eating and milling around, talking to one another. They seem happy. I don't let myself ask how much money we've raised. I can't stand to know if we didn't reach our goal.

"Not exactly," Inez replies, frustratingly vague. I'm starting to feel like I'm in another world, separate from the crowd, from the party, even from Inez. In my world, everything is nebulous. Nothing is certain. It all washes around like a watercolor painting in the rain, forming and re-forming futures faster than I can get used to them.

"Okay then." The raffle table is in sight. I can see George and Linda, looking around in what I hope is awe at the party, the crowd.

"There's the woman of the hour!" Linda cries when she sees me. "Honey, this is just fantastic!"

"Thank you!" I manage a big smile even as I feel more than half of me being drawn into the black hole of Inez's nonresponse. I'm starting to wonder what any of this matters without her. Who cares if we succeed if there's no *us* to see it through?

The one thing all this has proven to me is that I can't be just her friend.

George clears his throat. It's clear he's asked me something and is waiting for a reply, but I don't know what it was. "Sorry, I'm a little frazzled," I admit with what I hope is a charmingly self-deprecating grin. "Can you say that again?"

"I just asked if there's somewhere we can go to have a little chat," George repeats, smiling back. My stomach drops. After a lifetime of flophouses and cheap apartments, jobs that barely paid the bills, I feel like nothing good ever comes from your boss wanting to *have a little chat*.

"You can use the kitchen," Inez says to George, carefully not looking at me. "Cash knows where it is."

I want to tell her to come with us, that she's part of this too, but I'm so afraid to put any pressure on her that I just lead the way, leaving her standing by the table with that unreadable look on her face.

I open the front door despite the sign that says NO ENTRY. Inside the house, everything is much quieter. Everyone is outside enjoying the party. I lead George and Linda through the living room and into the spacious kitchen with all its kitschy farm accents left over from Granny O'Connor's reign.

"Can I get you two anything to drink?" I ask, hoping they say no. I have no idea what's even in this kitchen, and despite Inez's permission it feels strange acting at home here when things are so strained between us.

"That's okay, sweetheart, we can't stay too long," Linda says. Then she glances at George.

"I can't say how flattered I am that you came all this way for our little party," I say to forestall the inevitable bad news. "I hope you can stick around for the show, we got Sammy Espinoza to book us a headliner and she knows some really great bands."

"Oh, loud music isn't really our thing," George says. "We're mostly just here to chat with you about the future."

"Right," I say, heart sinking further. He's going to tell me they decided to sell the place. Or that they're retiring and giving it to one of their kids, who will want to be much more involved in the day-to-day. He's going to remind me that this place, as much as I love it, as hard as I've fought for it, isn't mine. That it never will be.

"Well, Cash, we hope you know how much we appreciate how hard you've worked for us these past years," he says, following the script of my worst fears. "And it looks like this fundraiser's gonna be a big success."

"Thank you, George. I did work hard on it."

"We know you did. And because of you, Joyce's is gonna be something brand-new."

"Why do I sense a *but* coming here?" I ask at last, unable to take the limbo.

Linda smiles guiltily, and it's clear I've hit the mark. "Well, honey, we've been talking and we're just not sure we're young and hip enough to know what a place like that needs. I mean, a music venue with *farm to table* food? We're just a couple of old fuddy-duddies."

If I still had a heart, I imagine I'd feel it somewhere near the toe of my shoe. I braced myself for success or failure when we started all this, but I never envisioned a world in which I succeeded so much that I lost the place anyway.

"You're gonna sell," I hear myself say. Barely more than a croak. Inez's happy, yellow kitchen hardly seems the place for all my dreams to die.

Another exchange of guilty looks. I want to scream that I did all this for them. That I pulled their business out of the toilet and made it into something that could compete with a franchise like Kings, all while making sure it still fostered the spirit of community Ridley Falls is famous for. I want to tell them they're making a huge mistake. I want to tell them to go to hell.

"We are gonna sell," George confirms. "But luckily we have the perfect person in mind to run the place. Someone with an understanding of what a place like this new Joyce's would need to succeed. Someone young and hip who cares about the community."

The way things are going, I think sourly, they're gonna bring Chase through the kitchen door. I don't say anything, I just let George finish tying the rope that my hopes and dreams will be swinging from any minute.

It won't matter who they bring in, or what *vision* they have, or how *young and hip* they are. Joyce's has been as good as mine and it won't be anymore. This new person will have their own ideas, and I'll just be their employee.

In the long pause before George speaks, I crack open the door to Gator's in Chinook River again. Just a little. Just to let the light in. If Inez loved me as much as I love her, she wouldn't have been able to keep me at arm's distance all day. If I'm gonna lose Inez *and* Joyce's then maybe Robin was right. Maybe it's time for a fresh start.

"So, what do you say, kid?" George asks, cutting into my bleak new fantasy where I walk away from Ridley Falls with a bandanna tied to a stick and Parker holding my hand.

"What . . . do I say about what?" I ask him carefully. "Bringing in a new owner?"

Linda laughs. The vibe is very surreal in here—like I'm missing a significant chunk of context. "No, Cash, about *being* the new owner."

26

MY MIND IS an utter blank. My expression must be something else, because George and Linda are laughing. Being the new owner of Joyce's. My own place. And I wouldn't even have to leave town.

"There's no way I could afford it," I say honestly, though my mind is already calculating how many more Jubilees it would take to get me there. Maybe George and Linda wouldn't mind waiting a beat while I tried for a loan . . .

"We thought you might say that," George concedes. "But we have a plan. No big down payment, you just pay us a chunk at a time out of your profits until you're all caught up and then we sign the paperwork. We'll have our lawyer get it all in order."

"That's so generous," I say, still feeling like I'm floating twenty feet above this conversation. "But why? I mean . . . why me?"

They laugh again. "Honey, we've always known you love the place more than we do, and you've done such a great job with it. But the real kicker came when Inez called us last night saying you might have a better offer. That's when we realized we better get our ducks in a row. You know we couldn't do it without you, Cash."

There's so much to parse in this statement, but of course my mind grabs one word and holds on tight. "Inez?" I ask. "Inez called you?"

"Last night," Linda confirms. "We were up north in B.C. but she said we needed to know you had another offer over in Chinook River and we'd better act fast if we didn't want to lose you."

"She's a firecracker," George says with a chuckle. "She made quite a case, not that we needed to be convinced. We'd been discussing the idea of passing the place along to you for a while. She just let us know we didn't have time to dillydally."

Inez called George and Linda, I think in a daze. Inez wanted me to stay badly enough that she called our bosses and convinced them to sell me a bar just so I didn't move an hour away.

"I don't know what to say," I confess. My thoughts are more tangled than they've ever been, but I know that I need to find Inez. I need to find her and ask her what it means that she fought this hard to keep me here.

"Say yes!" Linda replies, beaming. "And then get back to your party, we can work out all the details in the next few weeks."

I know there are things I should consider here. Like whether owning a dive bar in the middle of nowhere is really the soundest business decision. Like what the paperwork will look like and whether I'm equal to the task of keeping the books and staying on top of the permits and building codes, but right now all I can think is that I want this. That I fought for it. That Inez and I fought for it together.

"Yes," I say, smiling so big it hurts my face. "Okay. Let's do it."

Linda scoops George and me up in an impromptu hug, and I

laugh and pat them both on the back before disentangling myself. "I don't even know how to begin to thank you," I say.

"Just don't change the name," George says with a wink.

"I wouldn't dream of it."

Twilight is gathering when I make it back out the farmhouse door. I feel like my feet are floating an inch or two above the grass as I make my way through the crowd. Everyone stops. Smiles. Claps me on the back, or congratulates me, or thanks me for the party.

They don't even know, I think. But they will soon. There's just one more thing I have to figure out first.

Most of the Jubilee-goers have made their way to the field in front of the stage by now. As the light dims some of the kids run around with glow sticks and bracelets that I eventually track down to Mystical Moments' tarot booth.

"Nice touch," I say to Maeve, who hands me one with a smile.

The rest of the night has been turned over to Sammy and her band. I relish in the feeling of having pulled this off. Whether or not we raised all the money we needed, I know we're going to be okay. That Joyce's is going to be okay.

My own place, I think again, and I'm smiling again.

I'm scanning the crowd for Inez, of course, but part of me wants to stay in this moment just a little longer. The one where everything is pure potential and nothing has been decided just yet.

To that end, Sammy Espinoza takes the stage—gloriously pregnant—and beams out at everyone gathered. The cheering starts before she even speaks, and I relish in the feeling of being part of the crowd. Experiencing this event that we created instead of pushing it along its tracks.

"So, are you all ready to hear some music tonight?"

Everyone cheers even louder. A little ways away, I can see Parker with a bunch of her classmates, lovingly supervised by Gladys, Willa, and Brook.

"The band I'm about to bring out is very special to me, one of the first bands I signed to my label when I opened it. They're currently on a U.S. tour promoting their amazing new album, but I called in a favor for my good friend Cash and Joyce's—a Ridley Falls institution, right y'all?"

This prompts the loudest round of applause yet. A Ridley Falls institution, I think. I like the sound of that. It's something I can build on.

"Cash, are you out there somewhere?" Sammy asks, peering into the crowd. "Join me up here for a minute, would you?"

Everything feels very surreal as I make my way toward the stage, climb the steps, join Sammy in the light. She puts an arm around me and I smile and wave. My friends are out there. My family. It's an emotional moment but without things settled with Inez I don't even know how to process it.

"So, Cash," Sammy says. "A little birdie just told me that you're *very close* to your fundraising goal."

"Is that so?" I ask, because I really don't know. I haven't been able to let myself ask all day. I wanted to believe the community coming together and supporting us was enough even if we didn't get the money.

"It is, and I don't know if you knew this, but my husband's first time performing in a decade happened onstage at Joyce's a few years ago."

"Of course I knew," I say. "It's practically become an urban legend."

She laughs. "Well, the place is really important to me, and to my family. So I want to give you this."

Sammy holds out a little rectangular piece of paper. I take it with a shaking hand.

"It's ten thousand dollars to go toward the Joyce's renovation," she says, and the crowd loses their minds.

"I can't take this," I say away from the mic. "It's way too much. More than we even need."

Sammy covers her mic, too. "I may have some ideas about the stage's dedication."

Everything in me says to give it back to her, but this is what I've learned over the course of these past wild few weeks. I can't do everything myself. And if I'm going to be taking over Joyce's, I'm gonna need more help than ever.

"Thank you," I say, into the mic this time. "Thank you so much."

We hug, everyone cheers until I'm sure they'll all be hoarse tomorrow. My eyes well up and I don't even try to hide it.

"Well, don't thank me yet," she says. "I haven't even told you the good news."

"What?" I ask blankly, not bothering to perform.

"I happen to have a friend on the Ridley Falls city council," she says, to me and the crowd. "And they just let me know that as of today, Kings has *withdrawn* its proposed plan for a franchise in town."

I'm starting to actually feel numb to good news. How is this even possible? I'm full-blown crying now, but it's okay. The cheering from the crowd would have been too loud to talk over anyway.

Thank you, I mouth to Sammy. To all of them.

"Okay, y'all!" Sammy shouts. "Enough local politics—without further ado, here's The Walking Wild!"

My heart skips a beat. The Walking Wild? Parker's favorite band? Literal, actual famous people?

"I told you I'd come through," Sammy says to me as we make our way off the stage and the band greets the crowd before launching into their first song.

Somewhere out there, my child is losing her tiny mind with her friends, having the best night of her life. There is a famous band onstage rewarding everyone who came to this party and supported Joyce's. We exceeded our fundraising goal, and Kings is running off with their tail tucked between their legs, and Chase is fired, and right now absolutely all of those thoughts will have to wait, because when I climb down off the stage, Inez is waiting for me.

I approach her, away from the crowd, knowing that after an entire day of trying to track her down this is it. The moment I'll finally know, once and for all.

"Hi," she says.

"Hey," I reply.

"So," she begins, but I hold up a hand.

"Wait," I say. "There's something I have to say first, if that's okay."

Inez nods. Her eyes are wide, fixed on mine. She no longer looks angry. She just waits for me to speak.

"I'm sorry," I say. "There is no part of this that I haven't horribly mishandled. I've just been so worried for Parker's whole life that I wasn't giving her the childhood she deserved, and I guess I let myself get buried in trying to keep things as 'normal' as possible. But being with you that night made me realize so many things."

She smiles a little, and I sniffle, trying to keep it together.

"First of all that I'm, like, *so* gay." I chuckle. "But second, that it wasn't fair to spring all this on you. Yes, I love you, but I never want to make you feel like being your friend wasn't good enough for me. Because it's been the most important touchstone in my life since the day we met. And I never want you to feel like I value that any less because my feelings have changed."

"Cash—" Inez begins, but I stop her.

"If I don't get it out now I'll never be able to do it," I say, feeling every centimeter of the distance between us like a dare. Hoping. Wanting.

She gestures for me to continue.

"It was fucking childish for me to walk away from you the other night, and to plot to leave town because I didn't know how to talk about what was happening between us, or how I felt. So let me be totally clear: I'm not going anywhere. And not just because you talked to George and Linda, but because this—whatever it can be between us—matters to me enough to do the work to overcome this mess I made. Whether that's as friends or as more is totally up to you, but I accept whatever feels right to you."

This time, she doesn't try to stop me. But her smile is so beautiful, the relief behind it so palpable, that I know it will be worth whatever happens next.

"That's why I want your name on the paperwork with mine," I say finally, spreading my hands open, entirely vulnerable for the first time. "Fifty-fifty. Whatever happens between us next, you're my best friend. My partner. We built Joyce's into what it is together. We saved it together. You deserve every bit as much credit for that as I do, and I don't want to do it without you."

A bit of a smirk plays around the edges of her smile. I feel it low in my belly. The heat her mischief always brings to the surface. "So you'd really accept being friends and business partners?" she asks, stepping closer.

I swallow, hard. "If that's what you wanted, then yes. But to be totally clear, what *I* want is . . ." I trail off as she takes another step. I can feel her, like my skin is a magnet pulling her closer.

"You would work behind the bar with me, and stay up late crunching numbers with me, and never want to touch me . . . ?"

She reaches out one finger and runs it up my forearm. I shiver, even though the spring night is warm. "I can't make any promises about the wanting." My voice catches on the word. "But yes. If that's what it takes. I'd do it."

"Wow," she breathes, and her nose is an inch away from mine, her eyes peering up at me through her thick lashes. "You're a whole lot stronger than I am."

And then we're kissing, and the relief is so intense it makes me dizzy. Inez is kissing me. Knowing what I asked her. Knowing that I love her.

"Wait," I say, pulling away for a torturous moment, just to be sure. "I just need you to know I'm a mess. I've known I was a lesbian for essentially one second in the grand scheme of things. And I'm a single mom. And bars fail all the time and I might be awful at it and—"

"Cash," Inez says, clearly exasperated—but in an affectionate way. "I know what I'm getting into. You're a person. My person. You don't require a warning label. I'm all in. I've always been all in."

"All in," I echo, hardly daring to believe it. The band launches into their most popular song. The one that Parker sings every morning in the car. And I hear her say it again in my head, just to make sure: *I've always been all in.*

As I kiss her, the stage lights glinting in her hair, I realize it's the truth. Even when I was too stupid or stubborn to realize it, it's always been me and Inez. And now, maybe, it always will be.

EPILOGUE
One Year Later

JOYCE'S IS JUST as peaceful before opening as it's always been, but that's one of the only things that's still the same. I let myself in through the front door, still smiling about how cute Inez looked when I left her sleeping in our bed at the farm this morning.

It'll be a little while before Brook, our weekend chef and produce-providing mastermind, arrives to prep for Saturday brunch, so for now it's just me.

Next week is the second annual Joyce's Jubilee, and we're in full swing with the planning. The kitchen table at home is covered with notes, poster design rejects, budgets and projections, but here it's quiet.

Light streams in through the big windows on the east side, waking up the potted plants along the wall that Brook's wife, Willa, gave us as a grand reopening present. The white-painted stage has its little stack of speakers—no more wheeling the karaoke cart in and out—and a permanent mic stand. Next week, we're getting a Joyce's drum kit.

On the front of the stage, a little silver plaque reads: PALOMA ESPINOZA MEMORIAL STAGE. Sammy's only wish after her generous donation at last year's event—and one I was all too happy to grant once she told me the incredible story of her grandmother.

It would have been easier to gut the place, as at least seven contractors told me in no uncertain terms. To put something chic and marketable in its place. I'm sure anyone else would have. But me? I love it here. I always have. So we kept the dark wood tables. The long resin bar top with photos and coasters from the seventies wedged underneath. We got rid of the carpet—that was just a health concern—and the windows open now, but it's still unmistakably Joyce's.

The biggest change is through the little doorway behind the bar, and I drift back there now just to smile at it. A big, bright, clean kitchen with a shiny steel prep counter, six-burner grill, a refrigerator that can fit more than lime slices.

Brook runs a tight ship, and Eduardo, who's her second-in-command in the kitchen now, sticks to the program during the week. Personally, I'm just a tourist back here. I prefer to be behind the bar, listening to folks' troubles. Celebrating their successes. Contributing in my small way to the community that's given me so much.

"Knock knock!" rings a voice from the front door I left open. I smile, already knowing who to expect.

Madison's mom, Rachel, has both girls at the entrance. Parker is a little taller, though she still barely hits Madison's chin.

"Come on in!" I call, but Parker is one step ahead. Her rain boots thwap along the hardwood floor—we recently sized up, so they're a little floppier than usual.

"Mama!" she shouts, throwing herself into my abdomen without worrying about the impact. "I can't believe it's finally today!"

"Me, either," I say, ruffling her hair.

"Everybody behaved admirably," Rachel says. "We were on sleepover time last night so she might be a little loopy, but given the excitement of today I think that would have been the case anyway."

I grin. Rachel has become a friend over the past year, ever since Inez and I learned that the reason Madison was acting out at school was because her mom had recently come out and the extended family wasn't taking it well.

We, of course, started inviting her everywhere. Last I checked she and Mars were at the good-morning-texts stage of their burgeoning situationship, and Parker and Madison have been thick as thieves since the start of second grade.

Small towns are funny like that, I think.

"So, how are you feeling about today?" Rachel asks when the girls run off to play by the stage. "It's a pretty big deal."

I reach impulsively into my jacket pocket where a very conspicuous square box is, reassuringly, right where I left it.

"Everyone should be here by ten-thirty," I say, almost more to myself than to Rachel. "Inez will be here at eleven to make room for the stragglers. Brook has the French toast all prepped. The flowers are coming in about twenty minutes . . ."

Rachel's laugh cuts me off. "Cash?" she says. "I asked how you're feeling, not what's on your to-do list."

"Oh," I stall out entirely. "The to-do list has basically been keeping me upright the past few days."

But I take a second to think about it. How I'm feeling. Inez, warm and sleepy this morning as she kissed me goodbye. The life we've built together—not just since last year, but since the day we met. How it feels to have a partner in parenting, in Joyce's, in life . . .

I smile wide, in a way my face is getting used to. I tell Inez it's a brand-new smile—one that belongs just to her.

"I feel amazing," I say, truthfully. "I feel ready."

"I'm happy for you," Rachel says, and then her phone buzzes, and she's smiling, too. "Mars is on their way over."

"Already?" I yelp. "No one's supposed to come here for another hour and a half!"

"They say you forgot your clothes," Rachel informs me.

I look down. Sure enough, I'm wearing jeans with holes in the knees and my old Joyce's T-shirt—we've redesigned the logo, but I still feel most comfortable in the old navy blue. I didn't even bring the button-down shirt and blazer I planned to wear.

"Tell them thanks," I say, laughing again. A lot of things have changed, but the extent to which I prioritize fashion is not one of them.

"We'll be back when the fun starts," Rachel says, calling out to Madison, and then they're gone and it's just Parker and me.

"Well, pal," I say, sitting down next to her on the side of the stage. "How are you feeling about all this? Still on board?"

"Duh," she says, smiling. "Ruthie says weddings are a tool of the pastryarchy but I love parties, and I love Inez and you, so why not?"

I sigh. Ruthie's mom is going through a man-hating phase.

"I just want Inez to know how special she is to me," I say. "And we want to share that specialness and love with our friends and family and our whole community."

"*If* she says yes," Parker replies practically.

"Do you think she won't?" I ask, smiling. This is not one of my many anxieties this morning.

"Nah, she definitely will," Parker says, punching me affectionately on the arm like a football coach in an old movie. "You're perfect for each other."

"Nobody's perfect," I say. "But we love each other, and we both love you, and I think even if things get tough we want to face them together."

"If she says yes," Parker says again, crossing her eyes and sticking out her tongue.

I tickle her. She squeals. I relish in these moments of just the two of us. It's so much more special now that it's intentional, I think. Now that I'm not stubbornly clinging to the idea that I have to do everything alone.

Mars and Jaz arrive next—Gladys is coming over with Inez and Granny at eleven.

"Would you please put this on?" Mars asks, looking despairingly at my outfit as they brandish a garment bag. "We did all this work to bring you out of the closet, but sometimes I think maybe we should have focused more on your sense of style."

I laugh, swatting their arm and taking the bag. "Thank you," I say. "Life wouldn't be the same without you all in our corner."

As if drawn by the mention, Jaz drifts over, ethereal in a silk wrap dress. "We were on the fence about you for a long time," she says. "But you treat our girl right, there's no denying it. You just better not kick us out once the honeymoon phase is over."

"Are you kidding?" I ask, trying to imagine the farm, our life, without the friends that have become family. "We could never afford that place on our own."

Everyone laughs. Parker comes over and asks Jaz to show her how to use makeup. Mars bullies me into my outfit—slacks, a button-down shirt that says *Marry me?* in tiny font all over it, and a blazer that will hopefully make it subtle enough to maintain the surprise factor.

The flowers arrive, and soon after, our friends, fellow business owners, and community members start drifting through the doors. Parker greets them with the air of a professional hostess at a big-city restaurant. Incredible smells begin to drift out from the kitchen.

We're all gathered around the longest table when she walks in. Parker is on one side of me, Mars and Jaz on the other. Granny O'Connor gives me a wink from across the room but I barely see it because Inez is on her arm, and when I see her, everything else goes blurry.

I find the ring box in my pocket again, and I think that I can't imagine a moment of the past year where I wasn't perfectly, totally sure about this woman. This family. This life.

Inez looks confused at first, then her eyes find me in my fancy clothes and the wattage of her smile could get rid of the bar's electric bill entirely. I know, in that moment, that she knows what's happening. But it's okay, because I can see the *yes* in her eyes as they well up. In her steps as she quickens them to get to me sooner.

The rest of the morning will be for the people I invited here today, but in this moment, I know I didn't even need to ask. There's a buzz in the air between us, and I can feel it happening. The first day of the rest of our life has begun. A life that I once thought could only be a dream.

ABOUT THE AUTHOR

TEHLOR KAY MEJIA is the author of *Sammy Espinoza's Last Review* and the critically acclaimed young adult fantasy duology *We Set the Dark on Fire* and *We Unleash the Merciless Storm*. Their debut middle-grade series, *Paola Santiago and the River of Tears*, is currently in development at Disney as a television series to be produced by Eva Longoria. Mejia lives with their daughter, partner, and two small dogs in Oregon, where they grow heirloom corn and continue their quest to perfect the vegan tamale.

tehlorkaymejia.com
@tehlorkay

ABOUT THE TYPE

This book was set in Fournier, a typeface named for Pierre-Simon Fournier (1712–68), the youngest son of a French printing family. He started out engraving woodblocks and large capitals, then moved on to fonts of type. In 1736 he began his own foundry and made several important contributions in the field of type design; he is said to have cut 147 alphabets of his own creation. Fournier is probably best remembered as the designer of St. Augustine Ordinaire, a face that served as the model for the Monotype Corporation's Fournier, which was released in 1925.